To those who support any author by buying and reading their books, I salute you. I couldn't keep telling these stories if it weren't for you and for the support team surrounding me. No one works alone in this business.

THANKS

Beta Readers and Proofreaders - with my deepest gratitude!
Micky Cocker
James Caplan
Kelly O'Donnell
John Ashmore

SOCIAL MEDIA

Craig Martelle Social
Website & Newsletter:
https://www.craigmartelle.com

Facebook:
https://www.
facebook.com/AuthorCraigMartelle/

Also in series:

THE MAIN PLAYERS WITHIN

Ambassador/Major Declan Payne
Executive Officer/Major Virgil Dank
Mrs. Ambassador/Lieutenant Mary "Dog" Morris/Payne
CEO Tech Inc/Tech Specialist 7 Katello Mateus "Blinky" Andfen
Tech Specialist 6 Laura "Sparky" Walker
Tech Specialist 6 Augry Byle
Tech Specialist 4 Salem "Shaolin" Shao
Tech Specialist 4 Huberta "Joker" Hobbes
Mr./Combat Specialist 7 Cointreau "Heckler" Koch
Mx/Combat Specialist 5 Marsha "Turbo" Skellig
COO Tech In/Combat Specialist 3 Alphonse "Buzz" Periq

*"When one life ends, another begins, unless it's you.
Then you're just dead."* –From the memoirs of Ambassador Declan Payne

A ship, nothing more than a massive shoebox, moved slowly into the outer reaches of the PX47 system.

A space station loomed above the only planet in the Goldilocks zone, the distance from the star where water existed in a liquid state, which also meant the possibility of an oxygen-rich atmosphere and life. With less than one percent land mass, PX47 was the perfect colonization planet for the Rang'Kor.

The space station above had few on board, military who had been moved to the station from decommissioned warbirds. The military head had once captained an older frigate, but the war was over.

This station was nothing more than a communications and flight control center. It had been built by the Ebren for the Ebren, a race of tall, fibrous, humanoid beings. The Rang'Kor were cephalopods, multi-tentacled and rubbery when not fully hydrated.

The crew on the station was in ill humor because of it. Not enough water had been transported to the station to make it comfortable. They had brought water-lined space suits they could wear, but they never fit their bodies correctly, even though they'd been designed by Rang'Kor scientists. The suits impeded mobility, and the wearer couldn't eat with the thing on.

The comfortable answer was to fill the station with water, but the government said that was years away, although the engineering had been finished. The politicians had debated whether to build a whole new station before allocating the assets on one plan over the other. While they debated, the crew suffered, if nothing more than in their own minds. Floating the idea of better space suits had been met with silence.

Hauling mass quantities of water into orbit was a challenge, even for the advanced technology the Rang'Kor enjoyed.

"It's like a desert in here!" the creature at the scanning station complained. "Sorry, sir."

"Easy," the station commander replied. He was still getting used to not being on a ship. "It's at ninety-seven percent humidity. Maybe swim laps in the station's pool. You'll be fine." He wanted to be a positive force for his crew, but they all suffered from the lack of excitement and engagement. The commander stabbed a tentacle toward the main screen. "What is that coming toward us?"

"Initial indications suggest a flying box. Steady speed. Not the remnants of a planet. It appears to be of artificial construction."

"Energy scanners now, please." *Leviathan* had shared sufficient elements from the energy wave-scanning technology with the Blaze member races to help them see objects that were much farther away than normal scanners could pick up. It gave them no advantage over *Leviathan* should they return to a state of war against humanity, however. Lev had ensured the scanners were energy hogs, which prevented the younger races from keeping them on all the time.

The cephalopod tapped multiple screens simultaneously with its tentacles. "Now we wait," the operator said. "Two minutes."

They watched the blip and the extremely long-range image that showed the object with the unnatural shape.

"Course?" the commander asked. The rough linear display suggested it was headed for the water planet.

"Here. It's coming here. I wonder if it'll have anything for barter. Is that a Zuloon ship? Maybe they have water, and we could fill the lower decks. That would be something, wouldn't it?"

"Our comfort is the last thing on the mind of the Zuloon, but no. This isn't one of their ships. Databanks. Any matches?" The commander knew the answer but asked to get his demoralized crew to engage.

"No matches." The scanner operator leaned close to his screen. In a place where nothing happened, something was happening. "The alien ship is accelerating."

The station commander stared at the screen with his large, round eyes. "An old Rang'Kor saying comes to mind. Be careful what you wish for; you may get it. I was thinking how boring this was. Dampen your tentacles and send thanks to Rang. We got work to do. Consider this entity hostile until we can confirm otherwise. Comm, get me the fleet commander."

He pushed his tentacles close together to support his body and stretched toward the ceiling. Even at full height, his head didn't reach it since the station had been built for the much taller Ebren.

"Fleet is active," the communication officer replied.

"This is Commander Tre'Gesh of Space Station Superior

47. Intercept inbound spacecraft to ascertain its intentions. Weapons hold."

"Roger," the captain replied. "Intercepting flying box, designated FB-UFO-1."

"Good luck, Captain."

The captain responded by leaving the comm channel. The six Rang'Kor cruisers in orbit spooled up their drives, formed up, and disappeared as they entered faster-than-light speed.

"Time to intercept?" the station commander requested.

A crew member to his left delivered the answer. "Eleven minutes. Six hundred million kilometers at an average speed of three times c, the speed of light."

"Eleven minutes to showtime," the commander said. "Keep your eyes on that ship. I'm going to grab a bite since we don't know how long this engagement will last. There's time enough now for shrimp. I'll be right back."

The commander left the bridge. The Rang'Kor's biological clocks ran at different speeds, resulting in a standard approach of always having food available as opposed to set dining times. The crew was few enough on the space station that the support crew was able to maintain a living buffet.

In the command deck's galley, a semi-circular clear trough wound through the room. The ends disappeared behind the wall, where the tenders kept it stocked. Paddles forced the water and a variety of fish, shellfish, and crustaceans through to the next paddle, and they were moved along at regular intervals. The first spots at the feed end of the trough were well-worn. No one went to the far end by choice. Getting the other crewmembers' leftovers was less than appealing on the best of days.

The commander was the second person who'd decided to eat at that time. He took a spot next to the other and dashed two tentacles into the water to pluck a shrimp free as it tried to get away from the new shadow looming overhead.

Rang'Kor tentacles carried tiny razor-sharp barbs to impale their meals and bring them to their mouths, which were located near the base of their tentacles. The commander slipped the shrimp under his body and into his mouth as he watched for his next tasty morsel. The rippling of the water put him in a trance-like state, calming him and bringing peace to his soul.

A fish slipped past the paddle and into the trough in front of the commander. He darted a tentacle after it, then a second, spearing it on the third try. The Rang'Kor next to him bobbed his head at the capture.

"A worthy prey," he offered.

The commander stuffed the fish into his mouth. "Indeed, and that will be enough for now. The command center beckons as a strange ship approaches. Enjoy your repast."

The commander sighed as he left the galley, still hungry but less so. He had to leave the solace of the moving water and the natural Rang'Kor state of having wet limbs behind. He didn't want to, but he had his duty. A strange ship. It might be the only excitement on this entire hitch.

He had two weeks remaining before his alternate arrived and he could return to the sea.

The Rang'Kor fleet had not yet reappeared from FTL. The commander took his seat, looking with pride upon those who had mustered out of the space service but were still serving. They worked with the efficiency of a well-trained frigate crew.

———

Captain Pel'Rok counted down by tapping his tentacle on the floor. When the timer hit zero, the heavy cruiser came out of FTL. Two heavy cruisers accompanied him, along with three light cruisers.

There had been little excitement since the peace agreement

with the humans and members of the Blaze Collective had been signed.

The weapons remained powered down. Six ships against one. The stranger wouldn't want any of that. A show of force would be sufficient.

"Captain Pel'Rok of the Rang'Kor fleet. You have entered Rang'Kor space. Please identify yourself and your purpose."

"Please?" the ship's second in command whispered.

"I'm feeling generous and giving today, Dor'Rel," the commander quipped. "First contact. I've never had one before."

After a minute, the communication station re-sent the recorded transmission. "On all bandwidths," he clarified.

A crackling noise came through the bridge's sound system.

"Refine and isolate. Translate!" The captain waved tentacles at multiple stations.

"Working it," came the non-specific reply.

"Broadcasting language files," Comms reported.

The sound stopped. The ship continued to accelerate down the PX star's gravity well despite the Rang'Kor ships.

"Reverse course and match acceleration. Bring the weapons online. All weapons. Load the outer tubes with Shark's Tooth missiles and prepare to fire." The Shark's Tooth missiles were called Stiletto-class by the humans because of their ability to navigate narrow openings to reach their targets.

Dor'Rel leaned close. "You went from 'please' to 'prepare to fire' in about five heartbeats. What do you know that I don't, except that they don't speak a common language?"

"The ship is twenty times the size of ours. A lack of communication should be met with caution, and they should be slowing down. That alone is enough to make me want to blow them out of the sky." Pel'Rok expanded to fill the space in the center of the bridge.

"Message coming in from the alien ship," Comms reported.

The line crackled with the odd language they'd heard earlier before a mechanical voice kicked in. "Rang'Kor. We are Ga'ee. Peace."

The captain looked at his second. "What by Rang's whirlpool was that?"

"Comms. Open the channel."

"Captain Pel'Rok of the Rang'Kor heavy cruiser *DF41*. Slow your approach immediately, or I will be forced to fire. You cannot hope to stand against the firepower of six Rang'Kor cruisers. I say again, slow or be destroyed."

"Peace," the mechanical voice repeated. The ship was close enough that it filled the main screen with only a three hundred percent magnification. The sides of the box cantilevered upward quicker than it had appeared, and hundreds of small craft jettisoned through the opening that ran the length of the rectangular ship.

"Fire!" Pel'Rok shouted. "Damn your eyes, fire!"

The ship lurched under the simultaneous launches from all systems. Missiles leapt from their tubes on fountains of pressurized air. Rocket motors kicked in and accelerated the ten-meter-long Shark's Tooth anti-ship missiles at fifty gees toward the alien ship.

The tiny craft danced like fireflies in a night sky. They seemed to multiply on the screen, flooding the void with a cloud of hardware behind which the alien ship stayed.

"Close-in defensive systems on automatic," the captain ordered. Two button-taps later, the defensive operations controller acknowledged that the weapons were at one hundred percent capability and ready to fire.

"Ha!" Pel'Rok shouted. "Today is the day the Rang'Kor made first contact with a new alien race, the Ga'ee. And they thought the best answer was to fight us."

Dor'Rel squinted at the fog of tiny craft in a loose formation between the Ga'ee ship and the Rang'Kor cruisers. "The alien ship is slowing."

High-energy lasers pulsed at the enemy ship but didn't reach their target. Ion cannons accelerated atomic particles to near-light speed. The cloud of small craft popped with flashes of light as the ions tore them apart. The captain did not call off that attack. He needed to send a message to the aliens that aggression would be met with greater aggression.

"Small craft accelerating at..." the technician stared at his screen, "five hundred gees."

"Suggests there are no life forms on those craft. Scanners, talk to me."

"Small craft, silicon and duranium. No organic life forms."

"Silicon?" Could they be a silicon-based life form? The cloud headed for the outbound missiles from each of the six cruisers.

The resulting impact came quickly, and the missiles were scrubbed from the tactical board as transponders went dead. Not a single explosion registered.

"What happened to the missiles?"

"Taken offline, commander. They're gone while visually still there."

"The aliens killed my missiles?" The captain swelled again. "Continue firing with the ion cannon. Energy weapons at maximum cyclic rate. These drones are getting on my nerves. Take them out, please."

"Captain?" the weapons specialist asked. "All of them?"

Dor'Rel answered on the captain's behalf. "You heard the order. Destroy them all. Synchronize fire with the other fleet ships. Fill the void with heat and fire!"

A dazzling array of firepower spat at the approaching cloud.

"Little effect," the scanner operator reported. "Impact in fifteen seconds."

"What's their speed?" the captain wondered. "Never mind. Fast. Transition to FTL."

"No time," the pilot reported.

The cloud approached. "Brace for impact!" Dor'Rel shouted. Cephalopods were able to withstand significantly greater gee forces than their human counterparts.

The captain wrapped three of his tentacles around bars on the deck made for that purpose.

The craft rained on the heavy cruiser like as many impacts from Thor's hammer. The ship shook under the deluge, the sound as harsh as the roar of a hurricane. The lights flickered and went out. The ship groaned and lurched before losing artificial gravity. Emergency klaxons sounded.

The hull had been breached.

"Anyone who can maneuver, get out of here. Back to PX47 and warn them," Pel'Rok ordered in the hope that someone would hear.

"Comms are down."

Pel'Rok's message had not been transmitted.

"Flight control is down."

"Life support is on battery backup."

The captain looked at his second. "Take charge of damage control and get the engines back online. We need maneuverability first and foremost. And then we need to get out of here. Priority to FTL."

The main screens were down. No one saw the Ga'ee ship fly past the six dead and dying cruisers to recover its craft and close its outer doors. It continued on a straight line toward PX47.

[2]

"Is your problem nothing more than a pimple on your ass? The answer is 'yes' almost every time." –From the memoirs of Ambassador Declan Payne

"Come on, Dog, show some sympathy!" Declan Payne complained. He was lying on a blanket, looking at the stars outside the Vestrall capital city of Leeyaness.

"Sympathy. Because humanity won't call you 'Supreme Ruler of the Seven Races?' I offered 'Preeminent Supremeness,' but they didn't approve that one either. You're just going to have to live with 'Ambassador.' And we've been together for more than a year. Are you ever going to call me by my name?" Mary Morris was Payne's former deputy team commander and partner. She used the title Mrs. Ambassador because it made Payne antsy.

Payne tried to look hurt. "Beefy Supreme?" he tried. "Damn. Now I'm hungry for tacos, and Lev isn't here."

"Mrs. Beefy Supreme? No." She jabbed him in the ribs with a fork.

Kal'faxx, warrior and former Ebren champion, threw a

custom-designed ring that the Cabrizi, two long-fanged doglike creatures, ran after. He exercised them frequently. They weren't the type to live a sedentary life. Kal had sworn allegiance to Declan Payne, the only warrior ever to defeat him in hand-to-hand combat.

"When can we go home?" Mary asked as she often did. Neither considered Vestrall Prime their home, not even a home away from home. That was *Leviathan*, a massive battleship that was bigger than most dreadnought-class ships. It had been built as a doomsday weapon so terrible that it would force an enemy to sue for peace by its mere presence.

The ship's deep secret was that it was a pacifist. It would fight to defend itself, but Payne's challenge was the mental gymnastics required to convince the ship to remain in the fight for peace. Even if it meant making war.

Lev, the artificial intelligence that ran the ship, was also their friend. He'd gone to the portal at XK-175 to collect data on the final test. The portal in Earth's solar system was ready except for the final calibrations. Once the portals were online, the team could move back and forth without using Lev's ability to fold space, which always knocked him offline for three days.

With the war over, he was safe during his recovery. Still, a direct link between Vestrall Prime and Earth would change the nature of the relationship between the Vestrall and humanity.

Also, an active portal would allow humans and visitors from the five races of the Blaze Collective to visit Vestrall Prime.

As often as they wanted.

Payne looked forward to it. The Vestrall did not, especially the former Mryasmalites, those who had led the Vestrall before Team Payne raided their offices and forced them to surrender. It wasn't even one-sided. Payne had been true to his word.

"Mrs. Ambassador?" Payne blurted. "That doesn't bother you?"

"No. Why would it?" Mary leaned on her elbow to face Declan.

"Because we're not married. Maybe someday, I'll make an honest woman of you."

"Oh, really?" She dragged out the words, and Payne realized he was in trouble. "You are old-fashioned in some things. I enjoy your company Declan. From now until the end. Don't ruin it by thinking that you're in charge of this relationship."

"See! That's my point exactly." He stabbed a finger at the sky before rolling onto his side to face her. "I'm supposed to be the Supreme Pre-eminence of Awesome, and out of two people on this one blanket, I'm not even in charge. Maybe Earth authorities were right in making me an ambassador."

"They did that because they had to think *they* were in charge. It's hard to take credit for everything you did if they can't tell the people they ordered it."

"They didn't order it. Harry Wesson did, the fleet admiral. I wonder how he and Nyota are doing?"

Nyota Freeman was the Blue Earth Protectorate commodore who would have court-martialed Payne for being insubordinate had it not been for Lev. She and the admiral had run away together after the final battle.

"That still blows my mind," Payne added.

"What? People who have few peers falling in love? It was a beautiful thing to watch." Mary's look challenged Payne to argue, but he didn't take the bait.

The Cabrizi vaulted over them as they chased the ring.

"I guess Kal is ready to go," Payne commented.

Mary nodded and kissed Payne. "I'm already an honest woman. I'll tell anyone that you're mine and fight them if I have to."

"After a year of training, you'll probably be able to take all comers except for Marsha. Those throwdowns with Heckler.

12

I'm amazed they haven't killed each other." Marsha "Turbo" Skellig and Cointreau "Heckler" Koch, Team Payne's combat specialists, had married and started an extreme game and rugged-adventure shop.

Once they'd convinced the Vestrall they wouldn't die, the younger locals had started to participate. It had become a thriving business, even though it was looked down on by the older generation.

"I thought they were supposed to blow up a planet?"

"I think getting some on a regular basis calmed both of them down. I'm happy they didn't destroy Vestrall. It's been a good year."

"I concur. Probably one of the best years of my life. Ever since they assigned me to Team Payne."

"I wasn't a fan. You had no combat skill."

"If I were in your place, I would have protested, too. Vehemently. I held you back, but I was in Medical so much that it didn't matter a whole lot."

Payne laughed. "All broke up, nice and dirty. But no scars, Mary Morris. I promised you scars."

Mary tapped her chest. "My scars are in here."

"Damn, woman. That's deep. I wish my scars were only in there. My body looks like a bad case of Naugahyde."

"It does." Mary pushed herself to a sitting position, then stood. "But you look just fine in the dark."

Payne reached for her, but she stepped out of range. Kal stood nearby.

"Y'all are leaving? Already? If you must, I'll be right proud to carry your stuff. Come on, boys, vittles are waiting!" the Ebren drawled.

"We both know you don't have to talk like that," Payne said. "I can't believe Lev did that to you."

"I find a good Western movie accent as comforting as pigs in a blanket roastin' over an open fire." Kal hugged himself and smiled. Kal'faxx, all three meters and over two hundred kilograms of fibrous muscle of him.

Payne was still amazed he'd beat him, even after getting juiced by Lev to produce an exponential increase in his strength. "Have you ever had pigs in a blanket?"

"I reckon not. Can we get some?"

"Hey, buddy. Have you forgotten where we are?" Payne climbed reluctantly to his feet and picked up the blanket.

"Dammit!" the Ebren warrior said in a parody of Payne's common outbursts.

"We'll find something at home. Lev keeps us stocked pretty well." He whistled at the Cabrizi, and they came to him. "Get in, you filthy mongrels."

Payne activated the side hatch on the skimmer he'd had since the day they'd first encountered *Leviathan*. He called the tactical insertion craft *"Glamorous Glennis."* Now he used it for casual transport as if it were his personal car.

Being Earth's ambassador had *some* perks.

They flew to the top of the tallest building in Leeyaness and landed on the roof. The former Mryasmalite meeting space had been converted into quarters for the ambassador and his family, which included Kal'faxx and the Cabrizi.

The elevators had long since been repaired, making getting to the street level much easier.

There still weren't any restaurants worth going to except the one run by Laura "Sparky" Walker with help from the two best programmers in the galaxy, her teammates Katello "Blinky" Andfen and Alphonse "Buzz" Periq. The humans ate there six days out of seven, but today was the day they weren't open.

"It's my turn, isn't it?" Payne asked. Mary nodded.

Kal'faxx rolled his eyes. "I'll take care of me." He disappeared into the kitchen and returned a few moments later with a bucket of cereal drowning in reconstituted powdered milk.

The humans watched him disappear into his room, the one with all the windows and the best view of the city. After the Cabrizi joined him, he closed the door.

They wouldn't see him again until morning.

Payne strolled to the other side to look at the stars. "Space beckons."

"I kind of got used to being out there, too. It's hard being planet-bound like a commoner," Mary quipped.

"Maybe that's why we're anxious. We aren't common. We belong out there." He nodded at the growing darkness. "Even if there's nothing to do, there will always be something to see."

"You were never common, Declan Payne, although you are salt-of-the-Earth."

"Unlike you, an angel from heaven," Payne told her softly.

She pushed him but smiled.

A voice spoke into both their heads. *The portal to Earth is operational. Congratulations, Declan. You've taken a greater step toward intergalactic peace than any other being in history.*

"Welcome back, Lev. Are you saying we can go home, like, take *Glennis* for a quick trip back for some tacos?"

The portal is powered by a gas giant. Jupiter is beyond the skimmer's range, I'm afraid. You will have to take a real ship.

Payne deflated. "We don't have a real ship."

You do. I will take you to Earth as soon as the portal opens. Prepare to embark, Declan and Mary. I'll contact the others. You should all go together.

"I like how you think, Lev. But since you're in my mind, you already know how I think. Please don't tell anyone."

My lips are sealed, Declan.

"Hey! You don't have any lips." Payne kissed Mary on the

cheek and bolted for their quarters. "We're going home for tacos!"

"Is your stomach all you think about?" Mary called after him.

He thinks about many things, but two take up more of his mental capacity than anything else. Food is number one, but you are a close second.

"I'm not sure how thankful I am for that revelation, Lev. I can't tell if you're serious or not since you just said you wouldn't tell what Dec was thinking. We'll discuss it on the trip home," Mary warned.

[3]

"When the call comes, answer it. It could be your mom, or the universe asking you to come to its rescue." –From the memoirs of Ambassador Declan Payne

The team loaded into the skimmer atop the Vestrall tower. They filled it, leaving no space for anyone to move.

"This ship used to be bigger," Payne complained. "What happened to you people?"

Heckler scoffed. "I weigh the same as I did when we retired a year ago. Mars and I work out every day."

"Is that what you call it?" Blinky quipped. He lost his smile at Turbo's glare.

She laughed. "I still got it." She pinned the pulse rifle between her knees, freeing her hands to check her sidearm.

"What the hell is that?" Buzz asked.

"Desert Eagle. Old-school slug-thrower. Lev was able to make two of them from plans we snagged last time we were on Earth...a year ago." Turbo scowled.

Heckler elbowed her.

"Y'all need a bigger ship," Kal'faxx drawled while

scratching the necks of the two Cabrizi, who sat calmly wedged into small openings between the passengers. The inside height was two-point-five meters, just enough for the tallest team member wearing powered armor. Kal was a half-meter too tall, and too big for the jump seats down both outboard sides of the ship. "*Ugly* 4 sounds good right about now from where I'm sitting."

The team chuckled. Augry Byle, Huberta "Joker" Hobbes, and Salem "Shaolin" Shao worked directly for the ambassador. Joker was their communications manager, a role that had expanded to include what Payne called propaganda: a continuous stream of information targeted at the Vestrall to change their perception of humanity. Joker called it "Doctor Feelgood." She played music under the same name.

Along with Joker, the team's former engineer, Byle, and Shaolin canvassed the technological centers of Leeyaness, looking for advanced engineering that Lev didn't have. Discoveries the Vestrall had made after the Godilkinmore departed the system.

It would have been a slow process to acquire the advanced mathematics and physics necessary to understand what they found, but Lev had used his telepathic learning process to update them in a matter of minutes. They now had what they needed to recognize what was new.

They didn't find as much as they thought.

The Vestrall were also Godilkinmore, but the ones who hadn't been the scientists. The Vestrall had wanted to take over the galaxy, and they did, but they'd lost the engineering capabilities of their brothers. Over the centuries, they'd relearned them, then moved forward. An example was the portal system for travel. They were still working to understand the engineering behind those.

Payne called over his shoulder, keeping his eyes focused out the front screen as the skimmer took off, "Hey Joker, do you have a communique ready for when we reach Earth?"

"Of course," she replied. "To make sure we're on the same page, what would you have put in it?"

"You don't have one, do you?" Payne pressed.

"No. I just found out you wanted one eight seconds ago. I'm good, but you gotta give me at least five minutes." She ticked numbers off on her fingers. "Well, more like two hours."

"You'll have it!" Payne declared as the skimmer accelerated toward the upper atmosphere. "You people gotta cut down on the chow or PT more. Body fat is draining *Glennis'* tanks."

Byle and Shaolin looked at each other. They'd lived the easy life for the past year and were up about ten kilos each.

Payne had watched them and hadn't said a word. If that was how they wanted to spend their retirement, who was he to say anything? He left it to them.

They looked embarrassed next to the others.

Payne gestured with his head at Mary. She knew what he was thinking, so she eased her seat around and leaned forward. "Mandatory physical training the second we hit the ship. No chow until after a workout and a run. Secure your gear, and we'll get to it. Team Payne workout room, command deck."

Some nodded. Byle and Shaolin looked sideways at the skimmer's flight deck.

"It's in everyone's best interest," Mary continued. "Please?"

"Damn, Lieutenant!" Heckler howled. "I remember the good old days when people gave orders liberally peppered with fuck-bombs. I hope we don't have to go to war again. We've been gentrified."

Payne swiveled to face his former weapons specialist. "Where'd you learn a word like that?"

"We're respectable businesspeople now. We have standards to upkeep," Heckler replied.

"I like how you didn't answer the question. Let me see your piece." Payne snapped his fingers.

Heckler removed the hand cannon from its holster, dropped the magazine, racked the slide to the rear, and caught the ejected round. He looked at the chamber before handing it over.

Payne pointed the barrel at the deck and checked the chamber for a round, then sent the slide home before checking the balance. He aimed out the window. "I like the weight on this thing. Have one made for me, will you?"

"There's a price for these things," Heckler replied.

"Okay, Mr. Businessman, I'll fight you for yours in an open ring. Dojo, bitch."

Heckler had always been a fighter, but Payne had been taken to a completely different plane of combat capabilities to fight as humanity's champion. Even a year later, Heckler couldn't hope to stand against the former major.

"Fine, bitch!" Heckler shot back. He lowered his voice to continue. "I'll have one made for you."

"After PT, of course. Nothing like throwing iron and running kilometers to invigorate the soul." He couldn't help but glance at Byle and Shaolin.

"Fine!" Byle snapped, locking eyes with Payne. She ended with a smile. "When our saying of 'bring the Payne' has a whole new meaning, maybe Lev can hook us up with heating pads and massages."

"Does anyone remember when we imposed our will on the enemy? When we did hard things and did them well? Is that a memory or a dream?"

"Forever-long ago, boss," Blinky replied. "It's hard to keep that sharp of an edge when we achieved everything we fought for. Peace, right? We won the peace and have been paid our dividends. What's the big deal with working out? We're retired."

"When we hear 'live long and prosper,' we don't want to ignore the 'live long' part. That means staying healthy. I want you all to have great lives, just like Dog and I have."

"That's Mrs. Ambassador to you," Mary corrected.

The team laughed while shaking their heads.

"When's the last time we were all together?" Payne asked. He knew the answer. Once a quarter, they met on the top floor of the tower for a get-together. Those events were subdued. They were isolated on Vestrall, whose population had nothing in common with Team Payne. Personal relationships were sparse. Besides Declan and Mary and Heckler and Turbo, no one else was in a steady partnership.

It was wearing on them.

Payne was happy to take them back to Earth for R and R, rest and relaxation. Even though it wasn't his job anymore, he still felt responsible.

"PT!" he shouted. "Oorah, Team Payne!" At the lukewarm response, he increased the volume. "We will run laps around the ship until I hear some motivation. If that doesn't do it, then we'll go with the beatings. Kal will fight us one at a time, starting with me."

"Bullshit!" Buzz blurted, eyes wide. He stared at the side of Kal's head, which was as big as Buzz's torso. "I'm not fighting him. I'm a tech guy! And a civilian to boot."

Heckler groaned. "One used weapons specialist, washed up, no longer in his prime. For sale. Cheap."

"What I hear you saying," Turbo started, "is that he's first."

"Absolutely. Buzz is first. Any objections?" Heckler looked from face to face. Some nodded. Others gave the thumbs-up.

"I object!" Buzz shouted before banging his head off the bulkhead when Kal turned to look at him.

"I'll take it easy on you." Kal waited a few moments before adding, "Not."

Buzz's mouth fell open.

The view through the ship's forward screen showed *Leviathan*'s open hangar bay, well-lit and inviting.

"Just funnin' you, Buzz," Kal added. He turned his attention back to the Cabrizi and scratched their jet-black ears.

Lev guided the skimmer into the bay and deposited it next to *Ugly 4*, the latest and largest iteration of the egg-shaped stealth insertion craft Team Payne had spent a great deal of time within.

"When we return, we're taking *Ugly 4*," Payne stated.

The side hatch popped open. Blinky was first into the doorway while Buzz wedged against Sparky, trying to get out. He stumbled and fell.

"What happened to you people?" Payne wondered.

Heckler answered. "Peace happened to us. Different skills, Mr. Ambassador."

Sparky tried to help Buzz upright but was bowled over by the Cabrizi in their rush to get off the ship. She tumbled out the open hatch and landed on the deck, then moaned in pain.

Not the good kind, either.

Buzz crawled out, and the others followed in a more orderly manner.

Declan and Mary were the last ones out.

"Spool us up and take us to Earth, big dog!" Payne shouted once he was outside the skimmer.

"You know I can hear you even if you whisper. Even if you don't say the words at all," Lev told him.

"What fun would that be?" He took Mary's hand, and they headed for the last available cart provided automatically in response to the needs of the crew. "It's nice to be back, Lev. Thanks for staying with us."

"There is nowhere else I'd rather be, Declan."

"I thought you wanted to find the Godilkinmore. Go home."

"When the time is right. That is the challenge I have, and someday, I will reconcile it. Do I enjoy the peace for which I was built, or do I leave it behind? I don't have the answer to that. I have dedicated a significant amount of computing power to this question."

"And Davida can't help you?" Davida Danbury was a recluse genius from Earth who had bonded with *Leviathan* and lived somewhere on the ship. She had no intention of leaving, having decided to live her life in a veritable stasis. She'd turned her back on the outside world once she'd found the one who completed her.

Leviathan.

No one questioned it since they had met her. She was different.

Payne stood at the cart but didn't board.

"Can we see her, Lev?"

A quizzical expression crossed Mary's face. She waited for an explanation.

"Davida. She's fine. You didn't think about her because she wasn't like any of you. You're worried that made you something you're not. But she is, deep down, just like the rest of you. Very human. You didn't worry about her because you trusted both of us when we committed to our partnership. If you'd like to see her, she's in a life pod of her own design. I will take you there while I make preparations to fly through the portal. We're already underway to the gas giant in this system."

"Lev, it's like you're in my mind."

Mary pulled Declan into the cart. "Let's check on Davida and then go to the bridge."

Payne turned his head to look at her. "You said 'gym,' but it sounded exactly like 'bridge.' Weird. Lev must be in my head again."

"Yes, gym. Workout room. That's what I said," Mary agreed. "Lev, who else is on board?"

"I'm afraid there is no one besides Team Payne and Davida."

"Nothing to be afraid of, Lev. We're here now. The dark doesn't have to scare you," Payne joked. *Leviathan* was a massive ship, five kilometers long, a kilometer wide, and nearly as tall.

The doors opened and the cart accelerated into the corridor, only to come to a rapid stop when it found Kal standing in the way.

"Did y'all think you were going to escape?" Kal asked. He worked his way into the cart while fighting with the Cabrizi to keep them from squeezing in with him.

"Kal! There's no room," Payne complained.

Kal gestured dismissively in a very human manner.

"Someone is a bad influence on him," Payne remarked.

Mary pointed at Payne. "You have seen the enemy, and he is you," she intoned. "Lighten up. Going to Earth to celebrate yet another accomplishment brought about by He-Payne, Master of the Universe."

"They told me I was. Everyone was saying it." Payne stuck his nose in the air until Mary jabbed him in the ribs.

"Maybe we can stop by the medical lab. Just like old times when we were in there more than our own bunks."

"No!" Kal cried from the back seat. "Ain't got no hankerin' to see the inside of that barn ever again."

"Kal," Payne began but couldn't finish. The cart accelerated down the ramps integrated into the main corridor. Three levels down was the mid-ship location of the bridge, secure in the farthest point from the outer hull. They continued down one more level to a space directly below the bridge. It was in the secure zone, a shell that would protect those on the bridge from the catastrophic destruction of the ship.

Of course, that was where Lev would put Davida.

His soulmate.

The cart stopped. The Cabrizi danced anxiously outside the door that opened as Declan, Mary, and Kal approached. The animals refused to go in.

They entered into a surreal twilight. In the middle of the room, a tank filled with fluid contained Davida's naked body, but she was wrapped tightly in cables and tubes. She looked pale under the lights but otherwise healthy. Her arms and legs twitched with the shocks that stimulated her muscles.

"Declan and Mary. I'm pleased you two are together," Davida's voice sounded all around them. That meant she was in their minds, even though they swore they could hear her. Lev's telepathy was powerful.

The technology of the Progenitors, and now it was hers, too.

"It was meant to be," Mary replied. "How are you?"

"I am well. I have never been better. Don't worry about what you see. That's the meat wagon that hauled my mind into this space, where I have since expanded. Lev's knowledge spans our galaxy, and it's now my knowledge, too. You have no need to worry about me, Declan. I am exactly where I was meant to be. And I suggest you are, too."

"On board the ship or on Vestrall? Because I didn't feel like I was at home on Vestrall. I felt like a cat on a hot tin roof." Declan shifted uncomfortably and looked away from the body in the tank.

Mary stopped him from walking away and embraced him.

"Am I where I'm supposed to be?" Kal asked into the silence.

Declan leaned back to look up at the Ebren. "I never knew you had any doubts, buddy. I'm sorry."

Kal gripped Payne's shoulder in his oversized hand, his fingers trailing halfway down the human's back. "You have told me many times that I am free to do as I wish."

"And yet, you remain where you are in a role that you defined, doing what you have determined to do. If only everyone answered their calling with such zeal."

"I would be dead but for Declan Payne and Leviathan."

"Your life has meaning, Kal'faxx. No one could ask for more," Davida replied.

Declan approached the tank and put his hand on the clear composite. "Are you our spiritual guide?" he asked with a chuckle. "Don't answer that. You have my word that we will visit more often. I think your insight will be valuable to keep me from going insane."

"I suggest you know the answers to your questions, Declan Payne. I look forward to next time. We'll be transiting the portal to Earth soon, and your team is waiting for you on the bridge."

Payne turned to Mary. "It sounded like Davida did it, too. She made 'gym' sound exactly like 'bridge.' So weird."

[4]

"It'll work out in the end. If it's not working out, it's not the end." –From the memoirs of Ambassador Declan Payne

They transited the Vestrall portal with less disorientation than when Lev folded space. It happened almost imperceptibly. Had they not been watching the screens surrounding the bridge, they wouldn't have known.

"I am pleased with the experience," Lev stated. "How quickly do you wish to travel to Earth, Declan?"

"Quick as you can, Lev. I can smell tacos from here!" Payne declared.

"You cannot," Lev confirmed. "Twenty minutes to orbit."

"Workout is canceled, you slackers." Payne looked at his team, then opened his mouth to give them grief, but Mary stopped him.

"Easy, Mr. Ambassador," she whispered.

"Team Payne, prepare to disembark. We're taking *Ugly 4*, Lev. Hook a brother up!"

"I live to serve," Lev deadpanned.

"So, we're going back to the hangar where we just were?" Heckler asked. "What happened to you, man? You used to be far more efficient with our time." Heckler raised his eyebrows, expecting a response to his challenge.

"You fuckers are making me rethink my life choices. I feel like I should be twenty kilos heavier with a grizzled beard and the first choice to play Santa Claus at the annual party."

Heckler and Turbo faced each other and whispered quickly. "We want our major back," Heckler declared. "We don't know what to do with...this." He waved his hand at Payne.

Mary shook her head. "On your horses, slackers. To the hangar bay! Earth awaits. We have an appointment with destiny, and we'd best not be late!" She punctuated her orders with her best war cry, a strangled "Arghharoo."

Declan looked at her. "Don't do that. You're not good at it," he whispered. "How about this?" He let loose with the pent-up frustration and aggression that strangled his soul every day he wasn't preparing for battle. His mind had wanted peace, but he had the heart of a warrior.

The Cabrizi responded to Payne's fierce battle cry by howling. Their tails stood straight up and vibrated with the call to action.

Heckler and Turbo pumped their fists with the grim determination that was missing from their lives, too.

Kal jumped up and bumped his head on the ceiling. "Maybe we can arrange a little combat action while we're down there? Cattle rustlers on the prowl?"

"We'll see what we can do," Payne replied. "Now get your sorry asses in those carts. We're going back to the hangar bay, and if we don't get there quickly enough, we're coming back to the bridge and doing it again, but we won't be riding next time!" Payne spread his arms wide and herded the team back into the corridor, where they boarded the waiting carts.

Kal waited for Declan and Mary to board. The Cabrizi jumped in first. A second cart appeared.

"You ride with them," Declan told her. "They like you better anyway."

"If I must. Come to Mommy, my sweet babies," she cooed while clearing space in the back seat before the animal in the front vaulted over the seat and into her face.

"We'll be right behind you." The wrestling match got underway while Payne and Kal reclined in relative luxury in the following cart.

"Are you going to give a speech?" Kal asked in an unaccented voice.

"I hope not, but I better be ready. I'm okay if they wave me off. I don't need to be on any more newscasts."

It's been a year, my friend, Lev said softly. *Knowing humanity, I think you'll find schools and spaceports named after you. Everyone will want you to bless their child.*

"Don't even joke like that, Lev! Damn. Don't be a jerk."

I know it causes you distress, but I am serious. You should prepare yourself, so you don't come across as a jerk. Don't ruin humanity's view of you, Declan. You are a hero. Do your best to remain that in their minds. Soon enough, we'll leave again, and all they'll have is the impression you've made in the short time we'll be here.

Payne scowled, his thoughts dark and uncomfortable. He felt like jumping out and finding something else to do. Anything else.

His role in the universe was not to be an idol, but he couldn't refuse to embrace it. The cart accelerated up the ramps and to the hangar bay to deposit them near the stealth insertion craft he had designated *Ugly 4*.

"Mary," Payne called and nodded at a place away from the others. She had been the star of *Bikinis in Paradise* for three years. She would know how to handle swooning fans. When she arrived, he pulled her close and put his forehead to hers, noses touching. "Lev told me to be ready to bless people's children."

She caressed his cheek. "That bothers you, I know. Give them the time allotted. I'll be your handler to hurry you away from engagements. Always be positive and humble. *'You shouldn't have. I don't know what to say. All I can give you is my deepest appreciation.'*"

"We should have talked about this before now. We had a year. I like the quips. I can do that, but how do I ignore the looks of adulation? I'm not that guy. I'm not the face of peace."

Mary kissed him softly. "But, my love, you *are* the face of peace. You and your misfits. Don't bring them since they won't like being in the background."

Payne nodded as he stepped back. "I knew you'd have the answer. Thanks, Dog."

"Mary." She laughed. "You're going to get us all fired."

"That's the face of peace. Bring the Payne and his gang of misfits. If humanity only knew the truth."

"They know all the truth they need," Mary replied. "Don't mess it up."

Payne pumped his fist in the air. "Load up, people. It's time to go find tacos."

"Real-time communication with Earth is established," Lev reported. "I'll patch it through."

"Payne! Thank God you're here. Stay there; we'll be right up. While you wait, we're forwarding information to Lev. Read it." The voice sounded familiar, but the edge of concern in his voice was unusual.

"Admiral Wesson? Is that you? What's going on?"

"An invasion. It's good to hear your voice, Major. See you real soon."

"Major?" Mary wondered. She closed her eyes and blew out a long breath.

A dark cloud passed over his face. "This would be funny if it wasn't so serious," he told them. "Back in the carts. Back to the bridge. Lev, send them to us when they get here."

[5]

"Who are you willing to die for? That's your priority."
–From the memoirs of Ambassador Declan Payne

The team shuffled aimlessly around the bridge, waiting for the admiral to arrive.

Byle and Shaolin looked at each other before dropping into chairs. "What the hell did we do?" They groaned. "If we get recalled to duty, we're going to die."

Payne eased close to them. "We'll train, and we'll get back up to speed. It'll be okay. Start by watching what you eat."

"No shit, Major," Byle shot back. "I'm sorry, sir."

Payne returned to the raised chair where the ship's captain integrated with *Leviathan* but didn't climb in. Some of the experiences while being linked with the ship had been less than pleasant. That was for people like Davida and Arthir.

A steady tread announced the arrival of their guests, who were decked out in their uniforms. Admiral Harry Wesson walked with Commodore Nyota Freeman.

"Admiral. What's with the pomp?" Payne asked.

"We've all been recalled. Did you read the information we

sent?" At Payne's look, the admiral shook his head. "Never mind. You've all been recalled to active duty, and we've been directed to take *Leviathan* to PX47 on our way to Berantz space to investigate the loss of communication with a number of outposts."

"Loss of comms is a far cry from an invasion, Admiral. You must have more." Payne scowled. He knew there was worse to come.

A steady stream of individuals made their way onto the bridge. Most of them had been there before, but there were a few new faces. Those were easy to pick out since they stared wide-eyed at the majesty of *Leviathan*'s command and control center.

"Lev, show the video from the space station at PX47," the admiral requested.

A clear energy wave-scanning image filled the front screen. On it, a rectangular ship sent clouds of drones into the void to face six Rang'Kor cruisers. The cruisers launched a devastating attack with all weapons, most of which were intercepted by the cloud. The rest bounced harmlessly off an energy shield around the ship.

The cloud turned into waves that crashed against the Rang'Kor ships, killing their power. Killing *them*. The cloud returned to the ship as it passed and headed toward the water planet. The space station transmitted the information to an FTL cargo vessel that immediately departed the system.

When the screen went blank, it left the watchers in shock and clarified the admiral's sense of urgency. Humanity's leadership didn't want such a threat entering human space

"We haven't heard from PX47 in over a month. The Rang'Kor sent ships, but none have returned. And the Berantz have contacted us regarding this strange ship."

"Same ship?" Payne asked. He thought about asking Lev to

display the ship on the main screen and build a graphic of it based on what they'd seen, but he didn't need to say anything. The ship appeared and rotated for them to examine.

The massive ship seemed like nothing more than a carrier, a small fighter-launch ship. It had doors on both sides and drones—tens of thousands of drones that appeared to replicate in space before recovering when their task was complete.

"Lev, buddy, you up for a trip to PX47? The Rang'Kor have that planet because of us, and now I'm feeling a little guilty."

"I have no intention of taking orders from the human government," Lev announced.

All noise on the bridge stopped.

"Give us the room, please. Everybody out," the admiral requested evenly. He kept the commodore close to him. She'd be staying.

Payne wasn't going to leave either, nor Mary. And wherever Payne was, Kal would be too. Payne gestured at the vault-like hatch. His team headed out. Heckler and Turbo stopped and studied their team leader's hard expression.

"Take the team to the workout facilities. The easy civilian life is over. Bend them hard, Heckler, but don't break anyone. We have a long way to go."

"Aye, aye, sir."

They hurried out, barking orders at the team as they reached the corridor.

"Yes, Harry? I know what you want to say, but maybe you can say it aloud for the others' benefit." No one could keep secrets from Lev.

Harry Wesson faced Declan and Mary. The Cabrizi decided they didn't like being closed inside the bridge and started to howl.

"Kal, can you see to that, please?" Payne asked, but Mary was already on her way to the animals.

"We need Leviathan. You saw what that thing did to six cruisers." The admiral sounded like he was pleading.

Payne glanced at the screen, where a three-dimensional representation of the alien ship rotated like a display model.

"Admiral, I don't speak for Lev. You know that he won't take the war to an enemy. Yes, the Rang'Kor have been attacked. Maybe the Berantz, too. I don't even have to ask Lev to know that his recommendation will be to form a coalition, the Blaze Collective plus humanity, to confront whoever this newcomer is."

Lev finished his calculations, and the ship's dimensions appeared on the screen.

Payne stared. He pointed at it and turned to the admiral. "It's ten kilometers long."

"That's what our people came up with, too. They also counted the small ships that we assume are drones. You know how many there were?"

"Seventy-four thousand," Lev replied before Payne could fathom a guess. Clouds of drones that had defeated the Rang'Kor's defenses and killed their ships.

"I'd say drones. That's a big ship, but is there room for seventy-four thousand crew along with all their ships? I suggest not."

"Can we count on you, Lev?"

"I won't fight. This is an enemy that you'll have to deal with. I will take you to Rang'Kor and Berantz space to conduct an investigation but nothing more."

"That's all we're asking," the admiral replied.

The lights dimmed on the bridge, and a miasmic color barrage surrounded them. "There was a time, Harry, when you tried to mislead me, but you learned. Over the past year, that lesson appears to have been lost. Do not try to lie to me, Harry."

"I can feel your soul, Lev." Payne held his chest. "I know

35

you won't fight unless there is no other choice. Let's conduct the investigation, and we'll see what we see. We can make better decisions after we have more information. We will probably need to shuttle between the former Blaze to rally support if we find what I'm thinking we're going to find." He added, "You need to tell the government that they can't order Lev around."

The admiral remained tight-lipped, refusing to commit.

"Don't make an enemy of Leviathan, Admiral. He can't be strong-armed. You'll only get Earth ostracized and put humanity at risk." Payne studied the man who had been the bedrock of Payne's entire career. "What happened, Admiral?"

Harry Wesson sat in a nearby chair. Nyota Freeman sat next to him.

"The civilian world happened. Results were paramount, no matter how you achieved them." He ran his fingers through his gray hair and tried to stretch the tension away. "I didn't do well out there."

"I'm not sure I know how to respond, Admiral, but it sounds like the civilian world is a lot like the military. We were all about results, too." Payne leaned against a console and crossed his arms. He'd never thought he would be the one called upon to bring calm.

Is this what it's like, being an adult? he thought.

"Not like that. They'd kill each other to get what they want. We might have poked fun at Tamony Swiss, but corporate bigwigs are more like him than not. At least with him, you knew exactly where he was coming from. Others wait until the moment is ripe before stabbing you in the back."

"Sounds oddly specific. I can't believe they are all like that, just the ones wanting to trade on your name." Payne looked to Mary, who was still working with the Cabrizi to settle them down. "Makes me glad we weren't here."

With a final harsh command in strained Ebren, Mary returned with a Cabrizi leaning against each hip. She took Payne's hand, knowing she didn't have to say anything. Sometimes he needed support, and other times, he needed a different kind of support. This was the latter, where he would work it out for himself.

"What Harry is trying to say is that as horrific as a new war might be, it's where we belong," Nyota clarified.

"I'm still not convinced this will lead to war. We might have to jack up these newcomers a bit, but a war over PX47? The Rang'Kor can have it!"

"But they might not have it. If someone is conducting genocide across the galaxy. We have to stop it."

Payne recoiled while schooling his features to keep from wincing. "We killed a hell of a lot more than six cruisers. I'm glad no one looked at us as the purveyors of genocide."

A range of emotions crossed the admiral's once-confident countenance. "We need to investigate. That will help us understand our next steps. Other conversations will be nothing more than fruitless mental masturbation."

Payne snorted, and finally, the admiral smiled.

"Lev, can you please take us to PX47 to investigate?" Payne waited. "Please."

"For the investigation. If that ship is there and comes after me, I will not stay. I'll pick a point three days FTL travel from PX47. We will be there in six days."

"As we expect. Never jump into the middle of a firefight when you're low on ammunition and the gas tanks are empty," Payne stated. "Are you still loading people?"

Lev responded before the admiral. "I sent everyone in the corridor to the hangar bay."

"Even my team? They're supposed to be working out."

"Even your team, Declan."

Payne avoided looking at Mary when he heard her start to laugh.

The admiral looked less than amused. "Payne, you haven't changed one bit."

"It's an inside-team joke. We'll unfuck ourselves and be ready to deploy. We might have to go ashore. Lev, tune up our combat suits. And I hope you can get us a little bigger sizes for about half the team."

"I measured everyone the instant you stepped aboard. Your new suits will be waiting whenever you need to go. And for the record, it's more than half the team. Only Heckler and Turbo will fit into their old suits."

"Hey! I'm the same. Mary, tell him I'm the same."

"Lev, Dec is the same."

"He's not."

"Okay, I tried," she replied. "But I'm the same."

"You've lost weight, Mary. I'll prepare a high-protein diet. And Declan is right; Team Payne needs to spend more time in the gym."

"Ah." Payne looked at the admiral and the commodore, who still weren't smiling. "I've lost weight, too. Got it, Lev."

"You have not," the AI replied.

Payne scowled. The admiral scowled too, for far different reasons.

"When the universe is on the line, you can count on Team Payne to make inappropriate jokes at inopportune times and then save the universe. I used to be the leader of the seven races and then the ambassador when Earth officials thought themselves emasculated. And now, I'm just Major Payne."

The admiral's expression softened. "Which do you like best?"

Payne offered his hand, and the admiral took it.

"This one, sir. I like Major Payne." Declan Payne felt more

at home at that moment than he had for the past year.

"I thought so. Now get your damn uniform on. You look like a bag of hammers. And you, too, Lieutenant Morris. You're not much better."

Payne chuckled on his way to the corridor. The hatch silently opened to reveal a cart waiting outside.

"I go by Lieutenant Payne now, Admiral."

"Hang on," Payne called over his shoulder.

"No," the admiral replied, crossing his arms to defend his position.

"Yes." Mary crossed her arms as well.

Payne returned. "I thought we talked about this?"

"It is what it is, Dec. Deal with it."

His mouth twitched, but he knew what a good deal he had. "Lev, so let it be written, so let it be done. At this moment, Mr. and Mrs. Payne have declared their lifelong love for each other and are married by your hand as the ship's captain. Witnessed by Harry Wesson and Nyota Freeman."

"My first marriage. Thank you!" Lev declared. "Your chariot awaits. Sorry. I didn't have time to put out streamers or the ubiquitous cans to make noise as you drive away."

"Our chariot takes us to our quarters to consummate our marriage." Payne made eyes at Mary.

"Your chariot will take you to the workout facility," Lev replied.

Payne shrugged. "Maybe later, then. Have the team meet us at the gym."

"They're already on their way, and I'll tell you that they found as much humor in the back and forth as you did. I don't understand why humans would think being unproductive through multiple task changes is funny."

Payne took Mary's hand and headed for the hatch again. "Team Payne is back, baby!"

[6]

"If it's all hurry up and wait, you need to fire your plan-
ner." –From the memoirs of Ambassador Declan Payne

Payne reveled in throwing the iron, but it was a pale shade of
the mass he had been able to move when he was in Ebren-cham-
pion shape.

Mary worked out with Byle and Shaolin, who had shied
away from the others. Payne glanced at his new wife. She was
thinner, and he hadn't noticed. She had lost muscle mass, a
testament to how hard she had worked during her time in the
service.

Somebody punched him in the arm. "Hey!"

"Stop hogging the bench," Heckler snapped irreverently.
He and Turbo were waiting while Kal looked on. Kal hadn't lost
anything. He never missed a workout or gave it anything less
than his all.

Kal jogging through Leeyaness was a sight to see. Between
him and the Cabrizi, the Vestrall feared for their lives and dove
out of the way.

Even if they were operating hovervehicles, they never failed to give the Ebren natives a wide berth.

Payne climbed to his feet, feeling a good burn and tightness. He hadn't missed much, but it was enough to let him know his core was weak. He hopped on another bench and executed fifty dolphin kicks, grunting his way to the end.

Kal jumped on the bench after him, balancing precariously. He knocked out fifty dolphin kicks in forty seconds, then did another fifty for no reason whatsoever. "Your turn."

Payne felt the pain in his midsection. *Not a good idea*, he told himself, but climbed on and knocked out thirty-five before spasms rocked his core. He rolled sideways off the bench and curled up until the spasms stopped.

Kal hauled him to his feet. "That's how you should finish the final set of every exercise." He slapped Payne on the back.

"I'll try," the major mumbled. "Lev, when are we going to push off?"

"One more frigate is coming aboard. As soon as they're docked, we'll leave."

"Thanks for taking care of us, Lev. Getting us out of the vortex of doom that is humanity's government. Let's go take care of business. After that, Mary and I would be happy to accompany you wherever you go."

"You're going to abandon us?" Joker asked. "No way. You're not leaving me with those goofy bastards."

She meant the Vestrall.

"We're not splitting up again, *Major!*" Blinky shouted, using Payne's rank for emphasis.

"Is that how you all feel?"

The team nodded. Heckler grunted through his final rep. After he finished, he answered for the team. "We've been talking. That circle jerk back and forth between the hangar and the bridge sealed the deal. Where else in this galaxy can you get paid to have that much fun?"

"We were dying on Vestrall," Sparky added. "Just like you, despite you always trying to be upbeat."

Payne pointed at Heckler and Turbo. Turbo shook her head. "Us, too. The Vestrall have zero sense of adventure. Parents sent their kids to us to show them how good they have it. We had exactly one repeat customer over the past year, and that guy was a total nutcase."

"I thought you guys were doing okay?"

"We grossly overcharged everyone, so from a monetary standpoint, yes. But what is Vestrall money worth?"

"They don't use money," Payne replied.

"Exactly." Turbo fist-bumped Heckler.

Payne felt better. His team was covered in sweat and already rubbing sore muscles, even though the real pain wouldn't come for some time.

"Get cleaned up and into your uniforms. We'll fold space three days' FTL flight from PX47. You know the SOP. With Lev being combat-ineffective for three days following the fold, we have to jump into the middle of nowhere and make like a hole in interstellar space until his systems come back online. That gives us three days to not kill ourselves while making some improvements in these nasty civilian bodies of ours.

"Once you're cleaned up and dressed, get your happy asses to Medical. I'm sure Lev has something that will expedite the healing and muscle-building process. We don't have time for weeks of breaking our muscles down to build them back up again over another month. And then to chow. We'll talk next steps at that point." Payne gestured with his head. The team snapped to attention before running off.

Payne stayed behind to do another set of curls. Kal and Mary waited.

"I just realized that I haven't fired a weapon in a year." Payne grunted, feeling the power in the one muscle group he hadn't let go to pot.

"It'll come back to you," Mary assured him.

Kal shrugged. "Use a bigger gun that fires more often."

———

"Who the fuck are these people?" Buzz complained.

"I remember when we used to call you 'Fetus,'" Sparky shot back.

"Thanks to not getting anyone killed, we don't have a new team member to wear the nugget title. How about we celebrate that?" Payne asked.

"While we wait in line for chow," Buzz continued. The line stretched to the counter. It moved quickly, though. They'd have their food in five minutes. "Hey! Look who's here."

Buzz pointed at the cook behind the counter, who was berating someone who looked young enough to violate the child labor laws.

Cookie. The cook from the last deployment. "Turkey dinner!" Heckler shouted over the din of a hundred voices.

"You'll get nothing and like it! End of the line with you, heathen!" Cookie yelled back. He worked his way around the counter and the crowd to shake hands with his old friends.

"You made life bearable," Payne told him. "Thanks for coming back."

Cookie looked both ways before answering. "Earth is getting bad. There's nowhere I'd rather be than anywhere other than there."

He backed away with a growing smile. "Good to be back. Bring the Payne!"

"Bring the turkey," Heckler replied.

Turbo punched him.

"I'm still amazed you two didn't blow up a planet," Blinky mumbled.

Payne whispered into Mary's ear, "This group would rather go to war than spend another minute on Earth. We missed something, and it's not good."

Lev, download news and periodical files from the moment we departed. I'd like to look at them later, especially anything that would account for our people's discontent, Payne thought.

I've already done that, Declan. I noticed the same things you did. The new arrivals' thoughts are jumbled but filled with anguish. I will figure it out and get an answer back to you. There is a ship approaching with a delegation from the government. They've requested permission to land.

"How about we fold space instead of taking any more on board? Right now would be good, Lev."

The disorientation unique to the fold drive ran through every flesh-and-blood on board. Payne closed his eyes until the vertigo passed. When he opened them, he found Mary clinging to him. He nudged her.

"That was unpleasant," she muttered.

Those who had never experienced the effect were more incapacitated. Some sat with their heads lolling. Others fought nausea. Their bodies contorted as each waged their individual battle to recover control.

Payne stepped to the front of the dining area. "My name is Declan Payne. The effects will pass quickly. Don't attempt to stand or move until you're able. We have folded space to a location three days' travel by FTL from planet PX47. This ship, *Leviathan,* is on minimal power until it recovers from the energy drain of the fold drive which takes about three days. When power is restored, we will depart at faster-than-light speed for the Rang'Kor's water planet. We have six days of orientation, training, and downtime until we can start our investigation into what happened at PX47. Welcome aboard."

Every member of this group knew who he was. The military had made an icon of him. Maybe his name was on schools, too. That should be in news articles. He'd ask Lev later.

Then again, it was probably better not to know. It had zero bearing on their current mission.

Find the truth about the interaction between the Rang'Kor and the alien ship. Along the way, learn the fate of the water planet's settlers.

"Whoa!" a familiar voice called from the entry to the dining hall.

"Look what the cat dragged in!" Payne hurried to his friend. "How are you feeling, Virge?"

They embraced and held it there. "I'm doing better, Dec. I think the bad days are behind me. Any way I can snag the team's XO position?"

"The ol' ball and chain might have something to say about that."

"Hey, Mary," Major Virgil Dank called.

"Good morning, Virgil. And if you," she glared at Declan, "ever call me that again, I will kick you in the nuts so hard you'll need the Heimlich to get them out of your throat."

She smiled at Dank. "I'm glad you made it. You can XO all you want. You have a solid bromance with my man, but I'm not threatened. And a year off didn't make me any better than I was before. I was a shit XO."

"Damn, Dog! Firing a full broadside. I don't think Virgil's weak heart can withstand the truth missile."

"You call your wife 'Dog?' Way to go, Dec! You were always a class act." He looked at Mary. "Unlike you, who was always a class act."

"Clear as mud. Cookie promised us a turkey dinner," Payne continued.

"He did not," Mary clarified.

"Business as usual, Virge. We're all suffering from our first team workout. You need to get into that. Feel the pain."

"Bring the Payne! Team Payne." They returned to the line. Dank surveyed the filled tables. "Who are all these people?"

"You could pull out my toenails with pliers, and I couldn't tell you."

Mary made her best sour-lemon face. "You two belong together."

Payne grinned. "Nah. I traded up to get you."

"It just gets worse with every new word that tumbles from your mouth." Her eyes wrinkled and her mouth twisted as she tried to reconcile Payne's descent into madness. Marriage—the get-out-of-jail-free card.

Payne took her hand. She had been right a lifetime before when she called him smitten. They smiled at each other but briefly.

Declan's old friend wasn't completely better. Not yet. "You find someone, Virgil?"

"Kind of. Maybe. We'll see. She's somewhere on *Leviathan*. I'll catch up with her when I have free time."

"You wrangled your girlfriend onto the ship?" Payne glanced at his team. "What kind of asshole does that?" He tried to look innocent.

"I learned from the best." Dank's easy smile came back but quickly faded. They collected their meals and moved to a recently vacated table. Cleaning bots whipped through and picked up the refuse, sanitizing the table before they sat down.

The smell of turkey wafted past. Payne looked at the burger and fries on his plate. He tried to find the cook but couldn't spot him to give him the hairy eyeball.

"We're training hard, Virge. We'll probably have four hours of downtime, then go to the range. Most of us haven't fired weapons in a while, but then there's Heckler and Turbo. They have." Payne pointed with his chin at the combat specialists.

"Although we haven't fired the big guns," Blinky interrupted, "we've improved our digital game. Thanks to the differences between Vestrall technology and Lev's, we think we can jailbreak anywhere, anytime."

"Does that work on other Vestrall?" Payne asked.

"Not yet," Blinky replied.

"What if the newcomer is better than the Vestrall?"

Blinky smirked. "Anytime. Anywhere. They haven't run across me and Buzz. Sparky's got game, too. It's looking grim for the bad guys."

Bravado. False or not? Payne couldn't tell. Confidence was important. They'd be going into the unknown. They needed to keep their heads up and believe they could outwit their enemy.

"Lev said the Vestrall hadn't made many improvements since he last saw them."

"Not many is still a great deal more than what we had," Blinky replied.

Payne nodded. He wasn't convinced there was an enemy on whom to try out the team's new skills.

———

When the ship started moving, it did so without fanfare. Those who hadn't been watching didn't notice.

Payne was on the bridge, laughing at some miscreancy of the past about having done something that should have resulted in him getting tossed into the brig.

The admiral laughed only because Payne thought his story was hilarious. Wesson may not have been laughing *with* him.

"We are underway to PX47," Lev announced.

"How long until we get better data on what we'll find there?" Payne asked.

Leviathan had sensors that picked up engine vibrations transmitted outside normal space. Lev had found no discernible energy signatures from the PX47 star system.

"Without engines generating power for propulsion, the vibrations through the void are non-existent. We won't know anything until we enter normal space," Lev explained.

"Three days before we know anything, and when we do, it'll be too late to adjust," Payne lamented. "This sets the standard for going in blind."

"And we can jump out of there in a heartbeat if something isn't to our liking." The admiral watched the odd two-dimensional view on the main screen of the ship, which was traveling at faster-than-light speed. There was no feeling of a ship in motion. The images on the screen were cartoony in their appearance—unfocused points of light that represented stars from a time long past, however many light-years away they were.

Payne strolled around the bridge. Most of the stations had people sitting at them, tapping on the keyboards in the cases of those who hadn't realized they could access them from their minds.

He wasn't pleased. The old days weren't the old days when a small group of intrepid travelers had worked from within the massive ship.

"Lev, how many people are on board?" Payne asked.

"Over two thousand. Such a breath of fresh air, don't you think?"

"You know what I'm thinking," Payne replied. "And it isn't a breath of fresh air. Try to keep the lookie-loos out of my way. I have work to do."

He nodded at the admiral on his way off the bridge. Mary, Kal, and Dank followed. The Cabrizi snapped at various crew members as they passed.

"Get used to them, people," Payne called over his shoulder. "They were here before any of you. Maybe learn some Ebren since that's what they understand."

"What burr is under your saddle?" Kal drawled.

Mary stopped him from climbing into the cart. "No."

The answer to the unstated concern.

"It will take me a while to get used to these people," Payne mumbled. He pulled one of the Cabrizi to him and vigorously scratched the creature's ears.

"Lev, can you keep my husband away from the icky people?"

"Of course. I will move Declan and his closest friends to a deck where you are the only ones there. I'll activate the dining facility, workout facilities, Medical, and the combat range."

Payne admired his friends. Too often, he became immersed and couldn't see the root of what affected him. Mary and Dank had better clarity on the little things, leaving Payne free to think at a more strategic level.

"Are you throwing enough weight?" Payne asked.

Dank knew Payne wasn't talking to him.

"I don't think so. High reps keep a great bikini figure, but I lost too much strength. I'll get it back. Don't worry, Dec."

"I will worry. Three days to splashdown. It could be a nothing burger, but it might require Team Payne to deploy. How can you be ready in three days? Same goes for Byle and Shaolin."

Payne shook his head.

"I let everyone go soft."

"For fuck's sake!" Mary blurted. "We were supposed to be retired. You would have been the biggest dick in the galaxy if you tried to make everyone work out. A nebula-sized throbbing member. And they would have ignored you because they were *retired!*"

"Suits." Dank shrugged. "Put 'em in suits and let them operate like that for the next three days. The combat suit is the great equalizer."

"Sounds like we need to train while suited up. That'll make up for any shortcomings within our time constraints. Good call, you guys. Lev, is my fat-boy suit ready?"

Lev replied, "Yours is ready, although you are hardly fat, Declan. None of your people are fat, only reshaped with time. All the suits are ready and in your area of the hangar. I've moved the crews to the port-side hangar. You will be the only ones on the starboard side."

Payne smiled. "Now you're speaking my language, Lev!"

"I think I've always been speaking your language," the AI replied. "I'll send the others to join you."

Payne stepped aside to let Mary board the cart first.

A minor scrum broke out behind them as Kal wrestled the Cabrizi into the second cart. Dank and Payne climbed in quickly to get underway before the animals broke free and sought human laps for comfort.

The trip was short—up three levels to the hangar bay, where they found peace and quiet in the massive empty space.

Payne strolled across the deck away from the team's area. Mary didn't go with him.

"What's he doing?" Dank asked.

"Declan has been fighting to think like a diplomat for a year. He worked hard, but that's not him. It's not anywhere in his core being to placate people who look down on him. I think he's reveling in the return to normal."

"That doesn't look like reveling to me. It looks like he's moping. Is married life not suiting him?"

"Yes, but no. He needs this. The team, you, me, a crisis. He doesn't want to put me in harm's way, but that isn't his call, now, is it?"

"He's the team leader. Everything is his call," Dank countered.

The Cabrizi bolted past, heading toward the far end. Kal let them go.

Mary shook her head. "We merry band, a dozen strong and no more. Bring the Payne, even the score. Fight to survive, fight to win, end the war. We merry band."

"I expect there's music to that." The doors opened and carts brought in the rest of the team, depositing them in front of the gear cage where their suits stood in a neat line. Dank shouted, "Bring the Payne!"

The team repeated the call to arms.

"Come on, Dec. Let's do this thing," Mary called loud enough for him to hear. When he turned around, he was smiling. Together, they strolled to the team's changing area.

Mary hesitated, but Payne dropped his clothes in two seconds. The rest of the team stripped with equal alacrity.

"What's up?" Payne asked.

"I haven't been naked in front of anyone but you for the last year," she explained. Payne looked at himself as he stood in the buff, one hand on his combat suit. He scowled.

"The scars." His body had been through the war, burns, blast holes, and cuts. His was worse than anyone's except Kal's. The Ebren warrior had suffered more injuries than the rest of the team combined, although his fibrous body made it difficult to discern. Many of the scars had faded over the past year.

The team took turns showing their badges of honor and luck. Buzz pointed at his. "Those damn drone ships!"

The others chuckled. "You were two for two, Buzz," Blinky said.

Turbo and Heckler showed theirs, multiples on their torsos. They also had matching tattoos. "When the hell did you get those?" Payne wondered.

The sun rose behind a red planet. Words circled the image. "Team Payne ended the war. Mars and Coin, 1/1/1."

Payne made a face and held up a hand. "I don't get it."

Turbo rolled her eyes. "Team Payne, that's us." She rolled her finger in a circle to take everyone in. "We ended the war. Marsha and Cointreau—that's us, in case you forgot our real names." She gave him the side-eye. "We started a new epoch on the first day of peace."

"That's deep," Payne admitted. "I like it." He looked at the group standing about. "Stop fucking off and get dressed. We got shit to do."

The team went about their business. Mary held Payne's eyes as she dropped her jumpsuit. He didn't have to look for her scars. She didn't have any. Her injuries were inside: a busted knee, cracked ribs. Imposter syndrome, thinking she wasn't good enough to be on the team.

And she wasn't if she was only going to be evaluated by her combat skills. However, when it came to stability, she provided the foundation Payne needed. Despite his male desire to protect her, she would be in the middle of it, fighting with the rest of them.

She pulled on her suit, leaving her helmet off while she got through the initial discomfort of the suit connecting to her body.

"I have a proposal. Since you have an XO and since Buzz isn't filling the combat specialist role, I'll work with Heckler and Turbo as a combat specialist. I need to get better at fighting. Put me into the fight."

Payne clenched his jaw.

Heckler frantically looked from face to face. "Hang on a minute. Let's talk about this with cooler heads."

"Heads are plenty cool," Dank replied. "With Kal hauling the plasma cannon, that gives the team four primary combat specialists. That's a lot of firepower. Yes, Dog isn't big and burly like you, Heckler, but neither is Turbo. And none of you are as big as Kal. It's clear that size doesn't matter."

"Unless you're the one tasked with carrying the plasma cannon," Blinky offered. "Then size helps a whole lot."

"I'd say, 'Don't be insubordinate,' but it would be wasted on this mob. Get your helmets on and finish your diagnostics. No carts for us. We're running to the range, where we're going to blow the crap out of some shit. We move in three."

Payne continued with his sour expression. Dank explained, "XO's job is to assign the team members into the best positions that suit the mission. Blinky and Buzz working together in the digital sphere is optimal. Four combat specialists to secure our position and two experts in ship's systems to work with Blinky and Buzz and Sparky to make sure we always have comms. That leaves you and me to smoke and joke."

He locked his helmet into place and dialed up a direct link to the team lead, Major Payne.

"I'll watch over her, Dec. Nothing will happen to her without it happening to me first. I can't lose anyone else. I just can't."

He didn't have to say it would destroy him to see more team-mates sent to their final resting place in the nearest star.

Payne nodded. He would worry. That was the challenge of having his other half on the team. The Fleet had rules about fraternization, but those were tossed out the nearest airlock when married couples were recalled to duty.

He activated his team-wide channel. "Listen up, people. We're not the same steely-eyed SOFTies we were when we ended the war. Not on the outside, anyway. On the inside, there's none better. Who has more experience than us? No one, that's who. Who knows that every single member of this team will have their back? We do because we've all put our lives on the line for each other.

"I don't want anything to happen to Dog, of course. She makes me whole. And I don't want anything to happen to Buzz, or Turbo, or Byle, or any of you because you make Team Payne whole. We're practicing in suits because we aren't up for any actions without them, but we'll keep working on getting in shape because a soft body will succumb more easily to an injury. None of you wants me to go berserker because you got hurt. I'm too old for that crap.

"Measured engagement. The worst part about this upcoming mission is that we don't know what we're going to face. We're going in blind, which means we need to be ready for anything. And the worst part? We might never get off this ship, but don't let it be said that Team Payne wasn't ready. Our number has been called, boys and girls. Time to stand up and be counted. We run to the front end of the ship and back here, then to a deck that Lev is going to give just to us. Suits for the next three days except when you're sleeping or eating."

"You heard the man!" Dank shouted. "Four and a half kilometers to the bow. I'll give us eight minutes to get there. That's not even thirty-five kilometers an hour. And then eight to get back here. You shouldn't even be breathing hard."

Heckler and Turbo shouted their war cries and raced for the hatch, which popped open and stayed open. Kal wore his upper-body-respiration gear. He didn't need an environmental suit like the others. His body protected him from the extremes of space as long as he had air to breathe.

As physical and bio-engineered a specimen as Kal'faxx was, the team in suits running at full speed forced him to work hard to keep pace. The Cabrizi fell back after the first kilometer. They could sprint faster, but they couldn't maintain that pace.

Heckler grunted and growled as he led the pack.

Payne reviewed the team's vital signs. Everyone was struggling except Heckler, Turbo, and Major Dank. "Dial it back to thirty klicks per, Heckler. Everyone stay together."

"Weakest link..." Turbo started.

"Stow it! I'm the weakest link. What good is it if we get there fast if we're not combat-effective? Thirty is still pushing it. We have three days to reach thirty-five per, and we'll fucking do it carrying our gear. Shut your pieholes and concentrate on running. It'll all be over in fifteen minutes."

Which felt like two hours.

At the end, Payne felt like he was going to collapse. Mary was unable to talk, but she had made it, along with all the others. The first victory for the new Team Payne.

He hoped it wouldn't be the last.

[7]

"Silence isn't always golden. Sometimes it's a stealthy enemy on their way to kill you." –From the memoirs of Ambassador Declan Payne

Team Payne moved into *Ugly 4* in the most orderly manner they could manage.

"No, you have to stay here," Kal told the Cabrizi in Ebren. They didn't listen. They climbed aboard and moved into the clear forward area. Kal hopped up and ran off the ship, then yelled, "*Come!*"

He ran to the hatch and into the corridor. The Cabrizi finally followed him. Once outside, he dodged past them and back into the hangar bay, holding them off as the hatch secured.

"One minute," Lev reported. They were coming out of FTL, and Team Payne was ready to deploy. The two frigate crews were on board their ships and ready to launch as well, along with the two embarked Mosquito squadrons.

Payne wondered how they all fit in the other hangar bay but didn't waste much time thinking about it. He had his team, and in seconds, he'd have his mission. Kal ran back to *Ugly 4* and climbed into his seat.

"Secure the outer doors," Payne ordered, and the two sides of the egg-shaped craft slid into place and locked. The ship pressurized, but the team kept their helmets on. Both hatches became screens that would show the tactical picture. They were blank, waiting to populate the instant the ship's sensors operated in normal space.

"Admiral Wesson to all hands. We'll be dropping out of FTL in thirty seconds in the PX47 system. We are here to gather information and determine what happened. We have to find out whether this alien craft is an enemy or not, and then we have to take that information back to the allied races. Be ready to deploy. Do not engage unless fired upon first. Discretion is the better part of valor. Engines hot. Weapons tight. Stay on your toes, people. In ten, nine..."

He didn't continue the countdown. Everyone on board *Leviathan* would be doing it themselves. The emergence from FTL would be slightly disorienting but nothing like the transition through the fold.

The wave passed quickly. The team stared at the screens. Information started scrolling and tactical icons appeared in red, indicating destroyed craft. Usually, destroyed shipping was scrubbed from the board, but not today. They wanted to know where the debris fields were, along with any live spacecraft.

"No sign of the alien ship," Lev reported.

On the tactical screen, two frigates appeared outside *Leviathan,* and two squadrons of Mosquitos deployed into a DefPat, a defensive patrol.

"Their defensive assets have been eliminated," Payne muttered. He was talking to himself more than the team, but the comm channel was open. "What about the planet? Are the Rang'Kor safe?"

Leviathan accelerated toward PX47. They had their answer in less than twenty seconds. "The population of PX47 appears to be intact. Commodore Freeman has requested to speak with planetary leadership. I'll patch her through."

"We are happy to hear your voices," the commodore began.

"What happened?" the Rang'Kor demanded.

"An alien craft entered your system, and it appears to have destroyed your fleet and your space station. We are here to investigate and provide assistance."

"Contact our families on the homeworld."

"We will contact the first Rang'Kor vessel we come across and ask them to convey your message. Was there an attack on the planet's surface?"

"There was not," the voice answered in a clipped tone, an element of more than Leviathan's translation program. "We lost contact with our station a month ago. We sent a shuttle to the station, only to find it destroyed and all our people dead. The shuttle returned to the surface of the planet since it has no ability to travel in deep space. We request to send a delegation to you to represent our interests as you *investigate*."

Team Payne couldn't see the commodore but understood the expectant look she was giving the Rang'Kor. "Please send your shuttle with the greatest possible speed," she replied smoothly.

The communication closed with a confirmation of the request. The Rang'Kor hadn't agreed to send the shuttle.

"How's the space station?" Payne asked.

Admiral Wesson answered. "Since we probably shouldn't be seen investigating without the Rang'Kor representatives present, deploy in the stealth insertion craft immediately. Take a good look and check back in. You'll need to return as soon as the Rang'Kor are on board."

"Roger," Payne confirmed. "*Ugly 4* is a go."

The ship lifted into the air and maneuvered toward the hangar bay door. It flushed into space and continued at stealth speed, slow but indetectable.

Ugly 4 immediately began corkscrewing toward the target.

"What's going on, Lev?" Payne wondered.

"There is a quantity of debris in space. I will send the maintenance bots to collect it for reuse once you've cleared the field. I have the plans for this style of space station and will start the rebuilding process. If the Rang'Kor agree to the use of scrap material from their cruisers, I'll rebuild the station in its entirety."

Payne didn't care about any of that. "Are there any of those drones in this area?"

"I can't tell," Lev replied. "If there are, then they are blending in well with the wreckage."

"They looked to me like they used ballistic attacks, which means we should find parts and pieces of the alien devices. Follow everything you see from our helmets and let us know what we're looking at."

"Of course," Lev replied, an oft-used phrase.

"Looks like a spacewalk, people," Payne began. "Screen is showing no remaining atmosphere. All surviving areas of the station have vented to space." Payne stood as *Ugly 4* made its final approach. "Stay frosty, people. We don't know what we're going to find out there, but we're looking for what destroyed this place. Evidence we can bring back to Lev for analysis. XO, split the team into pairs and issue their geographic search areas."

"Aye, aye, sir." Dank dissected the debris field, highlighted the largest remaining sections, and designated the pairs. He questioned himself for only an instant about what to do with

Mary, but he put her with Joker and sent them to the surviving upper array.

Payne and Kal had to be together since Kal wouldn't have it any other way.

Heckler with Byle, Buzz with Blinky, and Turbo with Shaolin. Dank took Sparky, who, as the team's engineer, had always been the quiet one. She didn't have any use for being the life of the party, but she was good and had learned enough in the previous year with the Vestrall to be better than nearly all the high-priced engineers who had never left Earth.

Ugly 4 slowed to a stop, bumping the largest remaining section of the station. "We have arrived. There is no gravity or atmosphere. Don't forget where we docked, but I can always come and get you. Your suits are actively pinging."

The side doors slid upward to reveal the darkness of the void, sparkling with the system's K-Class star reflecting off millions of pieces of debris. *Leviathan* loomed nearby. On the other side of the ship, the planet dominated the view, blue on blue, with the typical fifty-percent cloud coverage. Wisps of white drifted lazily above the one ocean of PX47.

The team unbuckled and pushed into space, their HUDs guiding them beyond *Ugly 4*. Heckler and Byle entered the station directly beside the ship.

Mary and Joker headed upward to the communications gear on the detached top of the space station's spire. Payne waited, trying hard not to stare after his wife.

Dank pinged him. "You gotta get beyond that, Dec," the XO advised as if he were reading Payne's mind.

"On my way, Virge," Payne growled, more at himself than anything else. No one should have to tell him to do his job. "Keep your head up. Even casually floating debris could be a hazard, although the stuff around here has no momentum. We should be fine. Find me something I can put my hands on."

"Working on it. Dank, out."

Payne pushed out, using his pneumatic jets to gain a minimal amount of speed. A short tether gave Kal something to hang onto since he had no mobility assistance. The unit on his back and over his head only provided air for him to breathe, nothing more.

"We have to get that fixed, big dog," Payne told the Ebren warrior.

"Get what fixed, boss man?"

"Your ability to motorvate in open space."

"Wouldn't want to lack motorvation," Kal drawled.

Payne wasn't sure if Kal understood or if he was joking. The Ebren remained an enigma in many ways. Lev had never come clean about what he'd put into Kal's mind. Given the size of the Ebren's head, Payne suspected he knew a great deal more than he let on and that Lev had put that knowledge in his mind. On Ebren, Kal had been restricted to fighting and had not been given the opportunity to expand his intellect.

The far side of the core module was mostly untouched. Payne scanned the surfaces. "The attack came from the other side. This side is mostly clean. There are ruptures, but they blasted outward." He moved up and down the section to capture high-resolution images of the entire area before moving on.

When he finished, it was time to catch up with his people. He activated the team channel. "Report."

———

Heckler led the way into the oversized space of a shattered and empty corridor. It led to side rooms whose purpose was no longer discernible because of the damage from explosive decompression. He used the light on his railgun to scan the area. His suit lights provided general illumination, and his HUD provided the full scan experience, incorporating infrared and ultraviolet into the data filling his tactical display.

But Heckler trusted the Mark One eyeball—what he could see with his own orb. The wireline overlays showed framework, supports, and stanchions, things upon which equipment had been mounted before it was blasted into space.

Heckler pointed, and Byle followed as they entered what might have been a storage area. A quick trip around the area yielded nothing except the remnants of a trough and a second room behind the first that was just as empty. In the next room down the corridor, they found the heavy doors common on a command deck.

"Lev, you have the diagram of the station. Are we looking at the command deck?" Heckler asked.

"Based on reconciliation of the elements you've passed thus far—" Lev started.

"Jumping Jack Flash, Lev. Just say yes or no."

"Yes, this is the command deck, the bridge. This section survived as much as it did because it was heavily armored."

Heckler looked up and down the corridor. "This is all that survived from what was *heavily armored?*" He looked through the opening between the heavy hatches, then gripped one side with his hands, and with his feet on the other side, used the power assist from his suit to twist it out of the way.

Byle made to enter, but Heckler stopped her. "I'll go first." Looking down the barrel of his weapon, he stalked into the space.

Most of the equipment was in place, but the screens had shattered, and the lack of power made everything look old and cast-off. "Rang'Kor are octopus-like, aren't they? A little soft and squishy?" He knew what they were. He'd met them on *Leviathan.*

"Yes. They do not have bones."

"I think this is one, or at least a smear of one." Goo had splattered across the deck and frozen in place. Heckler directed his suit to scan the material.

"Yes. That used to be a Rang'Kor," Lev confirmed.

"It's frozen, but I won't step on it. I wouldn't have wanted to be them when those aliens attacked. Maybe you can recover this and what else is in here and reconstitute it for the families or whatever ritual the Rang'Kor have for their dead." He pulled himself away before kicking off the bulkhead to move farther into the surviving bridge.

"Heckler!" Byle blurted, staying clear of the remains. "You've grown soft."

"I always cared but never thought it worth mentioning. We had a mission to carry out. I focused on getting our people in and out since I didn't want anyone to see that I liked them. Don't repeat that, or I'll kick your ass."

"There's the Heckler Koch we know." Byle propelled herself toward a rent in the bulkhead, spun to arrive feet-first, and locked her magnetic boots down the instant she hit. She studied and scanned an object sticking out of the wall. "I think we have what we're looking for."

"Don't touch it!" Heckler called, pulling himself toward her.

"How stupid do you think I am?" She waved her hand at Heckler to keep a distance. A sword-like blade protruded half a meter through an armored bulkhead. One of three prongs faced forward, with a round mass behind the blades. "Looks like depleted uranium, breaking on impact to yield sharp edges and pyrophoric residue. Radiation levels are consistent with background radiation; nothing more toxic than that. I need to get a look at the other side. Lev, guide us around."

She moved her head to where she could peer through the opening.

"I think the other side is open to space." She switched to the team channel just as Payne requested a report. "Byle here. I think we have one, almost completely intact, wedged into the armored bulkhead of the command deck. Tagged it for Lev. Going outside to get a better look at the business side of this thing."

Turbo and Shaolin reported finding nothing but station remnants no bigger than a dinner plate. Buzz and Blinky requested more time to search where they thought the computer core was located. Dank and Sparky continued to explore a secondary section.

"I'm coming around to meet you," Payne replied. He followed the vector Lev provided. He approached the device, which was the same color as the station—a shade known as battleship gray.

It was also the color of an Ebren.

As Payne waited for the weapons specialist to appear, he examined the device from a safe distance, collecting data for Lev. Byle appeared, with Heckler close behind. He drifted away from the station as if providing oversight. Heckler faced the device rather than looking away. The threat was there, wedged into an exposed bulkhead, not in the void. *Leviathan* was at their backs. He would let nothing happen to them.

Heckler trusted very few people. As a combat specialist, he could never leave his people exposed. Fight hard. Fight to win.

He and Turbo lived by the same creed.

Byle moved close, angling around the drone to get scans from all angles. "Nothing is penetrating the outer layer," she reported. "That might account for how deadly they are as ballistic weapons."

She tentatively reached out to caress the smooth metal. "Can't tell if it's cast, machined, or three-D-printed. I suspect the latter. I think these are exhaust ports on the back side, like the pneumatic jets on our suits. Just enough to propel the unit forward." She was so close to the device her face shield touched it, so she backed up a centimeter. "Multi-directional exhaust nozzles for attitude control. Thrust and vector in one small package. No need for flight control surfaces. Suggests space employment only. The three points angling forward look to have the sole purpose of penetrating a target."

They looped from the outside of the rounded base to a point in front with a saber-like curve, a three-bladed space scimitar dealing death to the unwary.

Tens of thousands of them had been unleashed and delivered without mercy.

"Can you get it out of there?" Payne wondered.

Byle tugged on it without committing. "Seems wedged tight. Maybe Lev can deploy a few maintenance bots to recover it."

"Prudent." Payne was disappointed. He wanted his team to return triumphantly, carrying the enemy's weapon with him.

From the instant he saw the device, he had known this alien was an enemy. Anyone who would deploy such a weapon had no interest in making friends.

"Why did they attack the station after already neutralizing the cruisers?" Payne wondered. No one had an answer. Ebren space stations had minimal armaments, almost to the point of being useless. The Rang'Kor might have dismantled what was left on board, or the Ebren might have taken it with them when they turned the station over to its new tenants.

No matter what, the station shouldn't have been attacked. It was little more than Flight Control to coordinate traffic to and from the planet's surface.

Payne started to get angry.

There was a twinkle from the device, little more than the system's sun glinting off a speck of glass.

Byle recoiled and kicked off from the bulkhead to get away

from the device. "It's alive!" she shouted over the team's comm channel. It started vibrating and jerking in an effort to pull itself free.

"No, you don't!" Payne told it. He headed for it as it broke free from the station. It spun as he approached.

Payne instantly rethought his strategy since the device was a hundred times more maneuverable than he was. He maxed his jets to angle away from the device. It accelerated toward him.

A great figure pushed off the station and intercepted it, pushing it off-course. Kal'faxx wrapped a tether around one of the forward-pointing arms.

Payne activated his magnetic boots to pull himself to the station, jerking since he hit the metal harder than he expected. He pulled the tether in and twisted to set the device on an arc instead of straight toward him. Kal had one arm wrapped around the deadly business end while he reached behind the weapon with his other arm to redirect the exhaust. The weapon started to corkscrew through space. Payne froze, unable to find an avenue of escape.

With a final erratic move, the device lunged forward. Kal pushed off, redirecting it into the side of the station. The pinpoint of light in the after section faded to black, and it returned to being nothing more than a projectile.

Payne leaned back, his boots still magnetically coupled to the bulkhead. He let his helmet bump against the cold steel. "Thanks, Kal."

"I live to serve," the Ebren deadpanned.

"Lev, can you give us a tactical assist to recover that thing? And why in the hell did it target me? A whole bunch of us were floating around."

"What is different about your suit compared to the others in the area? And the Rang'Kor are on their way from the planet's surface."

"Command channels, feeds, scanners. Checking your suit. It looks like you also had IFF active," Lev explained. Identification friend or foe, a system to keep from being targeted by friendly forces. "And no one else did."

"I don't remember turning on the IFF." Kal offered a hand to pull the major upright. "Complete the search of your assigned sector, and then recover to *Ugly 4*."

"Need another fifteen," Blinky replied.

"Same here," Dank added.

"Keep the comm channel open, and if you run across one of those drones, stay the hell away from it. Mark it for recovery and move on."

"We're in!" Blinky cried it. "Take that, Diaper Drawers. You flea-infested quasar! You pustulant feculence. Navel-lint-eating, snot-gobbling…"

"*BLINKY!*" Payne interrupted. "Get on with it and stow the mind-numbing commentary."

"You just said to keep the channel open. We used to be free to speak our minds, but then we got drafted. Yanked from our beds in the middle of the night and run through the wringer. Do you know how much I've sweated in the last week?"

"I don't give a flying monkey fuck how much you sweated," Heckler noted. "The major is too nice to say it."

"I'm not, really," Payne interjected quietly. "What'd you find, Buzz, since Blinky is tongue-tied?"

"Looks like the original data on the cruiser attack, which we've already seen, but there's tactical data attached to this version. And then it includes the ship's approach to the station that took nearly four days since the ship traveled at ninety-eight percent of the speed of light."

"Nothing could survive that acceleration," Dank remarked. Payne had been thinking about it since the mindless drone went after him. If the alien ship could be penetrated and deprogrammed, Team Payne could stop future attacks without asking Lev to help. Minimal damage.

But Lev had helped before when attacks were conducted by drone ships. No life had been lost while defeating those vessels.

"Were there any other scans from the station to confirm the existence of life on that ship?" Payne asked.

"Inconclusive. They scanned until the last second."

"Look for silicon." Payne had a hunch.

"High levels of silicon," Blinky replied. "Transfer to Lev is complete. Returning to *Ugly 4*. How did you know?"

"What can survive five-hundred-gee acceleration? Or a thousand? I think we've found a life form that is not carbon-based. Break, break. Virgil, report."

"Attempting to access a secured space. Scanners tell me there is no air within, but there is organic matter."

"What do you think you'll find in there?"

"Bodies," Virgil replied. "Everyone deserves to be brought home, even if they're dead."

They had had to leave most of Major Dank's team behind during Operation Knifefight on E4135, an Ebren station identical to this one. Payne didn't stop him.

"Recover as soon as you can, Virge. Everyone else, *Ugly 4*. Lev, prepare to receive the dead."

"A maintenance bot has been dispatched."

The team returned to the insertion craft. Payne waited outside until Mary and Joker appeared from the farthest point away from *Ugly 4*. The comms gear was at the top of the station's spindle, and the majority of the pair's time had been spent in transit to and back from it.

The two inverted and touched down softly on the remains of a corridor they were using as an access platform for the insertion craft. Payne nodded at his wife before they headed into the ship. "Anything?"

"Dead metal and carbon fiber, shattered. Not a single usable thing left," Mary reported. Joker gave the thumbs-up.

"I wonder if they hit that first to cut the station's link? Although by the time the alien ship arrived over PX47, any communication from the station would have been meaningless."

"An ode to mortality. A cry for help that wouldn't come. Panic. Despair. Maybe the alien feeds off emotions," Mary offered.

"Interesting. I'm not sure. The Rang'Kor deaths came too quickly. If they wanted more fear, I would think they'd have drawn it out more. Many of the crew probably never knew what happened. We'll think on it and get Lev's take once he's looked at the station's data. We should snag the computer cores from the cruisers if they're still intact, and they should be. Those things are armored against catastrophic destruction."

Lev closed the outer doors, which brought the tactical screens into view. A shuttle from PX47 showed fifteen minutes until arrival. Lev had designated the port hangar bay for their reception. That left the starboard bay for Team Payne to return unnoticed.

Blinky and Buzz maintained a running dialogue about the station's records as they pored through the database. Payne was left to his thoughts as he tried to rationalize the alien's attack on PX47, and more importantly, what the next steps would be.

After ten minutes, the craft's outer door opened. Major Dank and Sparky hovered outside. They were empty-handed.

"Didn't get in?"

"We were able to get inside. Eight Rang'Kor, frozen solid. I tagged them for Lev to pick up."

Eight. The same number as were left behind on E4135.

"I'm sure they'll appreciate that." Payne had a hard time getting the words out. "I'll see to it personally, Virge."

"No, Dec. I'll take care of it. This one's on me."

Payne had never lost a team member. He hadn't had to suffer like Major Dank, who'd lost not one but two teams to make sure that Payne completed his mission.

Ugly 4 took off and accelerated along a seemingly erratic course as it navigated through the debris field. It stopped and floated as the Rang'Kor shuttle closed with *Leviathan*. *Ugly 4* continued once the shuttle was inside.

"Bring the bodies into this bay," Dank requested. Once *Ugly 4* landed, he walked in the opposite direction of the team. To a person, they watched him go. Mary held tightly to Payne's arm. He cracked the seal on his helmet and pulled it free before facing his team.

"Get your trash off and back into uniform. Heckler, Turbo, Byle, and Shaolin, give Major Dank a hand. Whatever he needs. Blinky, Buzz, and Sparky, go over that data. Give me something I can use to help us when we have to face that bastard. Joker..." Payne paused as he tried to think of what else needed to be done. "Do something important. Lieutenant Payne and I will do ambassador stuff."

The smiles at the title quickly faded as the team broke off to perform their separate tasks. The grim work facing Major Dank didn't call for jocularity but somber respect for the major and for the dead.

Declan and Mary dressed quickly and hurried into the corridor to get assaulted by the Cabrizi. Kal intervened, pushing them and playing.

"He saved my life," Payne told his wife. "That thing came after me, and Kal fought it in space, using a little of the super-structure for leverage."

"You've said he's the greatest warrior in the galaxy. He keeps proving it." Mary shrugged as if it had been nothing. "You better not die, dumbass. I'm too young to be a widow."

"You're hot. You'll find someone else."

She turned on him, fury in her eyes. "Don't even joke about that!" She clenched her fists, and her muscles tightened. Payne thought she was going to hit him, but she didn't. She closed her eyes and spoke softly. "You don't know how I feel, Dec. I've spent my entire life looking for you, only to find that you are the target of every alien out there. They all want to finish Declan Payne. We've only just started to live, Dec. Can't you be more normal?"

Payne bit his lip. "You didn't fall in love with normal. You got what you wanted. A man who fights other men while naked. The supreme leader of the seven races one day, and Major Dickhead the next. I think we balance those competing lifestyles well. It's a whirlwind, but it's the life we've been given. We don't have a choice to step away from it. That's not who we are.

"Now, buck up. We have to meet the Rang'Kor, and if you cry, they might try to wipe the tears with those spiky tentacles of theirs." Payne smiled while caressing the smooth skin of her face.

"Give me a good pirate's scar. Argh!" She looked away.

"We're going to survive. That's also in our nature, Dog. Stay sharp because I have a bad feeling about this one. At least with the Vestrall, I could see their shortcomings. The Progenitors gave us their foibles, and the Vestrall still had them. Thousands of years of evolution, and they still had their egos helping them make bad decisions. I could work with that."

"Firsthand experience. You're an old pro," Mary quipped. She took his hand and interlaced her fingers with his. "You frustrate the hell out of me, Declan Payne."

"Me, too. It's a gift. Now it's time to focus, Dog. Rang'Kor. Relations. Save the day. They can owe us. That kind of stuff."

The cart didn't take them to the bridge but to a meeting room one level up. It was the one they'd used in a previous meeting with the Rang'Kor, the Ebren, and the Vestrall. Lev didn't feel the need to show them any more of the ship than their people had already seen.

Or maybe he was trying to make them feel comfortable.

The Rang'Kor didn't look comfortable. None of them sat in the oversized chairs that would have accommodated their bodies. Payne hesitated at the doorway. They clicked and whistled, and Lev instantly translated their words into something Declan, Mary, and Kal could understand.

"We demand to know what is being done about the ones who attacked us," the leader began.

From Payne's perspective, he looked no different from the others except that he moved forward, using four of his eight tentacles for perambulation.

They know you've been to the remnants of the station, Lev told him.

Thanks, Lev. I shall adjust, Payne replied. The Progenitors had mastered the science behind telepathy, and it was built into the ship. Lev knew what everyone was thinking at all times. No one needed to call for anything besides having the thought in their minds.

Payne gestured for their guests to sit, but they didn't, so Payne continued to stand. "We found remnants of your people on the station. For some, their deaths were ugly."

"Once the body dies, the soul is released back to Almighty Rang. You can dispose of the refuse. It is meaningless to us."

Payne thought about how the team had avoided stepping on the frozen splatter out of respect. That was human faith, not the Rang'Kor's. He still had no desire to step on or in anyone's remains.

"We also found eight that appeared to be completely intact but frozen. Shall we dispose of them, too?" Payne wondered.

"Intact? No! They are still alive, then. We need to warm

them slowly within a vitamin-enriched water bath. Where are they?"

Lev, tell Virgil not to defrost the octo of octos, Payne thought.

Just in time, Declan.

"We need Rang'Kor expertise to bring your people out of their cryogenic state. Please, come with me." Payne walked briskly out of the room to find a cart for the humans and open carts that would be comfortable for the Rang'Kor.

The Cabrizi sniffed and snorted. The Rang'Kor ignored them. With razor-bladed tentacles and rubbery skin, they had no reason to fear the animals. Kal kept them under control, pushing them toward a second cart reserved for them. The Cabrizi were riding more often these days. Retirement had made them appreciate the finer things in life.

Life. Eight souls that didn't pass on. Hope danced on his heart and lightened his step.

"They're alive," he whispered.

[8]

"When you stop respecting the dead, you stop living."
–From the memoirs of Ambassador Declan Payne

"I hope the Rang'Kor come out of it all right," Mary said. It was hard to find hope within catastrophic destruction.

"If they can freeze themselves to survive... Lev, take us to the first engagement. There might be survivors on the cruisers."

"Harry and I both agree. Getting underway immediately. Additionally, I've asked the Rang'Kor for permission to use the cruiser wreckage to help rebuild the station, and they have agreed. We'll pull everything aboard to make it easier to examine.

"Sounds like some good news has bubbled out of a cesspool of evil."

"I think that's overly dramatic. We don't know the visitor's motivation for doing what it did," Lev replied.

"It didn't try to kill *you*, Lev. Even your medical mastery wouldn't have been able to save me if that thing had stabbed a hole through me."

"That doesn't make it evil any more than you. Why,

Declan? Why did it attack? We need to find the answer to this question. I will help, but I'm not at war with them."

"Not *yet*, Lev. I think you will be, soon enough. Any newcomer trying to eradicate the spacefaring is an enemy to the seven races. We're no longer constrained to our planets. Thanks to the Vestrall portal system, we're not even constrained to our star systems, even with the most rudimentary space travel."

"Do we *know* that they are trying to eradicate space travel? The information we have is far too limited to jump to such a conclusion, but I will continue to analyze the data from the station and from the intact device. We have time. We'll reach the cruiser debris field in fifteen minutes."

"Recall the team and have them suit up. We need to be ready to deploy. Did we recover the frigates?"

"Not yet. Harry suggested they remain over the planet. The Mosquitos are on board and ready to launch upon our arrival."

Payne stared into the distance, lost in thought. He didn't know what to say to convince Lev since he was the one who needed convincing. More data. How many more would have to lose their lives?

How many had lost their lives so far?

Combatants. Warships and a space station that managed the warfighters. No one on the planet had been harmed.

Payne. Attacked for reasons unknown. Or was it because he was the one giving the orders? The same as the space station.

End the enemy's ability to conduct war.

Cut off the head and the body dies.

The population on the planet had survived unscathed. They had not made war upon the alien ship.

"Dammit, Lev! Can't you let someone be angry?"

"You were angry, and now that you are not. You can see that I might not be wrong. But you might not be wrong either. We need more information to make a reasoned decision about this alien ship."

"What was its course? Were you able to project a flight path once it left the system, and does it have FTL?"

"The trajectory the ship followed into the system and past PX47 would have taken it toward Berantz space. Since we've not heard from the Berantz, the ship might have already reached them, which suggests the alien ship has faster-than-light capability."

"And then we'll have to decide if we follow them at FTL or try to jump in front of them, but calculating three days at best case could put us in peril if we guess wrong."

"That would be my concern should the alien turn out to be hostile," Lev replied.

"You're killing me, Lev. If it perceives us as a military craft, then it'll attack. Although you're a pacifist, you do have a great deal of weaponry on board. You replaced the two worldkillers, didn't you?"

"Those weapons are part of my standard complement."

"You don't sound as confident as you used to. What if this other ship is a doomsday weapon like you? Are you guys going to hang out, talk about the good ol' times, enjoy tea and crumpets?"

"I've never had a crumpet, let alone enjoyed it, but there's nothing like a good cup of proper tea," Lev replied. The carts pulled into the hangar bay, where maintenance bots were setting up a contained space to fill with water.

"Look at you, Lev! Making jokes during a life-or-death conversation. We can't fight that ship if it's a doomsday weapon."

"I am torn, Declan. I will contemplate this further. I will also get Davida's input on the matter. There are too many unknowns, but your theory about the alien ship is supported by existing data. *Ugly 4* is ready to launch."

The humans jumped from the cart. Kal ran after them, as did the Cabrizi. He detoured toward the corridor, but the Cabrizi were onto him. They stayed with the team.

The major and the lieutenant were the last ones dressed. Kal tried to collect the Cabrizi, but they were having none of it, dancing out of reach.

"Put them in the suits, and let's go!" Payne yelled before snapping his helmet into place.

Lev had made space suits for the creatures, but they had resisted earlier efforts to put them on.

The team captured the beasts as the two jumped into the insertion craft. They couldn't bite through the armor; otherwise, there would have been injuries. Payne put his helmet in his seat and got face to face with the Cabrizi.

"Settle down!" he roared, then grabbed them by their collars and led them out. Kal picked up one and carried him to the cage, and Payne carried the second one, counting on the power of the suit to keep him from getting away.

Mary ran to help.

They shoved the back paws into the suit legs, then folded it up the animal's waist. After a quick scrum to get the front legs in, they secured it around the beast's neck. Last on was the elongated clear helmet. Once they were done, they turned the Cabrizi loose. It stood stock-still.

"The corridor is looking pretty good right about now, huh?" Payne asked the creature.

They helped Kal with the second one. When both were suited up, they led their reluctant charges to *Ugly 4* and deposited them inside. Their whimpers and whines penetrated the helmets and filled the inside of the insertion craft. The outer doors closed.

"Tactical situation!" Payne snarled. The screens showed the area around them. There was little debris since it had scattered over the past month. Maneuvering vessels maintained momentum through their destruction.

"Energy signature, minimum power," Lev reported. *Ugly 4* lifted off and exited the hangar bay. An inset from the rear view showed the Rang'Kor delegation helping Major Dank deposit their frozen personnel in the water.

Payne turned his attention back to what was in front of them.

"Two by two, same as before."

Sparky raised her hand. She'd been with Dank.

"You're with me and Kal." Payne used his helmet's HUD to interface with the tactical screen, something Dank had done on the last mission. He highlighted where each group should go.

Four of the cruisers had suffered catastrophic damage that had to include power plants going critical, but two of the cruisers had major sections intact. Payne, Kal, and Sparky took the biggest one. He put Buzz and Blinky and Turbo and Shaolin on the main section and sent Heckler and Byle and Mary and Joker to the smaller section from the second cruiser.

"Lev will drop us first and then you four. Keep your eyes peeled for any of those drones. If you see one, tag it on the tactical display, and then steer clear. We don't need any more of those things on board *Leviathan*. If you haven't heard, the frozen Rang'Kor are still alive. If you find any intact, tag them for retrieval. *Leviathan* will return them to the tank, where they'll be defrosted and rehydrated."

"Dehydrated Rang'Kor. Does it make good jerky?" Heckler quipped.

"They are allies, Heckler. I'm sure smoked Rang'Kor, where the smoke is from a burning ship, isn't the safest thing to ingest, so no eating the people we've come here to rescue. Yes, I think they'd notice if a tentacle were missing. Stay frosty, people. We don't know what's out there but consider this a search and rescue mission."

The team gave their affirmatives as the side hatches popped open.

Kal looked at Payne and pointed at the Cabrizi.

"Fine, tether them to Sparky."

"Say what?" Sparky sounded less than amused. "Those things hate me."

"I can tether them to Kal, who's tethered to me. I have no desire to be a space bolo. At least they can't bite you."

Kal went to work attaching a tether to each and clipping them to Sparky's suit.

"You're going to owe me for this," she grumbled.

"Maybe they'll never want to come on a mission again. That is my hope, and if you are instrumental in that, I will be forever in your debt."

"And me," Kal agreed. "It's not safe for them out here. They're terrified."

"Be careful what you ask for, dumbasses," Payne told the creatures. "You might get it."

He pushed out of *Ugly 4* slowly. The Cabrizi tried to resist getting yanked into space, but they were powerless against zero-gee. Sparky jerked and twisted as she adjusted her jets to compensate for their inertia.

Payne hit the outer hull and locked his boots down. Kal flew into him, and the two tangled briefly. They freed themselves, and Payne took a step forward. Sparky hit the cold metal and immediately pulled the tethers hand over hand to bring the Cabrizi to her. They touched down much more gently than Kal had rammed into Payne. She pushed the animals out of arms' reach and wrapped the tethers tighter to keep them close.

"Thanks, Sparky. Those two are pains in the ass, but I like them."

"Me, too," Kal added.

Payne clomped across the hull to a massive gash across the metal, where the devices had hit it with deadly force at a steep angle. Payne leaned down to get a better look across the cruiser's remaining superstructure.

"See this, Kal? It's like the ship avoided taking any direct hits."

Payne led the way through the opening to find a double bulkhead that could act as an airlock. With Kal's help, they lifted the outer emergency bulkhead. Sparky limboed underneath, dragging the Cabrizi through with her. Payne went after her while Kal held the bulkhead. On the other side. Payne gripped it as well and used the power augmentation from the suit to remain steady. Kal eased underneath, and together they lowered the wall into place.

Sparky checked the panel that showed environmental status. "First, let me say I'm impressed this thing is live, but second, power is providing heat and air to the interior space. They must have some engineer in there. It's been a month?"

"And the ship is shredded. I hope they're alive since they've earned it. They won't be cryogenically stored with that temp since it's above freezing."

Sparky and Payne used their suits' air to equalize the pressure with that shown in the inner compartment.

When the panel changed from a crosshatch to a solid pattern, the inner bulkhead released but didn't lift.

"Minimal power." Payne took one side and Kal the other, and they started to lift. When the bulkhead was open half a meter, a laser beam from inside danced off Payne's armor. A second laser licked into Kal's leg. He grunted and dodged back, leaving Payne with the bulkhead's full load. Without the motors to drive it open, the default was closed. Payne fought the locks. The Cabrizi flailed and pushed off the bulkhead behind Sparky and shot underneath the open just before Payne let go.

"We're humans!" Sparky bellowed through her speakers. She dove to put her armored body between the opening and Kal's legs. "Cease fire! Cease. Fire."

"The Cabrizi!" Kal howled. The beasts were on the other side of the bulkhead. Payne started losing his grip.

More lasers licked at his armor. Kal kicked off the outer bulkhead but was stopped by Sparky being in the way. She crawled toward the opening.

The lasers stopped firing.

Kal pulled himself toward Payne using their tether. He braced himself where he could help lift the bulkhead.

"Stop!" Sparky yelled from the other side. "Thank you."

The bulkhead unhitched from the actuators. Payne and Kal slammed it into the ceiling.

On the other side, a gray Rang'Kor held a laser pistol in a tentacle that drooped farther each passing moment.

Payne stepped through the opening and removed his helmet. Kal nursed his wounds, but the Cabrizi wanted vengeance. "Settle down," Payne told them, patting their helmeted heads. "I'm Ambassador Declan Payne, and we're here from Earth to help. How many survived the attack?"

"I've put the others in stasis as there wasn't enough air or water for all of us. I've been trying to bring the engines online. Trying..."

The Rang'Kor relaxed, and his pistol floated free.

"I'm Captain Pel'Rok. I surrender my ship and crew to you." His eyes rolled back, then he regained control and forced himself back into the moment.

"No. You have saved your ship and your people. There's a

Rang'Kor delegation on board *Leviathan,* and that's where we need to go. Do you have a space suit?"

The captain reached into a nearby recess. "No air or water remains."

"We can pump a limited amount of air into your suit. You can do without water for a few minutes more, can't you?" Payne moved closer to the captain. The pallor of his skin suggested he was much closer to death than any of his frozen crew.

The Rang'Kor snorted. "I've done without for this long. What's a few minutes more?"

Sparky pulled herself close to him and hooked her suit to his to pump a minimal amount of air into the tank. Thanks to the Blaze coordination, their suits had the right adaptors for the connection. Lev had thought far enough ahead to make the moment possible.

Thanks, Lev, Payne thought. *Now, let's bring these people home. We'll depressurize this section and open the ship to space.*

"How many of your crew are on ice?" Payne asked.

"Forty-two out of a crew of two hundred and seventy."

"It's forty-two more than the other five ships, Captain. Whatever you did to keep the drones from slamming directly into your ship saved it and them. I'm sorry it took us so long to get here, but your plight and *Leviathan's* availability intersected at Earth a very short while ago. We came as soon as we heard."

"It is all right, Ambassador Payne." The captain had difficulty stuffing his hardened tentacles into a suit made for a Rang'Kor with more flexibility. "We keep to ourselves, usually. I'm surprised you found out at all."

Payne moved forward to help the captain. "You don't sound like a Rang'Kor."

"I've had a month alone to reflect on our isolationist and standoffish ways. We might not have chosen the best path for our people. Live alone, and you die alone."

With Payne's help, the captain suited up. He had enough air for fifteen minutes.

"We'll depressurize this section and then bring your people out. Where are they?"

"One section down. I put them there, moved the atmosphere to this level, and vented it to space. Without atmosphere, there was no explosive decompression. I have to assume they are still there. I have no way to check."

"Lev, one section down. It's already vented to space. Can you gain access?" A three-dimensional wire diagram appeared on Payne's HUD. The section was highlighted, and an arrow pointed at the opening. "Thanks, Lev."

Payne put the captain's helmet into place and secured it.

"I will have to widen the access but will do so momentarily."

Payne switched to the team channel. "Turbo and Shaolin, give Lev a hand opening that access point and moving the survivors to *Leviathan*. Location is on your HUD. We have forty-three survivors on the big section. Mary, what did you find on your end?"

"This superstructure is open to space. No pockets, no bodies. This is a dead hunk of metal. Four of us are returning to *Ugly 4*."

"Blinky and Buzz. Tell me you have the computer core."

"Not yet, Major," Buzz replied.

"Can you unlink the core so we can take it with us? We need to analyze the alien's attack patterns, along with all systems that were active during that time and anything else the data might show. We have the best people to look it over."

The Rang'Kor moved to the side of the corridor, where a computer access screen was located. He had trouble lifting a tentacle. Payne helped the captain.

"I'm going to vent this space and raise the bulkheads. Then I'll release the computer core. Your people will be able to pull it free with minimal effort." Payne secured his helmet with a glance at Kal, who gave him the thumbs-up, although a pool of blood floated around his injured leg.

With swirls and slashes instead of the human version of tapping keys, the air rushed from the space through vents overhead. There was no alarm. There was no warning of any kind.

The captain had operated this section at the bare minimum, but it had kept him alive. "How close were you to getting a propulsion system operational?" Payne asked while they waited for the bulkheads to rise. The light on the panel faded as the power drained.

"No engine. My solar sail depended on me spending more time in the suit than I had. I was dead in the water. I was trying to develop an electrostatic discharge to create a rhythmic locomotion like a Rang'Kor swimming in icy water, but I needed more power. I was not yet out of options."

"I admire the hell out of you, Captain Pel'Rok. Let's get you to *Leviathan* and into the water tank."

The captain fainted and would have collapsed had there been gravity. The Cabrizi moved aside as Payne pulled the captain through the opening and into space. Kal pushed off to put the minimal amount of drag on the tether attached to Payne's suit. With a Cabrizi under each arm, Sparky joined them.

Leviathan loomed large nearby. They skipped past *Ugly 4* and headed straight for the well-lit hangar bay. A line of bots streamed from the ship toward the wreckage. Payne touched his jets gently, hesitant to build up much speed because of the Rang'Kor's bulk and the Ebren coming in behind him. He didn't want the impact to spin them off-course or into *Leviathan*'s side.

Even with a tempered approach, they were coming in too high and too fast. "Need *Ugly 4* to intercept us, and we need it now." Seconds ticked by. Payne tried to spin and ended tangling

Pel'Rok in the tether and pulling Kal against him. Payne tried to orient himself to touch his jets, but he only pushed his threesome toward the top of the ship.

Lev used his ability to accelerate in any direction to adjust to Payne's flight path.

"Relax, Declan. I'll take it from here."

Payne tried to calm down. He couldn't see the ship since he had an Ebren wrapped around his head. The tactical orientation on his HUD didn't comfort him. He did the only thing left to him; he closed his eyes.

He bumped into something and opened his eyes to find *Ugly 4* filling his tactical display. Gravity sucked him to the deck as the insertion craft stopped their forward momentum at the threshold to space.

Kal jumped off him, hopping on one leg so he could unfasten the tether. Sparky swooped in and to the side, oriented to the gravity, and stepped lightly over the threshold, giving the impression of walking into the hangar bay from space. The Cabrizi hit the deck and tried to run. Trying frantically, Sparky couldn't get the tethers undone before they dragged her down.

Kal started yelling and hobbled after them.

"They never come on another mission!" Payne shouted.

Ugly 4 landed in its usual spot by the team equipment cage and discharged its passengers. Mary intercepted Kal to take responsibility for the Cabrizi, but Kal wouldn't get into the cart to go to Medical.

Major Dank appeared in a flash and helped lift the Rang'Kor upright. Two of the Rang'Kor delegation made their way to the captain and removed his helmet. They each took a side and half-carried him to the water tank, where they splashed water on his head and inside his suit.

While they waited for him to recover enough to leave his

suit, the first of the frozen crew arrived. The Rang'Kor delegation directed them into orderly rows of eight.

"I will expand the number of tanks," Lev offered. Almost immediately, the massive aft wall opened, and *Leviathan's* fabrication and construction equipment eased out and assembled itself. Drones from outside brought debris into the hangar bay, and the equipment went to work heating, shaping, and building.

"Go to Sickbay and get fixed up," Payne shouted and pointed at Kal. He ignored the major and stayed on the deck, working on getting the Cabrizi out of their suits.

"You took animals into space," the leader of the Rang'Kor delegation remarked while the others continued the process of thawing and rehydrating their people. Pel'Rok leaned heavily against the tank with two of his tentacles pulled out of his suit and draped over the tank and in the warm water.

"We did, but never again. They could have jeopardized the mission and hurt our chances to help your people."

"Appropriately so." The Rang'Kor drifted away to settle next to the tank and watch as his people were run through recovery.

Dank stayed with Payne. "You did good, brother," Dank whispered.

"That captain, Pel'Rok, did good. He saved a fifth of his crew."

The two watched the process in silence.

Blinky and Buzz flew in behind them and stepped into the hangar bay. Once inside, they took off their helmets. Blinky waved the computer core, which was little more than a box twenty centimeters on a side.

"Take it for analysis," Payne ordered needlessly. Blinky and Buzz were already on their way to the team area to change out of their suits.

"Why don't you go take care of team lead stuff?" Dank offered. "This one is mine if that's okay."

"It is, Virge. Sometimes, people survive the worst that can be thrown at them. It's the luck of the draw."

"And those Rang'Kor used up all their luck on this one. They probably shouldn't play the lottery," Dank joked. "Thanks, Dec. Figure out our next steps, and let's get to it. I think we're going to bump heads with that alien sooner or later. Let's do it the smart way."

"Let's do it the way where we all get to go home when it's over." Payne held out his armored fist, and Dank lightly punched it.

Deep in thought, Major Payne walked slowly to where Mary held his clothes.

[9]

"No matter how bad you think an enemy is, there's always someone worse." –From the memoirs of Ambassador Declan Payne

Once Lev had recovered sufficient raw materials from the largest sections of the destroyed cruisers, he transitioned into faster-than-light speed for a quick return to the area where he would rebuild the space station.

With the plans from Team Payne's trip to E4135 and the Rang'Kor upgrade plans showing a station with half-flooded passageways and spaces firmly in hand, he started construction.

Dank continued working with the Rang'Kor and the survivors.

Admiral Wesson had a decision to make that would affect all of them.

As long as Lev agreed.

On the screen that dwarfed the bridge, a parade of construction equipment moved raw materials into place and started the rebuilding process.

"We have eight hours to decide what we're going to do,"

Admiral Wesson stated as he watched Lev's efficiency. The AI had engineered the complete repairs of a horribly damaged dreadnought in that same amount of time, from a broken and warped keel to a destroyed weapons system. The only thing Lev couldn't fix was the loss of personnel.

Over one thousand had died on the dreadnought.

Over a thousand Rang'Kor had died between the space station and the cruisers.

"Who will staff the space station?" Payne asked.

The admiral pulled his attention away from the hypnotizing view of drones and bots in action.

"The survivors? More Rang'Kor from the surface? It's up to them to decide."

"Are you upgrading the weapons on the station?" Payne pressed.

"You know the answer, Declan."

"No upgrade. I understand. I'm not sure you could give them anything that would help them against these newcomers. Are you getting anything from the data that Blinky and Buzz brought back? Who is doing this?"

"There is nothing to suggest an origin for this ship," Lev replied. "I have dissected the drone you recovered from the station. It is a device with a five-gram silicone interface that is connected in the same way as a computer chip."

"Or a neuron," Mary suggested.

"Exactly. One part of a greater whole."

"Tens of thousands of neurons isn't a big number, is it?" Payne wondered.

"Not by the human standard, no. For a silicon life form, the mass drone attack suggests there is intelligence, but the attack was also brute force. Maybe tens of thousands isn't a great number for this alien either."

"You're confirming this is a new life form? A silicon-based form?" Harry asked.

"I am not."

"It sounded like you did." The admiral assumed the mariners' power stance of old: fists on hips and feet spread wide.

"That is my current working hypothesis, nothing more."

"Lev has become the wafflemeister. He's been hanging around with humans too much." Payne started wandering, hands behind his back, head down while thinking. The personnel on the bridge watched.

Faces and names Payne didn't know did things Lev directed them to do, all of which Lev could have done himself.

Payne only knew the admiral and the commodore.

No one sat in the captain's chair. The admiral wouldn't allow it since he didn't have his trusted strategist Arthir Dorsite on board. She was on her way to Berantz space with a small armada.

Wesson stared at the empty chair. "I think we had best get to Berantz space as quickly as possible."

"Do we take a chance at folding space to a random point three days away from the closest possible location of the alien ship and then FTL the rest of the way in? Six days. To get there with FTL is...what, seven, maybe eight days?" Payne said.

"Eight days," Lev confirmed.

"Show the star map on the big screen if you would, Lev." The admiral headed for the front of the command deck.

The map appeared.

"We're here," the admiral pointed at PX47, "and Berantz space is there. How many worlds are under Berantz control, and where is their home planet?"

Lev highlighted them.

The admiral made the distance calculations in his head. "Nine planets within a twenty-light-year sphere. If we fold to a spot at ninety degrees from BH01, we can react better to wherever the ship went. If the alien traveled at an FTL speed comparable to ours, they would have arrived twenty-three days ago in Berantz space. Then, if they dropped to sub-light speed to transit the individual star systems, they would have only transited six of the nine?"

"Seven if the ship transitioned to FTL after passing the system's primary planet. Five if the ship remained at sub-light until it left each star system," Lev confirmed.

"What if Admiral Dorsite's fleet was intercepted? That might not have happened yet." Payne put his finger on the line showing Fleet's approach to Berantz space. "We know the alien was not too keen on ships approaching it. Would it turn to challenge them or stay the course?"

"The Rang'Kor cruisers approached on its flight path, so we don't know how it would react to a lateral approach. We don't know what triggers its response." Lev had no information from which to speculate. "We must be prudent in case the alien is triggered by any warship."

"Good thing you're not one of those, Lev," Payne joked. "Otherwise, we might be on the wrong side of two goliaths going head-to-head. The titans throw down. The *kaiju* clash."

Lev remained silent.

"I know, Lev." Payne sobered. "Not your enemy."

The others nearby listened to the conversation as if Lev's words had come through their ears, even when those words were absent. The admiral took the commodore's hand.

"Why don't you check on our Rang'Kor guests?" He gestured with his head.

"Why don't you come with us?" Payne replied. "We can stop by Medical to check on Kal. Come on, you hairy butt-holes!" Payne stared down the Cabrizi. They ran past after their obligatory terrorization tour of the bridge crew, stopping and sniffing each person while showing their fangs.

Payne faced the group. "My apologies to anyone who lost a limb to a Cabrizi bite today. We'll try to do better tomorrow. Their training is going slowly, and I hope you'll bear with us during these trying times. Puppies! You know what I mean."

Mary herded him into the corridor.

The admiral and the commodore followed them out.

Harry Wesson looked at his hand as if it had betrayed him. "I used to be good at glad-handing."

"It's a learned skill like riding a bike. It'll come back to you," Payne said.

"Have you ever ridden a bike?" The admiral stared him down.

"If I had, then there is no doubt in my military mind I would have relearned its operation quickly. No doubt at all. Sir, can I ask you a personal question?"

"How personal?"

"What happened on Earth that made so many people happy to get out of there? And you seem to have lost your confidence. That bothers me more than anything. To answer your question, that personal."

"A new administration came into power with promises of broader opportunities with our Blaze allies, while at the same time decrying the alien invasion, all the while cutting the Fleet out of all conversations. As in, the Fleet had nothing to do with winning the peace. It made me angry, but I had retired by then. The destruction of the Blue Earth Protectorate forces? My fault. Nyota's fault."

"Why did they let you back in the service?" Payne wondered.

Harry looked both ways before crooking a finger for Payne to come closer.

"Don't tell me."

"Old friends are better than government dictates. The second I heard Lev was back, I knew what we needed. The old Fleet hands let us hop aboard the shuttle and come here. We're stowaways, Declan, which means we can't go back to Earth."

Payne crossed his arms and leaned against the cart. "Well, now..."

Mary stopped him. "Kal? Medical?"

Payne thought better of giving the admiral a hard time. "I don't give a flying monkey fuck what the administration says. I'm the leader of the seven races, and you're my admiral. So, stop goofing off and feeling sorry for yourself and get to work. Your chariot, ma'am." Payne stood aside for Mary to board first.

The admiral chuckled while doing the same for Nyota.

"You are one insubordinate SOB. Have you always been that way?"

"Far as I can remember, Admiral. SOFTies are anything but. Being an upstart makes it easier going behind enemy lines. Take nothing for granted. Take no shit. Accomplish the mission." He pumped his fist. "Let's see what Kal is up to."

"No!" Mary shouted at the Cabrizi as they tried to climb aboard. "You run."

The carts accelerated away, and the Cabrizi kept pace. Lev took it easy on the creatures as the carts headed up three levels and reversed course toward the bow a couple hundred meters until they reached Medical. The cart stopped, and the group burst through the doors in an effort to surprise Kal.

He stood in the middle of the room. "Lev said y'all were on your way. Let's go. I'm so hungry I could choke down a possum with a teaspoon of Meemaw's barbecue sauce."

The admiral raised one eyebrow.

"Lev," Payne started, "the best practical jokes are the ones you don't see coming. When we pull the trigger on the one for you, you are going to feel the anguish we've felt since you learned Kal good English."

"I don't say that. Y'all are funnin' me," Kal drawled. "Chow?"

"We're going to see the Rang'Kor first, and then we'll eat. I think we've earned some downtime. And you need to heal, so you stay in the cart."

"Anywhere that's not here is a better place. I've spent enough time getting poked and prodded by these damn machines." He brushed past them on his way out the door, took one cart, and filled it. The four humans looked at the remaining two-seater cart.

Kal hauled the Cabrizi inside with him.

"Lev, buddy, can you hook us up with another cart?" Payne asked aloud.

"I thought the best practical jokes happened when you were least expecting it?"

Payne's thought of getting back at Lev, who was always in his mind, lingered. How would he do it? Could he? "I might never get payback, will I, Lev? You are going to keep punking me until I curl up and die."

Mary took his hand. "I bet he can prolong your life indefinitely if he wants to."

"That's what I'm afraid of, Dog. How about if I concede that you have become the master of existential humanism? I bow to you and declare you the winner."

Declan bowed, and Mary curtseyed.

A cart cruised down the corridor and parked in front of them. "Thanks, Lev. When 'buddy' is only half the word."

"You should probably leave it alone," the admiral told him.

"When in a hole, stop digging," the commodore added.

"Words of wisdom."

Mary didn't wait. "Kal is hungry and ready to eat barbecued

possum. Maybe he can go straight to our private dining facility?"

"No way!" Kal called from the forward cart. "Let's get a move on."

They headed to the hangar bay and through the doors and aimed for the tanks in the middle of the open area. They found six additional Rang'Kor had been revived. They dripped onto the deck, where a small piece of equipment recovered the water.

The captain approached them. "I thank you again for what you did for my crew and me. To the giant Ebren, I apologize for shooting you. I wasn't in my right mind. I hope that you can forgive me."

"Nothing to forgive, Captain. You were defending your ship. I'd do the same thing. And I'm as good as new." Kal stood up, scattering the Cabrizi. He didn't put any weight on his heavily-bandaged leg.

"You are too kind." The captain raised himself to nearly the same height at Kal'faxx. "My crew has been assigned to the new space station. But I, with your permission, request to remain on board this great vessel to hunt down the alien who killed my ship."

"We're not about exacting revenge," Payne replied. "I'm good with you coming, Pel'Rok, but we're collecting information. We'll make a decision about what to do as soon as we're able. Until then, you are more than welcome to join us as long as the boss agrees."

The admiral cleared his throat.

"As long as Admiral Wesson agrees, and *Leviathan*, of course," Payne clarified. "Leader of the seven races! It's not an easy thing to forego."

"I agree. Once that station is ready and the personnel transferred, we'll be folding space. The FTL trip is more than seven days, so fold it is. Next stop, Berantz."

"If you start with nothing, it only gets better from there."
–From the memoirs of Ambassador Declan Payne

Leviathan materialized in interstellar space a full three-day FTL transit from the nearest Berantz planet.

"I wish he'd warn us," Payne grumbled. They stood in the hangar bay, from which they'd watched the shuttle carrying the last of the Rang'Kor depart for the space station. *Leviathan* had folded space the instant the shuttle was clear.

The admiral and the commodore leaned on each other. "We're usually sitting down for that."

Payne tried to shake off the disorientation. Mary stood still, eyes closed. He watched her until she returned to the moment. "What?"

"Didn't that bother you?"

"A little, but I'm fine. How about you?"

"For you, it seems to get easier, while for me, it seems to be getting harder." Payne rubbed his temple to try to alleviate the remnants of a headache.

"You're old. All you old people are suffering, it seems," she stated with a shrug. She walked toward the Rang'Kor captain. "Captain Pel'Rok."

The captain swayed drunkenly despite using all eight tentacles for balance.

"Are you sure you want to stay in here?" Mary asked.

"A tank of water and wide-open spaces? What Rang'Kor *wouldn't* want to stay in here?"

"I guess none. We have three days until we head toward the inner systems, and then it will take us three days to get there. We have roughly six days to kill. What do you want to do?"

"I want to learn about this ship," Pel'Rok replied. He steadied himself. "We will fight from here, no? We could have put a Rang'Kor cruiser in this hangar bay, ready to engage the enemy..."

His words drifted off. His dead ship and many dead crew weighed on him, even though there was nothing he could have done. The alien behemoth dominated the space around it.

"We will use this ship to collect data," Payne added. "Don't worry, Pel'Rok, there's another hangar bay just like this on the port side of the ship, and it contains two human frigates and two fighter squadrons."

"Put half of them over here! One lucky missile could cause you a great deal of grief," the captain advised.

"You heard the skipper, Lev. In our downtime, while we're waiting for the systems to recharge, let's balance our combat power."

"Of course, Declan. Although if you perform this change right now, a ship with my sensors would be able to detect the movement of the two ships."

"Even if they maneuvered only using thrusters?" the admiral asked, having gotten over the disorientation.

"No. If they could stick to thrusters only, then no one should see them."

"No one is going to see us out here, Lev," Payne assured the AI.

"The chances are low but not zero."

"Then we better be ready to fight. Weapons hot, thrusters only while outside the ship," Admiral Wesson stated. "I'll let them know, and I'll do it in person."

The admiral held out his hand, and Payne took it. "What's this for?"

"It's time to do my job like I belong here." He returned Payne's strong grip.

"You *belong* here. All of us do."

The commodore moved in. "All of us, Major. Thank you."

The two departed, leaving Declan, Mary, and Kal with the Rang'Kor captain. Another cart rushed across the hangar bay, carrying Major Dank.

"Virgil," Payne called. "Captain Pel'Rok would like a tour of the ship. Can you help him out?"

Dank gave him the thumbs-up. "Lev, can you hook us up with a different cart, please? We got places to go and people to see."

"Join us for dinner, Virge, Pel'Rok. Did we stock enough Rang'Kor food?"

"I think it is not the best, but it will be okay. If we get to a place where we can get fresh seafood, I will not turn it down. However, that's not why we're here. I'll eat table scraps if I have to and won't rest until I have my chance to take a tentacle off that alien beast."

Payne nodded. "We're collecting data," he reiterated. "*Leviathan* is a pacifist, believe it or not."

"But *Leviathan* destroyed our ships at the great Earth Battle, our final defeat."

"Lev never fired on your ships. He wouldn't. We used other means to win that fight," Payne explained. "We can hold our own, Skipper. Stay fierce, and we'll get our shot soon enough, if nothing else, to see this alien ship and then walk away from the encounter. Lev is not going to get killed by that thing."

"We can only hope," the captain replied ominously. The cart arrived, and Virgil climbed in after the Rang'Kor was settled.

Maintenance bots appeared and started the process of moving the tanks to clear space for a frigate and a squadron of space fighters.

Coming in hot on thrusters, Declan thought with a hint of sarcasm.

The transfer was nearly complete.

War was coming, even though Declan Payne had tried to accommodate Lev's concerns. A war with weapons designed to shred an enemy's ship. Smart weapons. Could *Leviathan* survive an attack from the alien?

Payne was less than confident.

———

Three days passed without incident. Lev's sensors picked up main engine signatures in three of the eight star systems occupied by the Berantz.

In a galaxy without the alien ship, there would have been movement in all eight systems.

"The big question is whether we come in behind it to evaluate the damage or get in front of it," Payne began. "I vote we go to BH01, see what it did to the Berantz homeworld, and then go after it."

"Going to BH01 won't save lives," the admiral replied. "I think we have to get in front of it. What are you willing to do, Lev?"

"I am willing to do either, but I will not engage that ship."

"Unless we find out it is consummate evil bent on the complete destruction of all life in our galaxy," Payne added helpfully.

"Then why did it leave the surface of PX47 untouched?" Lev countered.

"There might be holes in my hypothesis." Payne scowled. "Then why is it doing what it's doing? Scrubbing all ships and shipping from the systems it travels through?"

"That's why I recommend we get in front of it. The fact that I cannot see it on the energy scanners suggests its composition and drive are of a technology that I do not know. I have too many unanswered questions to draw any conclusions. The best way to get more information about the ship is from the ship, not what is in its wake."

"Didn't the PX47 station see it on their energy scanners?" Payne asked.

"The station saw the ship, but they were within thirty-three light minutes of it. I suspect it is able to dampen its signature at longer ranges. Whether intentionally or not is another unanswered question."

"Make it so, Lev," the admiral decided. "Put us in front of that ship, best possible speed. And summon the frigate and squadron commanders to the bridge. I want to talk with them about what's in front of us."

The admiral "heard" Lev send the request to the commanders to immediately board a cart for the bridge.

Payne, Dank, and the new Mrs. Payne stood nearby, with Kal standing close to the hatch. The Cabrizi ran up and down the corridor, chasing the flying ring Kal tossed whenever they returned it. But the Ebren kept his eyes on those nearest Payne, though Lev had vouched for all of them. Kal'faxx had committed to protecting Payne. It wasn't his job to trust people, so he didn't.

Payne had shared the greatest gift of all with him—the Cabrizi, a status symbol for the greatest on Ebren. Plus, he enjoyed their company. He called to them in Ebren and ordered them to stay at his side as he returned to the bridge with Major Payne and Lieutenant Payne for the briefing with the flight commanders.

They engaged in small talk that none of them were interested in until the group arrived.

Commanders Gordon and Appel from the frigates *Tempest* and *Shrew* were the first in, followed closely by the Mosquito squadron commanders, Woody Malone and Kilroy Wazeree. They approached the admiral, saluted without waiting for a response, and stood at ease with their hands behind their backs.

Their military bearing had not been lost. The admiral smiled, and Payne straightened.

"Lev is burning through the void to get ahead of the alien ship. It's five planets deep into Berantz space, including the Berantz homeworld. Our job at this point is to assess and engage, but not militarily. Your frigates will not leave *Leviathan*'s hangars unless it is deemed safe. The damage done to the Rang'Kor cruisers suggests you, your ships, and your crews would be obliterated. Two frigates and forty Mosquitos cannot stand toe to toe with this thing. Six cruisers were destroyed in less than a minute. Lev, do you have that drone for the commanders to look at?"

"I will have it moved to the port-side hangar bay. It has been rendered inert and encased in polymer to further seal it from external influence. We should reach the BD18 system in four days and two hours, although I cannot guarantee that the alien ship isn't already there."

"And we can't fold space, or we would die when we weren't able to protect ourselves. We have to hope for the best. If the alien ship has already left BD18, then we'll collect data. If it hasn't, we'll collect data. At this point in time, I do not see a tactical advantage. We will not engage the alien ship."

"We've seen the view from the cruiser," Commander Appel stated. "It wasn't pretty. If they are intelligently controlled from a remote source, can't we jam the signal?"

"That's information we don't have that we're looking for. How do the drones work? Are they networked or given instructions before they depart the carrier?"

"What else is on board that ship?" Gordon asked.

"Unknown," the admiral replied. "We don't know anything beyond what you've seen so far. We won't speculate further. We need information first and foremost, and then we will decide our next steps. Any questions?"

"That's not a lot to go on," Woody Malone said. "But it's right in my wheelhouse. Fly by the seat of my pants, making it up as I go. Kind of like we did on the last go, don't you think, Declan?"

"We might have done less advance planning than we let on, but it doesn't mean we didn't have a plan."

"We had mission goals. It's the best way to fight. Don't tell me how to do something. Just tell me what you need done."

"Fly, fight, win," Kilroy Wazeree quoted the space-fighter mantra.

"The Tricky Spinsters stand ready to engage, sir, ma'am." That was Space Fighter Squadron 317's name. Malone saluted and stepped back.

"Titan's Hammers are ready to fly," Kilroy added.

The admiral nodded. He'd ridden the bigger Fleet ships for his entire career. He had worked with the fighter jocks, but that wasn't his thing. He liked having a solid deck under his feet and megajoules of power at his command. Leading a crew into battle. Leading an armada, and then the entire Fleet. His exhilaration came not from his personal capabilities to manipulate a ship, like a space-fighter pilot's, but from his ability to get the most from his people and their equipment.

He felt the thrill all the same. Out-think the enemy. It was what drove him to this day.

"Lev, can you see Arthir's armada? They should be arriving any time now."

"They are on my scanners. They are headed for BHo1."

"Good. They won't get in the way as we move in front of the alien ship. They're better off where they are." The admiral issued his orders. "Get your people ready for the unknown. We will figure it out, and then we'll do right by the seven races."

"Sir, I have a question," Commander Gordon interrupted. "I've never seen a Berantz. Can we get a picture or something?"

"Good point," the admiral replied. "Lev, make sure the frigate crews and fighter pilots are trained on basic Berantz phraseology and cultural awareness in case the interpretation software takes a hit, so we don't inadvertently start a war while we're trying to help them."

Lev projected the image of a Berantz directly into everyone's mind. Humanoid, near-duplicates of humanity, except the homeworld, BHo1 was at the far reaches of the Goldilocks zone where little light reached. Their skin was translucent, nearly to the point of being transparent. They had larger eyes to better see in the low light.

"That's the stuff of nightmares," Gordon mumbled.

"Their heads are fifteen percent larger than that of the average human. Their intellectual capacity is comparably larger," Lev added.

"So, they're smarter, too." Payne shrugged. The Berantz were members of the Blaze and, like the Zuloon, had stayed back from the battles. The Ebren and the Rang'Kor had spent the majority of the war on the front lines.

As humanity had found out at the end, the Rang'Kor used

war for population control, and the Ebren were a warlike race. Fighting was in their blood. It made sense that they had borne the brunt of the Blaze's operations.

"Transparent humans. Got it." Malone tipped his head and walked away.

"I don't believe that's what I said." Lev sounded more put out than normal.

"Fighter jock, Lev," Payne explained. "They gin everything down to the simplest elements that make the most sense for them. Why use a megabyte of data when a few bits will do?"

"Human brains have enough capacity to work with the full picture and not a caricature."

"Yet here we are. Maybe someday you'll train us up right, Lev, but today is not that day. Our people are going to have a lot of things to do over the next few. Let's not teach them how to build a clock just to tell time."

"I shall endeavor to persevere," Lev replied without enthusiasm.

"Now you understand. Thanks, Lev. Team Payne, time to work out." Payne nodded at the admiral and headed for the corridor, with the others hurrying to catch up.

Once in the corridor, the commanders jumped in the carts to take them to the hangars, all except Woody Malone.

"What's up, Wildman?" he asked on his way to punch Payne in the chest. It wasn't a real question. "I haven't seen much of you since Earth. Hell, since last year."

Malone's fighters had been instrumental in the victory over the Blaze forces that had attacked Earth.

"It's been a bum's rush. Off to save the universe, and then we come back to find everyone running from Earth's unfriendly embrace. I guess I didn't want to hear more horror stories about my home."

"I'll spare you, then." He smiled warmly. "We have a new

mission. You've kept your ear to the ground. What's in front of us? What aren't we being told?"

Fighter pilots always wanted the "gouge." An ounce of gouge was worth a pound of knowledge. Transparent humans.

"I'll speculate for you. This alien is bad. It wants to eliminate the spacefaring for some reason. It's conducting a scorched-earth raid but in space. It doesn't go intra-atmospheric, so that's a way to survive its attack, but it's not leaving anything behind, which tells me all those drones are controlled from a central hub, which has to be that big-ass ship. It's twice the length of *Leviathan*. That concerns me a whole lot."

"What are we going to do against it? Mosquitos can't fly through a cloud of projectiles."

"That's why you're not leaving *Leviathan* unless there's a tactical advantage. Lev isn't going to fight this ship, so it'll be up to us."

"And we have no advantage that we know of," Woody replied softly.

"That's why we're going for a look-see. Lev can fold out of there if need be. We can't abandon the Berantz. Even if we haven't met them before, they are still our allies."

"We'll see." Woody stepped away after a quick handshake. A cart whisked him down the corridor.

"He's worried," Mary observed.

"We all are, but not all of us have twenty ships in space where each pilot has to make the right decision. He doesn't know what to tell his people. Just like me. I don't know what to tell ours either."

"There's nothing to tell. Team Payne knows that. They'll wait for more, and then they'll do what you ask of them. Have you seen that Byle and Shaolin are trimming down?"

"I haven't. Are they?"

Mary shook her head. "Men."

Payne threw his hands up. "Kal, help me out here. Have you noticed Byle and Shaolin losing weight?"

"Yes," came the deep voice.

"Dammit!"

"I noticed for you. Compliment them on it, and let's get to work."

They jumped into their carts, which took them one level up, away from the heavily occupied deck with the command center and beneath the level with the hangar bays.

They had everything they needed on the deck they solely occupied, for runs, for workouts, for range time, for food, and for downtime. Everything except answers to their questions about the alien ship.

[11]

"Trust your allies because if they betray you, you're all going to die together." –From the memoirs of Ambassador Declan Payne

"We come out of FTL in about fifteen. According to Lev, there are still ship energy signatures in System BD18. That means either the ship hasn't arrived yet, or the Berantz have made peace with it, or the Berantz have defeated it," Payne said, looking at their gear.

Combat axes, railguns, and the plasma cannon, optimal weapons for combat on board an enemy ship, were stacked neatly in the equipment cage beyond their combat suits.

No one questioned Payne's order to suit up and be ready to deploy. Even if there was no immediate order to depart, it gave them something to do. It was a lot easier to stand down than it was to gear up.

"Fifteen mikes, people. Suit up and load up."

The team started undressing. Payne glanced at Shaolin and Byle, then walked over to them.

"Thanks for working to get in shape," he told them.

"We shouldn't have let ourselves go," Byle replied without condemnation. "Just made it harder to get back where we should have been all along. Maybe Heckler and Turbo aren't the total psychos we made them out to be."

The three turned to see a naked Turbo hammer Heckler's shoulders with two fists before he took his turn. They proceeded to get dressed afterward.

Payne couldn't look at his team members. "Maybe not," he agreed noncommittally before tossing his overalls and climbing into his combat armor.

He ran through the checklist to ensure it was clean and fully charged and its active systems were nominal. They trusted Lev to keep the suits at optimal functionality at all times, but it was every operator's responsibility to double-check.

"My suit's a little too big," Byle told them with pride in her voice.

"Mine's not," Mary replied. She'd been working on adding muscle mass. They'd been at the twice-daily workouts long enough that she was starting to bulk back up. Lev's supplements didn't hurt.

"Me, too!" Kal'faxx said in a voice that drowned out all other conversation.

"Do you have any jets for extravehicular movement?" Payne asked, biting his lip to keep from laughing.

"Lev gave me these here doodads." He showed off two wrist attachments. If Kal held his arms to his sides, the small bursts would propel him through space.

"You'll want to practice with those before you try using them."

"I've watched you, boss man. That's right fine learnin'."

"Lev, buddy, can you fix Kal? He seems to be broken."

Kal tapped the side of his head with a huge finger. "Big head. Big mind, pardner."

He jumped up and ran for the corridor, calling the Cabrizi to him. They hesitated, and he yelled for Mary to pick up one of their suits. She obliged him and shook it at the creatures. They bolted straight out the door like they'd been hit with a cattle prod. Kal shut it behind them and returned to the team area.

Heckler and Turbo handed out the weapons. Axes for everyone, railguns for the humans, and the plasma cannon for Kal.

"Explosives?" Heckler asked.

"Normal complement," Payne answered. One kilogram in four bricks for each.

"And grenades. Open up and say, 'Ahh,' you big metal bitch!" Heckler shouted, followed by a maniacal laugh.

Blinky secured his weapons and grabbed a bag with half the equipment they needed to penetrate hostile computer systems. He stopped by Payne and whispered, "Don't sit me next to him."

"Take your spot, Blinky, and let him have his moment." Payne clapped him on his armored shoulder. "It's been a year in the making."

Blinky grumbled to Buzz as they boarded *Ugly 4*.

Payne embraced the familiarity of a team complaining about nothing important while waiting to enter the crucible of death, hoping they had the skill and wisdom to make it out the other side.

He one-arm-hugged his XO. "What do you say, Virge?"

"It's good to be back, Dec." Dank pushed off and jogged to the ship.

Declan and Mary headed in, took their seats, and secured the outer doors. The tactical display appeared, with a big clock counting down until they left FTL. Energy signatures continued to show within the system.

The clock hit ten seconds before entering normal space.

One of the ships winked out. The alien ship's energy signature finally appeared. The countdown clock reset to five minutes.

"What's going on, Lev?"

"I'm taking us farther into the system, closer to the inhabited planet and the proximity of the remaining Berantz ships."

"Does that ship know we're here?" Payne asked.

"It has not changed its speed or orientation from when it appeared on my sensors."

Lev's answer was precise but added no insight. "Admiral Wesson, can you hear me?"

Payne waited for Lev to connect them. "Maybe we can set a trap for this alien? As soon as we come out of FTL, dump *Ugly 4*. We'll float in space and wait for it to fly by. Then we'll try to get in. The footage from the Rang'Kor cruiser showed the cantilever doors remained open during their attack, and I assume the alien is going to continue their attack."

"That's high-risk, Major Payne, but high reward. We could end this thing right here, right now. Just like the drone dreadnoughts. Kill 'em from the inside. Lev, work out the best drop point, and let's do it." The admiral sounded confident, which was what Payne needed to hear.

"As soon as we come out of FTL, there will be turbulence. You will launch into that. Good luck, Declan." The ship lifted off the deck and eased toward the closed hangar bay door.

"Thanks, Lev. Come on, people, let's do this thing!"

Dank stood. "Helmets on and double-check."

The team secured their helmets, and the pairs checked each other. External life sign monitors showed one hundred percent. Payne verified on his HUD that everyone registered.

"Looking good, people. We'll make like a hole in space. When the time is right, we'll do what we do best."

Payne started to rock with the nervous energy that drove him before combat. He gripped the haft of his axe, ready to wield it to pry open bulkheads and shred metal to get access to panels and secured spaces.

Even the most advanced ships used lighter metals on everything but the bulkheads. An axe used with the power of a combat suit was capable of causing a great deal of damage. It would be like an old-school can opener, cutting its way inside.

A plasma torch would accomplish the same thing, but Payne preferred the axes when dealing with the unknown because they could be used in close-quarters combat, too.

He also thought they looked intimidating.

The countdown continued. Payne found himself incapable of looking away. The numbers mesmerized him. Put him in a meditative state.

Ugly 4 hovered close to the hangar door, centimeters from it, ready to fall into the wake of the big ship. Transmissions from the insertion craft were cut off. It could radiate nothing if it wanted to go unseen.

Two...one. The ship transitioned out of FTL. The door raced open, and *Ugly 4* bobbed into the wake. *Leviathan* sped away, accelerating toward two Berantz ships holding station in a high orbit over the habitable planet.

Lev sent messages to the Berantz to keep them from attacking him.

Behind them, the ten-kilometer-long shoebox-shaped ship bore down on the remaining Berantz ships.

"There's a problem," Lev sent. "The alien is traveling at ninety-eight percent of light speed. You will not be able to board it."

Then you're going to have to get it to slow down, Payne thought, hoping the ship was close enough to hear him.

Leviathan broadcast in Godilkinmore first to establish his place as one of the Progenitors. Milliseconds later, he sent a greeting in Rang'Kor since it had responded to them in their language during the conflict in the PX47 system.

"Ga'ee. This is *Leviathan*, the last Godilkinmore ship in this galaxy. I request a parlay. Stop your ship so that we may discuss a mutual way forward."

"Godilkinmore. Not welcome," the alien ship replied.

Payne screwed up his face. "I wonder if that will coax Lev to consider this ship as an enemy?" he asked using the external speakers to avoid emitting electromagnetic transmissions the Ga'ee might see;

Mary shrugged. "It's not looking good."

The alien ship slowed as it passed, doors open. Payne's butthole puckered for an instant; he knew the combat power within would destroy him and his team.

"Follow it at the best possible speed that won't get us spotted," Payne ordered. *Ugly 4* bounced ahead as the ship pulled away.

"Ga'ee. You have me at a loss. I've never heard of your race, but you seem to have heard of mine. Please explain why you think the Godilkinmore are not welcome here."

"No peace, Godilkinmore." The voice sounded mechanical —a translation program.

"What language is it speaking?" Payne asked.

"Rang'Kor," Joker replied. As the comms specialist, she had a different display showing on her HUD.

"So, it's not familiar enough with the Progenitors to know their language."

"Peace is a state of mind and always achievable. My name is Admiral Harry Wesson. I'm from Earth and represent humanity. I'd like to talk about your trip through Blaze Collective space. What are your intentions?"

A new voice entered the conversation. "This is Captain

D'graz of the Berantz Defensive Forces. You will leave Berantz space immediately, or you will be destroyed."

Payne shook his head. He was in the bleachers watching two starships heading toward each other, knowing that only one would survive and there was nothing he could do about it.

The screens showed the Ga'ee vessel coming to a stop. The drones didn't flush from the ship as they had in the Rang'Kor cruiser attack.

"Is it that easy?" Payne watched the screen closely, looking for any change, and listened intently for the conversations between the ships.

Although the Ga'ee side wasn't much of a conversation.

"Why was it asking about peace in Rang'Kor space while destroying everything in its path? And here it said no peace, yet it stops and doesn't attack. Does it mean the opposite of what it says?" Payne postulated.

"Wouldn't that be something?" Dank replied. "Let me give you a compliment. You suck."

Payne nodded humorlessly. "I don't think it would work from our side."

A data stream came over the comm channel. Joker explained, "Lev and the Ga'ee are communicating using binary."

"What are they saying?" Payne had expected a digital connection. "Does this mean that the Ga'ee is an AI like Lev, or are they so advanced they can stream binary?"

"If I can tap in, I can tell you," Blinky interjected.

"Can you do it passively?"

"I'll need a quick handshake to establish the protocol, but that's it. Nanoseconds. That's all we need." Blinky was confident.

"No. Nothing active from this ship. No signals at all. I think that thing is a nanosecond away from ordering the destruction of every space vessel in this system, including Lev. If it thinks there's any duplicity, we'll die right here. I don't *want* to die right here." Payne glanced from face to face. All helmets were turned toward him.

"Sorry, Major. As soon as I said it, I realized how stupid an idea it was. Any AI worth its salt would find us in nanoseconds. I'm convinced that ship is run by an AI."

"Maybe augmented by an AI?" Payne countered. "What about the silicon biomass as part of the drone?"

Blinky nodded. "Or thought. I'm not at my best today, am I? I'll shut up now." Buzz elbowed him.

"How long until we reach the alien ship at our current velocity?" Payne asked.

"Forty-two minutes," the kernel of Lev's AI that operated *Ugly 4* answered.

"Keep him occupied, Lev," Payne begged, even though he knew Lev couldn't hear him. "Everyone relax. We're going to be here for a while, but keep your helmets on just in case."

The team shifted in their seats in vain attempts to get comfortable.

Payne struggled with trying to think like the enemy, get inside its head. If it had a head. Or if it was alive. Or was an enemy, for that matter.

"Ga'ee," the admiral broadcast on the open channel after the binary stream stopped. "We would like to suggest a different route of travel to take you out of our galaxy. We are transmitting the star chart now."

Silence answered them.

Ugly 4 continued its slow approach on pneumatic thrusters, riding the gravity swells and the solar winds to increase its speed.

The cantilever doors of the Ga'ee's vessel remained open to

space, as threatening as open missile ports and cannons rotating freely on their mounts.

"Thank you for your language files," the mechanical Ga'ee voice said in unaccented English. "We are explorers, nothing more. Our systems are built to protect our humble ship from asteroids and space debris. Anything around it is automatically destroyed. We have been on our journey for so long that we have forgotten how to adjust the systems. We are flying blind, unaware of what is going on outside our vessel."

Payne pulled his helmet off so Mary could appreciate his scowl. "Are you buying this?"

She wasn't. "Seems hokey as Hogan's goat."

"My words exactly," Payne replied. He surveyed his team. "Blinky, Buzz, and Sparky, you three might get your chance if those knuckleheads are telling the truth. If they need help breaking into their own system, I'm sure you would be more than happy to oblige."

"That we would," Blinky agreed.

"I'm ready to go. I've spent my whole life getting ready for this. I say we break into their system in under an hour and have their ship under control in less than two. At four hours, we'll be on our way back to *Leviathan* while this big ugly bitch heads away from the seven races' space."

"Four hours? Are you drinking Mosquito lube? It took you two days to crack Lev's code," Turbo suggested.

"I don't think it took two days," Buzz replied. "Did it? I lose track of time during these things."

"Yet you're all-in on an hour. Do any of us know what an hour is?"

Buzz didn't have an answer.

Blinky did. "We calculate the set rate of decay of Uranium 236, which has a half-life of twenty-three point four two million years. We only need to measure the neutrons..."

"We get it," Payne interrupted. "Time is an artificial construct that we cannot see or touch, yet we agree it exists because it can supposedly be measured."

"Not supposedly," Sparky replied. "The passage of time can be measured with great accuracy and is fundamental in acceleration and speed calculations."

"Look at me." Payne stared at the reflective screens on his people's helmets. "Did you ever confuse me for a science guy?"

"Well, no," Blinky admitted.

"I'm jagging you so that we can make *time* go a little faster. It also accelerates."

"It slows down the closer one gets to light speed," Buzz argued.

Payne laughed. "Now we understand each other. If I keep you guys on your toes, then we have a better chance to survive whatever we get thrown into."

Mary removed her helmet and whispered into Payne's ear, "I don't like this."

"It feels wrong. If they were on autopilot, why would they only go to inhabited systems?" Payne gritted his teeth. As soon as they boarded the Ga'ee ship, he'd be able to do something. In the interim, he was helpless. He tapped Mary's helmet before putting his own on.

Ugly 4 jerked as something solid impacted it—an asteroid or debris.

The ship twisted and rolled, then returned to its course.

The broadcast channel went live with the mechanical voice speaking Rang'Kor. "We see you."

The tactical board showed drones exiting the massive ship in an unrelenting wave.

"If it feels wrong, it is." –From the memoirs of Ambassador Declan Payne

"Lev, get us out of here. Best possible speed to the surface of BD18," Payne ordered.

The ship changed course and accelerated, but it was nothing like the acceleration of the drones. They looped in an arc to get around the insertion craft. The uglymobile started angling and jerking through void space in an attempt to foil the drones' targeting.

"Handshake and go active, Blinky. Try to find the network frequency. Lev can jam it." Payne knew he didn't have enough time, but they had to try.

"On it!" Blinky called. He snapped open his computer and stared at the screen as he used his new neural interface, another gift from the Vestrall. Lev should have given him and Buzz those, but he hadn't. "Lev is already flooding space with signals, looking for the frequency."

Payne gripped the rails of his seat. "Access and shut them

down. You don't have an hour, Buzz. You have about thirty seconds."

Buzz didn't bother speaking. He worked with his system at the speed of thought.

A tidal wave of drones headed toward *Leviathan*.

The drones hesitated, and their tight formation lost its coordination. Payne relaxed as Lev shot *Ugly 4* through a small gap and accelerated down the gravity well toward the surface of a jungle planet that was nothing like the Berantz homeworld.

The drones recovered and regrouped as they chased *Ugly 4*, a massive cloud of intelligent projectiles homing on Payne. His throat tightened as he felt them coming for him to rectify the earlier attempt Kal had stymied. They were coming for him, too.

All of them.

Ugly 4 jerked from an impact as it hit the upper atmosphere. The descent angle was steeper than normal, bordering on unsafe. The stealthy insertion craft didn't have massive heat shields. Lev adjusted the trajectory as the heat build-up became too great. More impacts.

The drones had come into the atmosphere after them.

They shouldn't have.

There was no paradigm for how the Ga'ee operated. Random and extreme violence. How did one fight such an enemy?

The ship's flight smoothed as it entered the upper atmosphere and continued accelerating along a nearly vertical descent path.

The tactical board showed the live view behind the ship. At least five drones had made it through and were closing on them.

"I think we're going to die," Joker muttered softly without judgment or fear.

Heckler snorted. "Maybe we can snap off a few shots before we hit the ground?"

"Lev, fire whatever missiles we have at them. Release and blow."

The two anti-ship missiles came out of their tubes and almost immediately exploded. *Ugly 4* raced away from the blast.

The view showed an expanding cloud and fire, something that didn't happen in space.

The drones tumbled through the shock wave and continued toward the ship.

"Tactical exit."

"You cannot slow before impact," Lev advised. "I will pull up, and your team can jump at that point."

"Thanks, Lev." Payne unbuckled his seatbelt and stood, then seized the rail over his head and secured the combat axe to the side of his suit's leg. He brought his railgun up to his chest and held it tightly with his free hand. "Get ready to jump."

The team stood and assumed their pose, waiting for the radical maneuver and the doors to open. Kal hunched since he was too tall. He held the plasma cannon low to keep the portable jets attached to his wrists facing downward.

The time it took to get from an altitude of five thousand meters to one thousand was not much longer than the blink of an eye. The artificial gravity of the craft was strained to the extreme as the ship pulled up.

The side doors popped open, and the team vaulted out. Payne and Dank were the last to leave. Payne accessed his rear camera as three drones slammed into *Ugly 4*.

———

Admiral Wesson growled, "Those duplicitous bastards. Fire all you have at that ship!"

"I will not," Lev replied. "They saw our ploy as an attack even though it was not. They are only defending themselves."

The admiral tensed. "Are you going to die to prove you're a pacifist? That's okay if you don't take us with you."

"I am attempting to jam the signal that coordinates the drones. It is a brute-force effort, but I wish no harm to the Ga'ee, only that Declan and the others are able to escape."

"Any luck?" The drone clouds flowed through space with intelligent design and murderous intent. The admiral fought with his desire to flush the frigates and the Mosquitos and send them into the fray. To fire at the inbound enemy.

To try to hold back the tide with a broom, the challenge seemed so overwhelming. Even standing inside *Leviathan*, the greatest ship ever built, he felt fear. He knew how the cruiser captains had felt as the drones bore down on them. He had seen the video of the ships firing everything they had, to no avail. Drones died and were immediately replaced. They were so many they blotted out the stars.

They had hit the cruisers with the momentum of a comet, and they were headed this way. *Ugly 4* was nowhere to be seen in the much smaller cloud of tri-tipped drones headed their way.

The massive cloud split in half, then split again as the two Berantz vessels became targets along with *Leviathan*, even though the battleship stood between the Ga'ee and the Berantz.

Every ship in the system had become a target the instant the Ga'ee decided to attack.

"Are the drones capable of light speed?" the admiral asked.

"They are not," Lev confirmed. "But the Ga'ee ship is, based on how quickly they transited interstellar space between the Berantz worlds."

"Give me an open broadcast to the Berantz ships and to Major Payne and his team, please."

Lev confirmed the channel was open. "All ships in the BD18 system. You cannot stand against these drones. Run for your lives. You can do nothing here. Transition to FTL and regroup in System BD23. Major Payne, save yourselves any way you can."

Harry Wesson said those last words to make himself feel better. He saw the drones heading for where they suspected *Ugly 4* was located.

One Berantz ship disappeared off the tactical screen as it transitioned to faster-than-light speed. The other advanced on a trajectory around *Leviathan*.

Lev kept the ship where it was, neither moving nor defending himself.

Harry Wesson wrapped his arm around Nyota's shoulders and closed his eyes.

"Dying here proves nothing, Lev," the commodore began. "We have not yet collected sufficient data to make a decision about the entity known as the Ga'ee. We cannot end our role here before then, can we?"

"Compelling thoughts, Nyota," Lev replied. "I will collect data on the viability of their weaponry against me. *Leviathan* is a rather robust vessel."

"Just don't kill us in the process," the admiral pleaded.

"Of course." *Leviathan* angled the ship to meet the inbound drones on a broadside.

"Is he going to fire at them?" the admiral asked the commodore. She shook her head. They found themselves reaching for their consoles to steady themselves as the wave came for the ship.

Leviathan bucked and lurched from a thousand impacts, followed by a thousand more.

On the screen, the Berantz ship came apart as if its reactor had gone critical, but there was no expanding cloud from an explosion, only a widening debris field heading into the void of space.

A hideous screech tore at their eardrums, the grinding of metal on metal. The hatch to the bridge closed and secured.

The admiral held his breath through their final moments.

But they weren't final. Lev transitioned to FTL speed. After three seconds, they dropped out of FTL into normal space.

"I'm afraid my drives are damaged. I have deployed maintenance bots to make repairs."

"How much time did we buy?" Admiral Wesson asked.

"The idea of time as a transaction is interesting to me. I have studied this question for a thousand years, and the Godilkinmore studied it for far longer. Three seconds at light speed bought us very little time since the Ga'ee ship can accelerate to ninety-eight percent of the speed of light rather quickly. Their drones, on the other hand, cannot attain such speeds. Once they recover the drones, the Ga'ee can be here in three seconds."

"That is disconcerting. Can your sensors still pick up the ship and the drones?"

"I have refined the detection parameters based on the information I was able to collect. I can, and the drones have completed the destruction of the Berantz ship and are returning to the mother ship. The carrier, as you called it."

"Have we seen any weapons from the main ship?"

"Nothing from any of our recorded encounters."

"Next time, we'll have to make sure they keep those outer doors closed. Any update on the armada?"

"They have changed course. They are en route to the BD18 system."

"Launch a communications buoy immediately with everything we know and warn them not to interfere with the alien ship. If the box starts squawking right away, the signal should still be traveling through space when they arrive."

After a few moments, Lev confirmed that the comm buoy had been sent into space.

"Any idea what happened to Team Payne?" the admiral wondered in a voice that wasn't confident.

"I have no information from them. The drones going in that direction headed toward the upper atmosphere of the planet before returning to the Ga'ee vessel."

"There's some hope that they made it to the planet, then. We'll treat them that way. Carry them as MIA for now. Missing in action. We'll return when we can to search for them."

"I would like that very much," Lev replied. "They were first on board and the first to share their thoughts with me after a thousand years of silence. I think of them as my family."

"Me too, Lev. Payne is the pain-in-the-ass son I never had." The admiral frowned while watching the board. Arthir Dorsite was going to bring her ships into normal space right on top of the Ga'ee.

"What else can we do?" the admiral asked.

The commodore answered in a whisper, "Pray."

"No. There has to be something concrete," the admiral countered, shaking a fist at the screen. "We could deploy the frigates and the fighters to get in front of the Ga'ee."

"They wouldn't even slow that ship down. We'd lose everything and everyone," the commodore replied, saving Lev the effort. "I know something about that. I also know something about not committing your forces before they can make a difference in the battle. We have no strategic reserve. It's just us, so we need to shepherd our assets. Hold them tight until the moment they can affect the outcome."

"Sounds like you learned the right lessons at the BEP," the admiral replied.

"I think they were hard lessons learned in the hardest way, and most of them were right here. I'd hate for that experience to go to waste." She stepped out from under Harry's arm and away from his subconscious effort to protect her. It would make no difference. If the Ga'ee wanted to destroy *Leviathan*, they would. As long as Lev didn't protect himself, there was nothing Harry Wesson could do to save anyone.

The admiral leaned against the captain's chair and scanned the bridge. The crew at their stations watched him.

"Winners pick the battlefield!" he shouted. "We'll make sure we're ready next time, and there *will be* a next time. We're not going to cede our galaxy to Count Boxenstabby!"

A couple of the crew chuckled.

Nyota spoke softly. "Payne is a bad influence on you. 'Boxenstabby?' Is that the official designation of the Ga'ee ship?"

"It should be Gulf -Uniform-Oscar, the Ga'ee unidentified object, but maybe we'll stick with 'Count Boxenstabby.' May we cross swords with this big bastard without letting him pummel us. Those body blows are a real bitch."

Lev put a repair estimate on the screen. It showed five minutes and counting down. Even that small number was far more than three seconds, the time it had taken *Leviathan* to travel there from the impact area created by the drone cloud.

The Ga'ee carrier had almost completed its recovery of the drones. Once the alien ship started to move, *Leviathan* would be at its mercy.

It had shown no mercy in any previous engagement.

They waited impatiently to see what Fate had in store for them. The tension grew heavy and breathing became a challenge.

"Is the air handling working right, Lev?" the admiral asked.

"It is. Pulse rate and blood pressure among the crew has increased significantly in the last minute."

The board showed four minutes. The seconds ticked painfully by.

"When people see a countdown to their death, they tend to tense up," the admiral noted.

The clock disappeared from the board.

"Thanks, Lev. Is the Ga'ee ship moving yet?"

"It has changed course and is now traveling at point-nine-eight c. It will intercept the armada in fifteen minutes."

Admiral Wesson grew tenser as the crew relaxed at the news that their deaths were no longer inevitable. Not today, anyway.

A dozen ships from Earth and her allies, along with their crews, were going to die. That didn't make anyone feel better. Heavy pits invaded their stomachs.

"Lev. We need to get in front of the Ga'ee so we can tell our people to scatter. Don't give the Ga'ee a group target. And we'll meet up at BD23 unless the Ga'ee are there. Then we'll rally in the final Berantz system at planet BD27."

"I've updated the message on the comm buoy, but it will arrive far too late to help the armada."

The admiral spoke out loud but not to anyone in particular. "Three minutes before we can start moving. Fourteen minutes before the Ga'ee intercept Arthir and her people. They have energy sensors and should be able to see us once we hit the gas. They'll know it's us because we're the biggest ship out here that isn't them."

"Will they?" the commodore asked. "They had already left before we arrived at Earth. They don't know we're here."

"Lev! The sensors they installed. Can they tell it's you?"

"Yes. My signature is unique, like most capital-grade ships—your dreadnoughts, the Ebren behemoths. They will know it's me."

"Then, as soon as you can, light the fires and best speed to BD23. We'll show our people that we're leaving. They might not see the Ga'ee until they return to normal space, but when they do, they'll add two and two and realize that even we had to run from the alien ship."

"Like lighting a flare that says 'follow me.'" The commodore nodded with her words, hope creeping into her voice.

"It's the best we have. Lev, that's the plan. BD23 as soon as we're able, but first, let's try sending a message via the energy sensor..."

[13]

"If it's worth fighting for, then what are you waiting for?"
–From the memoirs of Ambassador Declan Payne

Admiral Arthir Dorsite sat in the fleet commander's seat in the interior command center of the Kaiju-class dreadnought *Cleophas*. Captain Ezekiel Smith sat nearby. Smith was in charge of the ship, but Arthir controlled the armada.

Two Boriton-class Ebren battlewagons, two Whale-class human battleships, two Rang'Kor heavy cruisers, and five Eagle-class human heavy cruisers rounded out the dozen ships in the tactical armada deployed to Berantz space.

To stop an incursion by an unknown entity calling itself the Ga'ee.

"Ten minutes to normal space," Flight Control reported.

Arthir took another sip of her coffee. A steward nearby, waiting to serve the admiral and the ship's captain—an ensign wearing a name tape that read Lord. Arthir drained her coffee and handed the cup on the saucer to the young man.

"Another, Admiral?" the ensign asked.

Arthir shook her head.

"Captain," the sensor specialist called before transferring the information to the tactical display. "*Leviathan* just left this system. They are behind a smaller signature, looks to be cruiser-class. Both en route to BD23. No other ship signatures remain in the BD18 system."

"What do you think it means, Zeke?" Arthir asked. She had an idea and was confident she was correct.

"The alien ship has been here," the captain replied.

"But where is it now?" Arthir asked.

"Sensors aren't showing anything. Maybe it's the ship registering as the cruiser."

"That ship was ten kilometers long," Arthir replied. "I can't see it registering as a cruiser." Arthir chewed her lip and watched the screen. How many ships had been in this system before *Leviathan* departed?"

The sensor operator replayed the previous twenty minutes of data. It showed two ships moving from behind the planet into the place where *Leviathan* would later appear. Two cruisers. One disappeared, and the other departed at FTL. Shortly afterward, *Leviathan* appeared. It flew for three seconds, then disappeared, only to reappear five minutes later.

"I'd say that looks like two Berantz cruisers and *Leviathan*."

On *Leviathan*'s reappearance, it moved in a jerky manner—three short hops, followed by three longer hops, followed by three shorter hops.

"Your orders, Admiral?" Captain Smith asked.

"Replay *Leviathan's* departure from its five-minute stop," Arthir requested while watching the countdown clock.

She had five minutes to decide.

After watching the sensor data a second time, it dawned on her. "That's a message from my old friend Harry Wesson. *Leviathan* must have gone to Earth first and picked him up. Neither here nor there. It's Morse code—SOS, which is an emergency signal. It's a message in the only form he could send it to us. Prepare a message for Task Force Hammer. Proceed to BD23 at FTL immediately. Transmit on my command. I recommend battle stations, Captain. I think we're coming into a hot zone."

Smith accessed the ship-wide internal communication system. "All hands, battle stations. Prepare the ship for combat. Defensive systems are weapons-free. Department heads, report status in four minutes or less. Mark."

The admiral stood and stretched her legs. She remained standing as the clock counted down to zero. She clenched her jaw as the ship exited FTL speed within the BD18 system. The rest of the armada appeared around the dreadnought nearly simultaneously.

At point-blank range before them, they found the Ga'ee ship with its outer doors open and its drones streaming into space.

"Target that ship and fire Rapiers, tubes one to forty-eight," Captain Smith ordered in an even tone.

"Send the message," the admiral called.

"Sent," the comm officer confirmed.

"Captain?" Arthir asked with a sense of urgency. "It's time to go."

The drones accelerated toward the lead ships in the formation, one Rang'Kor and two human heavy cruisers. The Rapiers arced out from *Cleophas* and headed for the Ga'ee ship.

"A moment, Admiral. This battle might be over soon." The captain stared intently at the screen.

"No shit!" the admiral shouted. "Get us out of here!"

The crew watched in horror as the three cruisers were scrubbed from the board in a matter of seconds. The ships came apart with puffs of lost atmosphere, with explosions stifled by the near-vacuum of space, with the ships ripped from the bones of their superstructures.

"FTL to BD23 now, now, *now!*" the captain ordered.

The ship started to turn away from the incoming drones.

An Ebren battlewagon was next in the path of the unrelenting drones. It lit up with outbound munitions, chain guns fired, railguns and plasma weapons cycled at their maximum rates of fire, and every available Rapier anti-ship launched into space.

The cloud descended, unperturbed by the volume of fire directed at them. Small explosions marked direct hits, but the empty spaces were instantly filled by more three-pronged drones accelerating on a deadly path toward their intended victim.

"All ships, FTL to BD23. Execute," the admiral ordered over the fleetwide broadcast channel.

A Boriton-class battlewagon was an impressive vessel. Two kilometers of armor-plated ship, bristling with weaponry, whose sole purpose was to fill the void with destruction. The Ebren tried, but the Ga'ee overwhelmed them.

The first explosions came from amidships, where the superstructure cracked and the ship split. The drone cloud blasted in through the opening to rip the ship apart from the inside out.

Pieces of the ship drifted away as the Ga'ee drones ended the battlewagon's existence.

They turned their attention to *Cleophas.* The captain and the admiral weren't the only ones holding their breath as the ship came around to clear space before transitioning to faster-than-light speed. "Faster-than-light" didn't mean one could fly through obstacles during the critical transition period. It was a calculation that ensured life.

A cloud of drones was in the way.

Thrusters were at maximum, forward pushing from the starboard side and aft pushing from the port side to spin the ship.

But *Cleophas* was a big ship.

"Accelerate through the edge of that cloud, or they will over-whelm us." Captain Smith jumped out of his seat to point out the route he wanted to Flight Control. It was close to the desired direction for BD23. They'd have to adjust further before transitioning.

The dreadnought's main engines fired and launched the big ship away from the kill zone being established by the drones. The surviving escorts behind *Cleophas* had already gone into FTL. Their maneuverability had saved them from having to perform the unnatural act *Cleophas* was attempting.

"All weapons, fire straight ahead to fifteen degrees star-board. Clear that cone. All you've got, even the Rapiers."

Firing massive anti-ship missiles at drones a tenth their size wasn't the best return on weaponry investment, but the prospect of dying required a dramatic approach to the employment of firepower. Weapons cycled and sent depleted uranium rounds, ions, lasers, and plasma into the void in front of the big ship.

The drones sparked and died under the onslaught, but more came, and more. They adjusted their courses, looking to deliver tens of thousands of impacts on the ship's flank, create gaps to exploit, and rip the ship apart. The Ebren battlewagon had lasted less than twenty seconds under the Ga'ee's attack.

With reactors at a hundred and twenty percent, redlined to send power to the engines, *Cleophas* surged forward into a wing of drones attempting to envelop the dreadnought. The ship screeched and groaned under the impacts.

Defensive weapons continued to fire. Offensive weapons sent the entirety of their capital-grade stock into a narrow section of the cloud, exposing the flank.

"Clear!" Sensors shouted.

Flight Control punched the button, and the ship protested

for only a moment before it transitioned to FTL. The resulting wave of nausea passed quickly, to be replaced by the relief of survival.

"Significant damage to the bow," Engineering reported. "We'll close the breaches and isolate compartments open to space. Forward firepower is gone. Two of our heavy railguns and all four plasma cannons. Eight Rapier tubes are damaged beyond repair."

"We're lucky to be alive," the admiral said to one man, the ship's captain. Arthir glared at him.

He met her gaze. "Care to come with me to inspect the damage?" the captain asked.

The admiral nodded, and they left the bridge. Before the admiral could unload, Zeke Smith offered his resignation. "Those few seconds could have lost the whole ship. I was wrong. I'll step down immediately. The XO is good. Put him into the big chair. He's ready for it. I'll join Engineering and work to fix the damage I've caused."

"As much as I'd like to tell you that it happens to anyone, it doesn't. It can't. We cannot risk losing *Cleophas,* and when I give an order that is meant to save lives, I expect it to be followed. I accept your resignation. Join Engineering and fix this ship. We haven't even started to fight this alien, and we're already down four ships, with significant damage to a fifth."

The captain hung his head. "*Leviathan* will be waiting."

"The fact that *Leviathan* didn't attempt to fight that thing was all we needed to know."

"The first salvo was clear of the drones. They had to hit home on that ship. It would have been nice to see how effective they were to help us with future engagements."

"We'll have a better plan for that when we choose to mix it up with the Ga'ee. When *we* choose, Zeke. Have your XO Captain Buto report to me in my quarters."

———

"Twelve ships appeared in-system, coming into normal space right on top of the Ga'ee ship. Eight were able to achieve FTL, including the dreadnought. Three cruisers and one battlewagon were lost," a faceless individual reported from a seat on the outer edge of the command deck.

"You did the best you could," the commodore offered.

Admiral Wesson wanted to argue but couldn't. *Leviathan* continued to collect data.

I know that's frustrating you, Harry, Lev said. *I can't go by a gut feel. I have to use empirical data when I cannot see inside the mind of one who might be my enemy. Empirical data suggests the Ga'ee ship is only protecting itself while exploring each of these systems. Maybe it is looking for a place to live and keeps moving on as each system with a planet in the liquid water zone is inhabited.*

If that were true, Lev, then we could find a mutually agreeable solution. Why haven't they given us a chance?

Maybe they met an alien race who took advantage of their willingness to talk and tried to kill them. They would be hesitant. Shooting first is a learned behavior.

Why did the Ga'ee treat you differently? Is it because they are AIs?

I can't tell if they are AIs or not. How did you learn that's what I am?

Payne told me, the admiral answered. There was no sense in trying to lie to Lev. *What did you learn during your conversation?*

I learned that they are probably from this galaxy, based on their designated time of flight. Intergalactic travel, even with advanced FTL drives, takes a long, long time. I think they exist in a part of the Milky Way that the seven races have not explored.

This galaxy has a billion stars that have one hundred billion planets, and an estimated three hundred million have planets in the habitable zone. And that's just for carbon-based life forms. A silicon life form could have completely different parameters, adding to or subtracting from the totals. It's a staggering amount of space to explore.

Are they silicon-based life forms? the admiral tried to confirm.

I believe so. That's why I wanted Team Payne to board that ship. Meet them in person. That would be the quickest way to deescalate the situation.

A heavily armed team secretly boarding their ship as a form of de-escalation? I don't see it, Lev. But they would have put us in a position to sue for peace, just like they did with the Mryas-malites. But it's all moot now. Team Payne is gone and we're flying blind, wondering if that big bastard is going to follow.

I don't want Team Payne to be gone, Lev admitted.

You should have thought of that before you decided the entity who would try to kill them wasn't our enemy, Lev. You are right; that frustrates the crap out of me. Peace through superior fire-power! We don't need to use the worldkiller every time we get into a pickle, but we need to not discount its use. All options need to remain on the table at all times. And the Ga'ee? If anyone is rated to get up close and personal with the worldkiller, it's them.

I will think about it more, as I have already. Recriminations are not useful except as an intellectual exercise to better evaluate the variables when it comes to future decision-making.

That was an awful lot of words to say that you'll try to do better next time.

There will always be a next time, Harry.

That's what I'm afraid of. How long until BD23? The admiral headed for the corridor.

"Two days and four hours to reach BD23," Lev replied so everyone could hear.

"I'm going to stand down the crew, have them get some rest and recharge. Time to get something to eat."

The commodore joined him as they left the bridge. In the corridor, he leaned against the cart. It settled to the deck to better support him.

"We'll rally at BD23. At some point, we're going to have to stand and fight, but we can't go toe to toe with the Ga'ee."

"Guerilla tactics, like we did with the drone dreadnought. A worldkiller lying in wait when it comes out of FTL, ripping into it before it can launch its clouds."

"Count Boxenstabby?" Nyota tried to lighten Harry's mood. Not having Team Payne around weighed heavily on him. He wanted to believe they were only MIA but feared the worst.

"It's hard to think of that thing as anything other than hell's spawn." He scowled, and the darkness of a new war crossed his face. "Once more into battle to win the peace. One ship against many. I don't like finding myself on the run. We can't distract it, and we can't stop it, but we will because we have to."

"Logistics. How is it building new drones to replace the ones lost in the attacks? Ripping ships apart destroys a lot of drones," Nyota asked. She ignored the cart and started walking. The dining facility wasn't far away.

"That is a good question. Hit and run to force it to use resources it cannot replace, as long as we can figure out where it's getting its construction materials from. Asteroids? It'll be hard to destroy all the asteroids in its path, but we could mine the asteroid field..." Harry's thoughts drifted into conversations about area denial when space was so vast. But lucrative natural resources were not. Few asteroids had the materials necessary to build a modern spacecraft, even if that craft was only a small drone.

"Sometimes, the best you can hope for is that you don't die. Everything after that is gravy." —From the memoirs of Ambassador Declan Payne

With his jets at maximum output, Payne still hit the ground harder than he wanted. His boots embedded a good third of a meter deep, part of the way up the suit's calves. He pulled himself free before he checked the area. The others had hit before him and were scattered nearby in an open area between trees and rolling hills.

Payne checked his HUD. Everyone showed up except Kal. "Kal'faxx, are you out there?" The Ebren's suit's helmet was tied into the team channel, but it showed as a dead link.

"Anyone seen Kal?" Payne asked.

"He was spinning out of control, trying to carry the plasma cannon while working those crazy hand jets. I last saw him at three hundred four degrees magnetic."

The suits' compasses had calibrated to the planet's magnetic pole.

"We need to find Kal."

The team moved toward him to rally around their leader. Everyone walked without issue. The health status for every member showed green and one hundred percent.

"Supplies, send me your counts," Dank requested as part of his duties as XO. After twenty seconds, he reported the bad news. "We're a bit light on food. We need to see what's left of the uglymobile and the rations inside."

"Roger," Payne confirmed. "Joker, see if you can contact *Leviathan*, although I expect they're gone. Next up is to contact the planet's leadership to see if we can get the hell out of here and find a way back to our ship. The armada from Earth should be arriving soon. If the Ga'ee are out of the system, then we'll be able to catch a ride on *Cleophas*, assuming they know we're here."

"You heard the major," Dank added. "Tactical formation, wide V, Heckler on point. Turbo left flank, Dog right flank. Form up in between and stay sharp. Even though this is the planet of an ally, we don't know how they'll react to us appearing here. They might consider us illegal immigrants. Wouldn't that be funny?"

"No, sir," Blinky replied. "That wouldn't be funny at all."

The technicians took the right flank with Mary, lined up with their weapons slung but facing forward. Without a system to break into, they were nothing more than pack mules.

Byle, Shaolin, and Sparky took the left flank. Dank moved up front by Heckler. Payne stayed centered in the rear of the formation, where he could see his team members to make any adjustments required by a changing situation.

"Pick up the pace, Heckler, but stay frosty," Payne sent over the team channel. "Looking for Ebren life signs. He needs us to find him sooner rather than later."

Heckler stayed alert. He walked point as he always did.

He'd never been on this planet and had never dealt with the Berantz. He didn't know if they were hostile.

Unexpected humans wearing combat suits and heavily armed.

There was no reason to think Team Payne wouldn't be met with resistance or outright hostility.

They traveled a kilometer, then two. They passed through a meadow of wild grain, then scrub brush, and started climbing a rocky hill.

Movement ahead. Heckler raised his fist and took a knee. The others dropped and covered their fields of fire.

Up ahead, an imposing figure waved from the top of a boulder.

"It's Kal," Heckler reported. He waved his arm and hatcheted toward the Ebren. The team continued up the hill, where Kal had collected the fragments of the plasma cannon and the cracked helmet.

"I hit kind of hard," he explained.

"Are you okay?"

"I'm fine. Ebren don't get hurt by trivial things like falling out of a spacecraft traveling at five times the speed of sound."

Payne snorted. "It wasn't that bad. Look at us! None the worse for wear."

"What do we do with this junk?" Kal asked.

"Virgil?" Payne redirected the question.

"Blow it in place. Leave nothing for anyone to reverse-engineer. Then again, the Berantz are allies, aren't they?"

Payne waved for Sparky to look over the equipment. She dug through it, snapped off two chips, and pulled the power supply. "Without this stuff, they won't get it to work. No need to do anything else. It's useless," she reported.

"We'll call it good," Payne stated. Dank gave the thumbs-up in agreement.

Kal pointed up the hill. "You'll probably want to see this." They followed him up. He walked with a slight limp, noticeable because he never showed physical weakness. He didn't complain, and Payne wasn't going to press him on it. They couldn't afford to have people hurt. They needed to get off that planet and back to *Leviathan*.

Beyond the crest, grass spread nearly to the horizon. In the distance, wild animals grazed. Payne was instantly hungry.

Closer, a heavy scorch mark scarred the field. At the end of it, *Ugly 4* looked partially intact. "Our food," Payne noted. He made to walk downhill, but Kal stopped him.

"Wait."

"What am I missing?"

Kal pointed and watched.

Behind the stealth insertion craft, a metal arm raised and lowered. "Don't tell me one of those things survived." Payne stared until he caught the movement again. It appeared to be digging.

"I think we need to go down there and kill that thing." Payne received unanimous agreement from his team. "Heckler, carry on. Lead us to the promised land."

Heckler pumped his fist and pointed down the hill. He headed out with Dank beside him. Although they focused on the impact crater, they looked elsewhere, too. They weren't in a hurry to walk into a trap.

The team kept their railguns up. Kal walked next to Payne with empty hands. Payne drew his boarding axe and gave it to the Ebren. "You look naked without a weapon."

"You've seen me naked without a weapon." Kal spoke softly out the side of his mouth while watching the way ahead.

"And you lost that fight. Now, you can't lose because you have clothes and a nice piece of gear."

"That cuts me deep, boss man. If the plasma cannon had

survived the crash, I would have already taken care of this." Kal nodded at his claim.

"No sweat, Kal. I'm glad you're okay. Those hand jets?"

"Suck hairy buffalo balls."

Payne nodded. "Close it up a little bit, Turbo. You're going too wide."

The combat specialist adjusted her course.

At the bottom of the hill, they formed into a perfect V for the final approach to the impact crater. Heckler looked down the barrel of his railgun, thumb ready to click it off safe. "Get ready with a grenade," he told Major Dank, who had the best throwing arm of the whole team.

"I'll use two just to be sure."

"I like it when we're sure," Heckler agreed. He slowed when they closed to twenty meters and activated the team channel. "I can hear it digging."

"Why don't you let it know we're here, Virge?" Payne asked.

The team readied to fire. Major Dank tossed the first grenade high so it would take longer to reach the hole and sent the second in on a lower trajectory. The first one clanged off metal an instant before it exploded. The second blew immediately afterward.

Heckler charged. Before he reached the hole, a Ga'ee drone leapt from the hole and raced skyward, corkscrewing upward as it foiled Heckler's aim before diving low to the ground and flying away. Heckler continued to the hole. He jumped back, snap-firing into the hole before easing forward to continue to pour fire into the space.

Dank jumped in beside him as Blinky and Shaolin showed up. They also fired into the hole.

"What the hell are you shooting at?" Payne ran a few steps until a big hand grabbed him mid-stride to hold him back. "Kal, let me go!"

The Ebren didn't. Dank called a ceasefire. "Dec, this could be the most fucked-up thing I've ever seen."

Kal finally let go. Payne hurried forward to find a number of silver fish-shaped objects at the bottom of the pit.

"What am I looking at?" he wondered.

"They were wiggling and slithering. Creeped me out," Dank explained.

Mary looked into the hole. She was the team member who had studied biology. "Gentlemen, what you're looking at are baby Ga'ee. I think each of the drones is capable of reproducing, which means every planet the ship passed could be infested with these things."

"We better tell the Berantz that one got away," Payne replied. "Any luck getting hold of anyone?"

"None. I'm not sure how close we are to any population centers," Joker replied. "If we can get some altitude, I'll be able to set up the array. That will increase my comm range exponentially."

"Virge, recover what you can from our ship."

"Byle and Buzz, in you go," Dank ordered. The two smaller team members worked their way into the pit, keeping their distance from the smoking nest. They crawled through the missing aft end into the ship.

"We have jerky!" Buzz declared. He reached out and tossed a bag to Dank. Two more bags of protein bars followed, which was the extent of the emergency rations kept aboard *Ugly 4*.

Despite their small size, those rations would extend the life of Team Payne by two weeks if they didn't find anything else to eat. Payne had his eye on the creatures grazing in the distance.

"Looks good on the food front. Heckler and Turbo, are you up for a hunt?"

They started walking without waiting for an order. "Who's afraid of a little blood?"

"I'll go with them," Mary offered. She held up her combat axe. "Not exactly the best for cleaning and skinning, but it'll do."

Payne gestured for her to follow them.

"Joker, you, Shaolin, Buzz, and Major Dank head to the top of the hill we were just on and try to make contact with the Berantz. I'll stay here with Blinky, Kal, and Sparky to see if we can figure out *anything* related to these things."

Heckler kept going, with Turbo and Dog in tow. Dank led the way toward the hill with his comm team.

Payne stood with his hands on his hips. "This changes everything while confirming one thing. They *are* a silicon-based life form."

"But they like the Goldilocks zone, based on two data points," Blinky clarified. "The first is that this is where we found them, and the second is that the Ga'ee vessel went to each system with a planet that could sustain carbon-based life. Whether they breathe air or need water or prefer the warmth, here they are."

"Which also means we need to backtrack and visit every system the Ga'ee have gone through." Payne stared into the pit as he ran his suit through the active scans available to it. He'd let Lev analyze the results. "Did anyone see Lev get away before we entered the atmosphere?"

Blinky and Sparky shook their heads. Payne looked at Kal.

"Sorry, but no. Who will take care of the Cabrizi without any of us there?"

"Somebody will. Cookie. The admiral. Lev will make sure of it. He knows what those animals mean to you and what they mean to me."

Blinky jumped into the hole, along with Sparky. They prodded the nest with their axes. Blinky raised his axe and brought it down with all his augmented strength, then again.

Sparky joined him, rhythmically hammering the baby Ga'ee into the ground.

"What are you doing down there?" Payne demanded.

"Coming out!" They didn't bother trying to climb out. He and Sparky activated their jets for a quick lift out of the pit. The second Blinky hit, he pulled out four blocks of explosives, wrapped them together, added a detonator, and prepared to toss it in.

"Blinky!" Payne stopped him. "Report!"

"Sir, what you see on the top is just scratching the surface. There's a bunch more of those things underground. It's like a snake pit down there." Blinky's armored hand shook.

"I'll do it." Payne took the explosive and set the timer for ten seconds. "Clear out. Fire in the hole." He changed to the team channel. "Blowing the nest. There were a lot more of those things beneath the dirt."

After his people had jogged away, he tossed the explosive in and sprinted toward them.

The explosion shook the ground and sent a small mushroom cloud skyward. "Do we have any motion detectors?" Payne asked.

Sparky nodded. She took one out of her kit, activated it, and dropped it into the pit. She stomped on the ground to make sure it registered. Once she was satisfied, she gave the thumbs-up. "If they survived the explosion and are able to move out of the hole, we'll know about it."

"I'm not sure I want to know if they find their way out of that hole, but worse is if they spread out underground where we can't see them. I'm not sure ignorance will provide any kind of respite or feeling of safety."

"What will they do to this planet?" Blink asked.

"Nothing good. The Ga'ee didn't seem too keen about shar-ing. Not space, and I expect not the planet, either. Come on, let's find a way off this rock. Break, break. Heckler, return to the hill. We don't have time for hunting."

"On our way," came the disappointed reply.

A strange but familiar sound approached. Payne dialed his sensors to the max. "Incoming!"

[15]

"School your expectations. Life is a lot easier that way."
–From the memoirs of Ambassador Declan Payne

After the Ga'ee carrier had retrieved the drone swarms, it moved slowly toward the planet designated BD18. The ship kissed the upper atmosphere, where a small formation of drones deployed.

The big ship set course for the nearest system with a habitable planet.

BD23.

The drones separated as they transited through the upper atmosphere. The fireballs were short-lived, and the drones cleared the barrier and headed toward the planet. They rejoined each other to fly in close formation. Their engines screamed during the descent.

Not to impress the locals. Not to proclaim their presence.

They weren't optimized for intra-atmospheric flight because this was a one-way trip.

———

"The Ga'ee ship has resumed FTL flight. It is headed toward BD23," Lev announced.

"How much time will we have with our fleet before the Ga'ee arrive?" Admiral Wesson asked. He put his fork down. Commodore Nyota Freeman put hers down, too. They were the only ones eating, although the admiral had given the order for everyone to stand down.

"Twenty-two minutes."

"And we arrive twenty minutes before that. Enough time to convince the Berantz to leave the system."

"What if we send the Berantz back to BD18?" Nyota asked. At the admiral's look, she explained. "Looks like the Ga'ee are on a one-way trip. What's to say we can't backtrack it?"

"That is genius. Why run in front of it when we can let it skip past us and keep going. Avoid confrontation altogether." Harry resumed eating. After chewing for a long time, he swallowed. "Once you say it out loud, it makes sense. We have enough ships to stay in front of it for at least the BD23 and BD27 systems. After that, who knows where it's going? We can be in front of and behind it."

"That means if we want to fight it, we need to decide in the next two days. Then we have twenty minutes to get everyone to buy into the plan to make a stand at BD27."

The admiral nodded as he continued to chew.

"But I'd rather be out here with this problem than back on Earth, even though we just lost four ships and their crews. The Berantz and the Rang'Kor have suffered significant losses. I should feel more for them."

"Your gift. Your curse," the commodore replied. "You do feel for them, but more for those who have not yet been impacted. You can't save them all. You can't be in charge if you can't keep the emotions out of it. You said that."

"I said that in a former life." The admiral pushed his tray to the side. "The first food trays were used as early as the seventh century before the common era but didn't come into vogue until Earth's world wars. Stainless steel serving trays with six compartments to keep the food separated."

Nyota glanced down at the tray on the table before her. Six compartments. "Your point?"

"My point is that we don't need to abandon the past to move forward into the future. When something works, it's okay to stick with it."

"You have a plan, don't you?" The commodore pushed her tray away. Cleaning equipment whipped by and picked the trays up for recycling and reuse.

"The skeleton of a plan is starting to form. I'm going to ask a lot from our people." The admiral stood and stretched to his full height. Despite the burden of command, he was getting back to himself. His people believed in him. Nyota believed in him. Declan had believed in him. He owed all of them his best.

Because that meant the best for humanity, plus all its allies.

The Rang'Kor captain entered, with the Cabrizi nipping at his tentacles. He slapped at them, but they dodged out of the way.

"Those creatures will not leave me be," he started.

The breath caught in the admiral's throat. He choked on the words.

"We'll take care of them," the commodore replied. She crouched, and they came to her as if they knew.

"What of Major Payne?" Captain Pel'Rok asked.

"He's gone," the admiral replied with a cold edge in his voice.

"When will he be back?"

"He won't, Captain." The admiral moved closer to the Rang'Kor. "You said you wanted vengeance. Do you think you can fly one of our Mosquitos?"

———

Payne dove into the grass. The others followed an instant before the first rounds landed.

Artillery.

It fell around them and the remains of *Ugly 4*. The rounds exploded on impact, shaking the ground while sending dust clouds skyward. The explosions walked back and forth across the area, turning the serene grassland into a cratered wasteland.

"Cease fire, cease fire," came Joker's calm voice. "Berantz forces. You are firing on a crashed human spaceship. We request assistance. I say again, cease fire!" The suit's computer translated the message to broadcast a repeat in Berantz.

The barrage ended as quickly as it had started.

Payne stood, then checked those in his immediate vicinity before accessing his HUD to verify that the whole team had come through unscathed.

"Up the hill, people." Payne pounded ahead. "When nothing is going right, why would we expect a break?"

They made it twenty steps before the second salvo arrived.

Joker repeated her message.

Payne crouched as the new barrage landed beyond the crash site.

"What in the hell are those people doing?" Payne grumbled. "Come on, Heckler. Get your people over here."

The hunting group ran, using their suits to augment their speed. They'd practiced on *Leviathan* and were able to hit forty kilometers per hour now. They raced past Payne's group and surged ahead.

When the third salvo arrived, they were well out of the impact area.

"Firing blind," Dank stated.

"Did we land in a firing range at a most inopportune

moment, or are they actually shooting at us?" Payne wondered. No one had the answer.

Joker continued her efforts to reach someone from the planet. "Berantz planet Bravo Delta Eighteen, please respond."

"What do they call this planet?" Mary asked. She looked from face shield to face shield. "Nice. We don't know what they call their own planet. What happened to cultural awareness training?"

Payne shook his head. He loosened his helmet, took it off, and motioned for Mary to do the same.

"Not a good look, Dog. Complaining about what we should have done doesn't help us. We're on our own, and we need to figure it out."

Mary frowned, but she understood. She nodded tightly. "Won't happen again, Dec."

He took a deep breath. "Clean, but we better stay suited up. We don't know where the next barrage is going to land."

"Active scan shows inbound aircraft," Sparky reported. "I've never seen their like."

"Berantz intra-atmospheric fighters?" Payne ventured. "Everyone wave and play nice. If they fire on us, do not shoot back. If we're to enlist their aid, killing them won't improve our chances at hitching a ride."

"We don't have anything non-lethal," Heckler noted.

"Doesn't matter," Dank interrupted. "They're not the enemy, even if they're shooting at us."

"Twenty seconds," Sparky reported.

"Spread out. Don't give them an easy target, and keep your heads down," Payne commanded.

The team scattered to the four winds, using rocks for cover where they could or going face-first into the dirt and trying to become one with the ground.

The inbound flight of four delta-winged craft screamed like

banshees as they raced overhead, then dipped into the valley before going vertical. They rolled over the top and zeroed in on the hilltop where Joker made call after call, spinning through a variety of frequencies and modulations.

Rockets leapt from the cylindrical fuselages and pounded the hilltop. Joker disappeared within multiple explosions. Near Payne, Mary erupted with the ground as a missile buried itself beneath her before exploding. Her twisted combat suit landed nearly in the same hole.

On Payne's HUD, her life signs redlined.

Payne's vision clouded. He jumped to his feet and raised his railgun. Kal appeared at his side. He pushed the railgun down. Payne resisted the movement but quickly lost his will to fight. He dropped his railgun.

The flight of ships banked and returned on a vector a hundred and eighty degrees from their first attack run. The Ebren stepped to the top of the hill and waved his arms while shouting, "Take me!"

Joker's voice returned on the channel for a space emergency beacon. "Listen here, you motherfuckers. You come at us once more, and we're going to rip you out of the sky and tear your bodies apart with our bare hands. We're humans, and you've made a mistake in treating us like your enemy. Fix your shit right fucking now."

The craft zoomed by without releasing more munitions.

A voice replied on the same channel, speaking Berantz. The translation voiced over nearly instantaneously. "What are humans doing on Brayalore?"

"We crashed while trying to defend your planet from an alien invader. We're sorry we tried to help," Joker snarled.

Payne vaulted to Mary's side. A huge rent in the side of the suit seeped blood. Her face shield was dark. Her vital signs monitor was missing. Payne unlocked her helmet, carefully twisted it free, and removed it. Mary groaned at him.

"I think I got my scar," she mumbled.

"We need to get you out of there. Your suit is damaged and hasn't deployed foam into the wounds like it should have," he cautioned. The pool outside the suit was growing. "You're losing too much blood."

He used his suit-augmented strength to bend the twisted metal outward. Mary cried out. He rolled her on her side to undo the suit from the back. Kal's oversized hands reached past to pull the suit apart to free Payne's hands to remove Mary and put her naked body on the ground. He kept pressure on the wound that traced from the back of her hip around her side and to her breastbone.

They each had emergency foam inside their suits. Payne couldn't get to his, but Sparky pulled herself free and handed the can over.

Payne's hand shook as he sprayed. A bare hand took the can from him to finish the job. Sparky kneeled next to him. She used her fingers to wipe the blood off. They didn't have a rag or any material.

Buzz offered a handful of dry grass. Sparky did what she could before checking her pulse. Mary's eyes rolled back in her head as she passed out. Payne pulled his helmet off so he could lean close and see her with his unshielded eyes. Her skin was pale and slightly gray.

"It's cold out here," Sparky noted. "We need to keep her warm."

Payne stepped back and removed his suit. He wrapped his body around hers to provide warmth.

"Get to the ship and see if any clothing survived or an emergency blanket, stuff like that," Dank requested. Heckler and

Turbo bolted, leaping over rocks and accelerating down the hill toward the cratered area and the crash site.

They held their railguns at the ready because of the creatures in the pit. No one knew if they had survived. The motion sensor had triggered during the Berantz bombing as the data shared across team HUDs but not since.

Dank rested his hand on Kal's back as the Ebren hovered protectively over his two favorite humans, but only for a moment.

"Establish a perimeter." Dank gestured at Blinky. "Joker, get me the Berantz."

She reset her portable array, checked it twice, and gave Major Dank the heads-up.

"Berantz forces. This is Major Virgil Dank from Earth Fleet. We request immediate medical assistance for a severely injured team member. We request transport for twelve to your city and further transport to space. The supreme leader of the seven races is here, too. Please expedite."

"Is that his official title?" Joker asked.

"Maybe they know Major Payne by that title. The least they can do is show a little remorse, if not any respect."

"This is Brayalore Planetary Defense. A recovery team has been dispatched."

Dank waited for more, but there wasn't any.

"Thank you. Team Payne is standing by." Dank tried to maintain the decorum that Payne had demanded before Dog got hurt. Declan had seen it coming, and he was right. They needed the Berantz more than the Berantz needed them.

At least when it came to BD18.

Brayalore. They now knew its name, but that didn't make any of them feel any better.

Two minutes passed before Turbo and Heckler returned from *Ugly 4*.

They handed out the team's spare jumpsuits and two emergency blankets. Sparky situated the first blanket while Payne pushed himself free. Together, they wrapped Dog within it and added the second blanket for good measure.

Payne dressed in his jumpsuit rather than climb back into his combat armor. He kneeled at Mary's side. "Kal, your job is to take care of her so I can deal with the Berantz. As long as I know you have her, I can do what I need to do to get us out of here."

"I swear on my life, Declan. She shall not leave my sight."

Payne gripped the Ebren's forearm tightly. "Thank you, Kal. I owe you."

"You owe me nothing, pardner," Kal drawled and winked. "She's going to be just fine. She's strong, probably stronger than you."

Payne chuckled briefly. "Probably, my friend. Don't worry about the Cabrizi. Lev won't let anything happen to them."

Kal nodded and sat cross-legged next to Mary. Sparky gave her a sip of water.

Payne stepped up the hill to the top, where Dank stood next to Joker.

"Thanks, Virge."

"You'd do the same for me."

"I would. What's our status?"

"A Berantz recovery team is on their way. No ETA. I have no idea what any of that means, but we have positive comm with planetary defense. No guarantee that'll continue. Hey, Dec?"

Major Payne glanced at Mary and then at the horizon. The sky was clear. "What do you need, Virge?"

Dank removed his helmet. "Do you think Lev knows we survived?"

"I doubt it. We weren't squawking. We were surrounded by bad guys, then we were burning through the atmosphere. If they knew what was good for them, they would have headed out of here at FTL."

"I don't suspect they'll be back," Virgil continued. "My friend is on board. She'll think I'm dead."

"I reckon. You know what they say. Absence makes the heart grow fonder. We'll do our best until we can get word to them. We'll send out messages on every ship as soon as we're able. Our message will catch up with them. They'll come back for us."

"If they can," Virgil said softly. "The Ga'ee are like nothing we've ever seen. Relentless. And they're leaving their seed behind. We need to go back to every planet where they've been and burn them out, but there's the rub. We're not sure how to kill them."

Payne faced his XO. "Delivered with all the subtlety of a worldkiller. I fear you're right. All that means is it's up to us. We don't have the crutch of the greatest ship in the universe."

They watched for the Berantz. It was ten more minutes before the ship arrived, a boxy transport like an oversized ambulance for intra-atmospheric flight only. The medics that stepped off the ship were all business.

"The victim?" the one at the front of an empty stretcher asked. Byle pointed.

Team Payne stayed on their toes. The Berantz had brought six armed security, but they were wearing uniforms, not combat suits. Team Payne grossly outmatched them if it came to a shooting match, which wasn't what Payne wanted.

He closed with the final party to come off the transport, a silver-haired individual with purple spots on his translucent skin. His oversized eyes carried a gray tinge. The major began, "I'm Declan Payne."

"Mr. Ambassador." The elder Berantz bowed his head. "We don't usually get unannounced visitors, but these are strange times. An alien ship entered our system, followed by *Leviathan*. And then nothing but white noise. Can you enlighten me?"

"We crash-landed, following the attack by the Ga'ee. Their drones chased us in, and I fear the drones also seeded your planet with their silicon-based life form. You'll find samples in the crater behind the remains of our ship. Whom do I have the honor of addressing?"

"I am the governor-general of Brayalore." He stepped back to call two of his security team to him. He directed them to the crater to collect a sample of the creature Payne had described. The two Berantz hurried down the hill.

Kal stayed closer than the Berantz medics were comfortable with since they kept glancing at him. Mary Payne lay naked on the blanket, her body exposed to the cold while they inserted needles in both arms and hooked up two bags of clear liquid.

Payne called over his shoulder, "Rally the team to me, Virge."

Dank summoned the team. Sparky put her combat suit on. Payne debated but decided against it.

"Byle and Shaolin, carry my suit, please."

The two ran to where his suit was parked and tipped it over, catching it between them as it fell. They carried it to the Berantz ship and wedged it into a corner between the seats and the fuselage.

The medics added heating packs, then wrapped Mary in the two emergency blankets again. They carefully lifted her and placed her on the stretcher. Team Payne moved in to take the handles, and the medics let them. The group hurried to the ship parked at the top of the hill.

Dank counted heads, checked his HUD, and reported to Payne. "All present."

"Mr. Ambassador," the governor-general said. "My medics report that the victim will survive."

"My wife, Governor-General. Your attack injured *my wife*."

"Had you contacted us before your arrival, all of this could have been avoided."

Payne clenched his jaw as the blood rushed to his head. Major Dank stepped between the two. "Governor-General. We were busy trying to save your cruisers and your system from the alien. Had we known we were going to crash, we would have sent a communique, a courier, and probably chocolates. Have you heard from your ships since the attack?"

"We have not. We thought the enemy had won the fight. We've mobilized to repel the invaders."

Dank turned to Payne. "He has a point, Dec."

Payne nodded. "As much as I'd like my kilo of flesh from the Berantz for hurting Mary, I understand. And from what we've seen, they have every right to be afraid. My apologies, Governor-General. Save my wife's life, and we'll do our best to save what's left of Berantz space, but first, you have a bug problem right here on Brayalore."

"You never run as fast as when you're running for your life." –From the memoirs of Ambassador Declan Payne

"We don't have much time from when we come out of FTL until the Fleet ships arrive, and we have to assume there's even less time until the Ga'ee show up. We have two questions we need to answer. The first is what do we do to save as many lives as possible, and the second is how do we engage the Ga'ee ship?"

The squadron commanders sat around the oversized table, relaxed but focused on the admiral. Captain Pel'Rok perched on his tentacles at the end of the table.

Commodore Freeman was there, too. She had once commanded a fleet whose sole purpose was to defend Earth, something none of the others had done.

Lev was there, of course, as he always was, even though this wasn't his fight.

"We know what doesn't work, and that's anything that smacks of being aggressive. It seems to also hold true when we're defending ourselves."

Woody Malone spoke up. "It set a trap for the armada. Four ships were scrubbed in seconds. Less than a minute out of FTL, and they lost a third of their ships."

"What's good for the goose..." the admiral started. He looked from face to face. "But how can we lay in wait without exposing ourselves?"

"Mines. We fill the sky with things that go boom."

"Lev, do you think that will have any effect on the Ga'ee vessel?"

"Thank you for asking," Lev replied pleasantly. "No. That ship's drones will clear the space around it. To destroy that ship, you'll need to get inside it. A missile that flies through the open doors. At ten kilometers long, finding the vulnerable points will be based on lucky guesses unless I get more data."

"Which in itself is problematic," the admiral replied. "Can we deploy buoys and remote sensors?"

"That is the only option. I'll begin construction immediately. We have thirty-six hours before our arrival in the BD23 system. I can have two hundred available."

"We'll deploy them throughout the system along the Ga'ee's inbound trajectory. We'll task one ship to stand in the way to draw the alien out of FTL. *Cleophas* is big enough."

"Will *Cleophas* be able to escape?" Commander Wazeree asked.

"If she transitions to FTL the instant the Ga'ee vessels starts opening its side doors. *Cleophas* can flush her launch tubes and make sure every munition available to her is in the void, ready to impact that ship when it enters normal space. The buoys will be deployed in a three-dimensional checkerboard pattern. We need to fly one or more into the Ga'ee's hangar bay once their drones have launched. Those designated to infiltrate the Ga'ee ship run silent while the rest are actively scanning."

"I concur with your recommendation. Their small size will

limit the other ship's ability to discover them until they go active."

"How much time do you need?" The admiral closed his eyes and tried to visualize the optimal encounter while planning for the worst possible engagement.

"A second or two. The sensor buoys will vastly increase our knowledge of the Ga'ee ship."

"That's what I want to hear." The admiral scanned the faces at the table. "A hit-and-run. Rally at BD27, using what we learned from BD23 for an engagement to resolve this."

"Are we going to kill it?"

"If we were, then we'd send a worldkiller right down its throat." The admiral pounded a fist into his hand.

"Then why don't we? Why the games?" Commander Appel asked. "That thing is a killer. We tried to talk to it, and it attacked us."

"When we tried to talk to it," Lev answered, "we were employing a certain amount of subterfuge in trying to infiltrate Team Payne into that ship. They only attacked us after that."

"What about the Rang'Kor?" Pel'Rok slapped a tentacle on the table. "Tell me, great ship, what about us? It entered our system and attacked without mercy. We only tried to defend ourselves. What about our space station? They didn't even have weapons!"

"I can see your angst, Pel'Rok," Lev agreed. "The space station is an anomaly that I can't account for."

"The answer is easy. The Ga'ee are the enemy of civilization. They enter star systems unbidden and destroy all the ships within them. Why? Maybe they are sociopaths. No remorse. The only time they hesitated was when you talked them, AI to AI. Why are we treating them as something other than a broken machine?"

The ships' commanders nodded while looking at the admiral for direction.

Guidance they agreed with—destruction of the enemy.

"Lev, is there any way we can get one of those worldkillers?"

"I'm afraid not, Harry. Let us collect more data, and then we will revisit the question."

The admiral frowned. "We need to send the Berantz cruiser back to BD18. The Berantz ships in BD23 need to depart immediately for BD27 or join the survivor from BD18. Those ships cannot be there when the Ga'ee arrive."

"Unless they join us," Commander Gordon countered. "We need all the firepower we can get, judging by what I've seen so far. I'll take my ship right up the gut of that thing as long as you can keep those drones away. Lev stopped them for a second. Can he do it for longer?"

"That's a good point, Andy. Do you have insight into whether you'll be able to stymy their networking?"

"I refined the parameters immediately after the apparent interruption, but they didn't respond to that or variations in the frequency and amplitude. I would not count on my ability to slow their drone attacks."

"You said 'apparent.' Does that mean they might have spoofed you? Given you false hope that you can disrupt the drones? That's a galactic-level disinformation strategy." The admiral stared at the opposite wall as his mind ran through the variables. "I need Arthir Dorsite to cross-deck to *Leviathan*. We're taking command of the armada, and I need her counsel."

"It will be nice to have Arthir on board," Lev replied.

Then-Captain Dorsite had integrated with *Leviathan* through the captain's chair. It had taken its toll with long hours and a lack of sustenance, but Arthir hadn't complained. She had slept for long periods afterward. Admiral Wesson had promoted her to the rank of fleet admiral to manage the war while *Leviathan* traveled deep into enemy space to win the peace.

Fleet Admiral Dorsite was formally in charge of the entire Fleet. What had made her take a personal role in leading the armada was probably the same driving force that had sent Harry and Nyota back to space: the desire to get away from Earth's toxic leadership.

"And if Arthir tells you she's taking *Leviathan* into her command?" Nyota whispered.

"I hadn't contemplated that, but you're right. Then we would do what Lev is willing to do. Hang on for the ride or be in charge. I have to admit that I've never thought about not being in charge. It's been so long. Maybe Arthir *is* the right person."

"Or not," Nyota countered. "We have to be ready for both possibilities."

"What about the deployment of sensor buoys?" Commander Appel asked. "Can we help?"

"Lev? It would give us a broader reach where we don't have to do all the heavy lifting."

"I will share the first one hundred as soon as they are ready."

"That'll give you plenty of time to load them and prepare a pattern for deployment. Work directly with Lev. This is all about collecting data. Give us the greatest chance with the broadest spread. If we use *Cleophas* as a blocker, we'll improve our chances of forcing the Ga'ee ship out of FTL at a location more beneficial to us. But we also need to assume that the Ga'ee will be expecting that, so we'll need to drop the sensors farther away, toward BD18," the admiral explained. "I'd like to see the Berantz vessel drop them off on his way back the way we came so it won't look like we're doing what we're doing."

"What can I do?" the Rang'Kor captain asked.

"All you need is to be ready to go. Woody, teach Captain Pel'Rok how to fly a Mosquito."

The commander nodded but didn't understand why. His place wasn't to question the order, so he didn't.

The admiral wanted to say more but left it unspoken. He stared at the table and fought tears. There had already been too much loss, but there would be at least one more if they could find a way in.

When seeking revenge, dig two graves, the saying went.

———

Captain Buto sat stiffly in the command seat. He'd been the executive officer long enough that he knew what to do, but the circumstances surrounding his ascension to the big chair didn't sit well with him.

Admiral Dorsite calmly sat next to him, watching the screens but not seeing the information on them. She was lost in thought, wargaming the days ahead. How would contact with the Ga'ee play out? What could they do to shift the odds in their favor? The answers remained elusive, but ahead of them, *Leviathan* would be waiting.

"A moment of your time, Admiral," Buto requested.

Arthir turned her head slowly and stared at the captain until her eyes focused. "Of course."

Buto left the bridge and waited in the corridor beyond.

"Yes, Captain?" Arthir had the time. She needed the ship's skipper to be confident.

"Captain Smith needs to be in that chair, not me."

"Aren't you ready?" It was a leading question. He would have never been made XO if he hadn't been ready to command the Kaiju-class dreadnought.

"I am, but the circumstances are all wrong. Zeke showed us all how lethal these Ga'ee are. And ruthless. He also tried to show us they weren't invulnerable, and it cost us. No one is beating themselves up more than him. And yes, we lost people, good people, to the attack, but what the war taught us is that sometimes people die. It's the way of the Fleet. And most often, the people who die aren't the ones who made any mistakes. Hell, you could do everything right and still die. I doubt the Ebren battlewagon was happy to die. They flushed all their weapons. They went down fighting, just like we did. We got away. They didn't."

"Is that how you feel?" Arthir asked.

"It is." Buto stood at attention.

"Who's your XO, and is he or she ready to take command?"

"My XO is Commander Tran Ving, formerly of Engineering. And as much as I'd like to give him a ringing endorsement, I can't because I don't know. He is the next most senior individual on board."

Arthir crossed her arms while she kicked absentmindedly at the deck. After an uncomfortable twenty seconds, she moved to the computer interface on the bulkhead. "Please have Captain Smith report to the bridge."

Buto sagged, relieved of the burden he'd been carrying.

"Captain Buto, sometimes it takes a lot more to say, 'I don't know,' than to say what you think I want to hear. I concur. I'll also tell you that no one knows better about instant obedience to the few orders I give than Captain Smith. When it comes to the armada, that's my responsibility. This ship is one of eight now when it used to be one of twelve. We must shepherd our resources until we're ready to strike. We'll meet up with *Leviathan,* and then we'll determine our way forward. If I understand the data properly, we'll have about twenty-five minutes before the Ga'ee arrive. Help Zeke prepare the ship and the crew. We don't know what we're going to do, and we better be quick about it."

"That's the strangest order I've ever received."

"You will make a good captain when opportunity knocks your door down. Until then, be ready for whatever *Leviathan* asks of us. They have been planning since they left the BD18 system. I'd like to say that I've been planning, too, but I don't see a way ahead besides running in front of this monstrosity."

"Scatter. Don't give the enemy a target. And create an FTL codebook for short messages just like the one warning us of the Ga'ee. If only that had been more clear."

"Develop that codebook, Captain. We'll transmit to *Leviathan* the instant we come out of FTL. Short and sweet. Everything needs to be said in three characters or less, but we can modulate our time in FTL to the millisecond. That gives you thousands of options. Put in everything you can and give them a time in FTL. It would be nice to communicate over extreme distances."

Buto saluted and hurried away.

Admiral Dorsite returned to the bridge and resumed sitting and staring at the screen. The situation was playing out as she had thought. She needed her most experienced captain in that chair, but he needed to be more aware. They had been lucky not to die at the hands of the Ga'ee.

It hadn't been their time. Lev hadn't resurrected her so she could be overwhelmed in a surprise attack that hadn't been a complete surprise.

[17]

"Create the conditions for success and the rest is anti-climactic." –From the memoirs of Ambassador Declan Payne

Payne waited outside the surgical theater of the Berantz medical facility. Kal stood next to him but their Berantz escort sat. The governor-general didn't try to conduct the planet's business. He was a politician and deferential. The Berantz galaxy was coming apart. Travel to the stars wasn't possible without ships in the system.

And no ships remained, here or in the other systems. Only BD23 and BD27 were left, but they were outliers. The bulk of Berantz shipping had been at BH01, and Payne had shared that no ships remained after the Ga'ee attacks.

Payne finally gave up his spot next to the window and took the seat next to the governor-general.

"We have to end that infestation, but we don't know what will kill these things," Payne started.

"Don't you want to get back to your ship?"

"As soon as there's a way, yes. Until then, we can't let those things get a foothold. And we need to get word to the other planets in the Berantz sphere of control to look for the Ga'ee. We never realized what they were doing. We only thought they were killing ships. That's one small part of the colonization of the seven races' part of the galaxy. We cannot let them establish a presence on this planet."

"I understand," the governor-general replied. "We have deployed our forces, looking for those ships."

"The one ship," Payne corrected. "It escaped the area of our crashed ship."

"Five more ships entered our atmosphere a short time after your arrival."

"We need to find them and eliminate them."

The Berantz leader displayed no emotion but dealt with the attack in space and on his planet in a matter-of-fact manner. Payne could appreciate that.

"We are ready to assist. We have significant combat power at our command."

"Do you have nuclear weapons?" the governor-general asked. He fixed Payne with an intense gaze.

"No. Why would you ask that? We're not going to irradiate the surface of Brayalore. This is your home."

He studied Payne's expression before replying. "I believe you." He returned to staring at the wall.

Payne couldn't see Mary from the window, only the tops of the medical team's heads. Two of them moved toward the door and disappeared. Two seconds later, they walked into the observation room.

"How is she?" Payne asked, but the team only spoke Berantz. Without his suit and the computer within, the words weren't translated.

The governor-general leaned forward to stand. Payne offered an arm and helped the elder Berantz to his feet.

"They said she'll make a full recovery. The wound was deep, but none of her organs were impacted. Her greatest threat was from blood loss," the governor-general explained in near-perfect English, which Payne hadn't realized he was speaking while they had been talking.

The doctor spoke quickly while Payne waited.

"She has what you refer to as O negative blood. This is the most common type on Berantz. She is part-Berantz."

"I'm O-neg," Payne offered. "She's what? We're part-Berantz?"

"Yes, of course. The Progenitors used a standard model when engineering races with the potential to become sentient. The Berantz were developed ahead of humanity, but the hostile environment of Berantz Main held back our progress." The governor-general addressed the medical team in Berantz. They shook hands afterward, and the doctors left.

"O blood types are part-Berantz. Nothing personal, but I'm glad we didn't get your skin, too."

The governor-general smiled. "I won't take it personally. There is much to be said for the human side of our evolution." He made to leave. "The doctors said that she'll be in recovery for a while and then needs rest. You can return in four hours to see her. Until then, let us talk about removing this infestation."

Kal headed toward the doors through which the doctors passed. "You can't go in there, Ebren," the governor-general warned, waving his hand to get Kal's attention.

Payne stepped between them. "Kal is my personal representative, and his entire purpose is to protect my wife while she's not capable of protecting herself. He's going to go where he can watch over her. Please let him do this, or he'll tear your hospital apart to find her."

"That isn't allowed."

"I don't care," Payne shot back. "You broke her. You fixed her. And it's Kal's responsibility to guarantee her recovery."

"The doctors will do that. You can trust us."

"I trust *you*. Is there any anti-human sentiment on this planet? Do you trust every single Berantz who works here? You don't need to answer those questions because they are moot. Kal is going to guard her. It's not up for debate, Governor-General."

"Yes, Mr. Ambassador," the old Berantz replied. He shuffled to the doors to summon an individual from the other side. After a spirited conversation in Berantz, he opened the door and pointed. "Follow him to the recovery area."

Kal ducked to get through the doorway, leaving Payne alone with the governor-general.

"Thank you. Now, let's see what we can do about the Ga'ee."

———

They returned to an airfield reminiscent of those relics on Earth, places where a nation's forces trained and deployed from to threaten violence upon another. It seemed incongruent on the Berantz planet.

"Why do you have a military like this?"

"Our alliance as part of the Blaze Collective was fraught with mistrust. We expected the Ebren would try to overrun our planets the second the humans were defeated. We had to be ready. Instead of committing one hundred percent of our military to the space forces, we kept half back for land forces. We tried to build air defenses, but those systems never worked right, which left us with a mix of aircraft and a land army."

"That's information we would never have learned. It's nice to exchange information. Your English is excellent, by the way. May I ask where you learned?"

"All diplomats were required to learn the language of humanity, so when we enslaved your race, we would be able to give direction to complicit human overseers."

"That's disturbing," Payne replied. "What do you think, Virge?"

"Everyone has a plan, although humanity had no designs on enslaving another race. But then again, we were more than willing to destroy every alien we came across. I'm glad we avoided that future."

"Thanks to you, Mr. Ambassador," the governor-general countered. "Can your suits translate Berantz?"

"They can. We'll suit up." Payne twirled his finger in the air before he realized that he was the only one not in his combat armor. "Fine."

He hurried through getting dressed and the power-up sequence. Payne snapped his helmet into place and gave the governor-general the thumbs-up.

The elder Berantz passed control of the briefing to the senior ranking officer and departed, walking slowly from the edge of the airfield to a waiting vehicle.

"Where were we?" Payne prompted.

"I am Colonel Ombaras of the Berantz Defense Force, Seventy-Fourth Division. I command the units on Brayalore. It has been brought to my attention that we have a bug problem. Silicon bugs. Do you know how to kill them?"

Mary was going to recover, and Kal was watching over her. Payne could fully commit to helping the Berantz.

"I like how you got right to the point," Payne replied. "We tried railguns with limited effect, grenades, and then explosives. I think the explosives finally achieved the result we were looking for."

"Fine, then we bomb them," the Berantz colonel stated.

"Let's return to our crash site first to verify. We'll need an excavation tool of some sort."

"You mean, a shovel?"

Major Dank laughed.

Payne shook his head. "I mean an industrial-sized piece of equipment. We're not going into that hole until we have a better idea what those things are capable of."

The colonel didn't see the humor since he wasn't trying to be funny. He waved an aide to him and spoke in hushed tones. The junior officer ran off, shouting at a group of soldiers nearby, which was instantly galvanized into action.

The colonel watched them, his expression neutral.

Still, there was a hint of pride. An army that maintained its discipline after the war was long over was a force to be reckoned with.

"Do you have any flamethrowers?" Payne asked. "And acid, like sulfuric acid?"

"Flamethrowers, yes. But sulfuric acid? We don't have that in any great quantity, I don't think. Hey!" he yelled to the aide.

The two conversed with a lot of headshaking before the colonel turned his attention to Payne. "We will bring what we can. Thirty minutes and we'll depart."

"In the meantime, let's detail where those other ships went down. By my count, we have six ships to find."

The colonel took in the group of ten armored combat humans. "My count is six as well. We will have our air support flying overhead at all times. They are carrying one-hundred-kilogram high-explosive bombs, and we have the locations. I'll have them transmitted to your systems."

Payne consulted with his team.

"Fuck this guy," Heckler started.

"Stop!" Dank replied instantly. "We have a job to do in the greater interest of human and Berantz relations. And we're stuck on this planet for now, so stopping whatever the hell the Ga'ee are doing is probably best *not* left undone."

"Exactly that," Payne agreed.

"Sorry," Heckler grumbled. "Not flamethrowers but more like plasma torches. I concur with the acid. That should do a number on a silicon-based life form."

"It does a number on carbon-based. Be careful handling it," Payne warned.

"If those things are planted and grown, or seeded, or whatever the hell they're doing, what kind of threat are they? That last bunch was like a nest of worms and no more dangerous."

"Then why did you jump out of the hole and scream like a little girl when you saw them?" Turbo prompted.

"People," Payne interrupted. "What other ways might there be to kill those things?"

Joker raised her hand. Usually she was the quiet one, so when she spoke, the team listened. "Sonic disruption. We might be able to hit them with vibrations from our suits if we space our speakers out properly and max the amplitude."

"What if we just capture them and secure them?" Sparky suggested. "We don't know how they're multiplying. From a single bit of silicon to a colony? Do they clone or what? Are we safe leaving any behind, even after they've been blasted?"

"You're making too much sense," Payne agreed. He turned to their Berantz liaison. "Colonel Ombaras, bring a plasma torch and an acrylic- or ceramic-lined container to put the remnants within. Let's not leave any Ga'ee refuse behind."

"I'll order another shuttle," he replied.

Payne was satisfied. The team took off their helmets and relaxed while the Berantz troops loaded a variety of tools and weapons into the shuttles. One was dedicated exclusively to an excavator that looked to overload the cargo space, but with tinkering, they were able to get it inside.

Getting it out would be another matter altogether.

"Not my problem," Payne muttered. He walked from team member to team member and stopped at Heckler and Turbo. "You two scare me."

The couple beamed. Payne shook his head and moved on. Byle and Shaolin stayed quiet. "You two are looking good. Keeping up. Besides that, what's bothering you? If it's chow, none of us will get Lev's fine programming for the near future."

"That's it," Shaolin blurted. "They don't know we're alive, do they?"

"I reckon not. There will be ticker-tape parades and much cheering when they find out we survived. That's us. Survivors."

Byle asked, "Will Lev survive?"

"He's Lev. He always survives," Payne replied more dismissively than he'd intended. "With the admiral on board, too? And Woody with the Tricky Spinsters. The deck is stacked in their favor. It only looks like we're outgunned by the Ga'ee. Lev has been right all along; we need more information. Once he has it, he won't let those bastards get inside the wire."

That was an old Earth reference to when an enemy penetrated perimeter defenses.

"They're already inside the *wire*."

"Then he won't let them stay here once he figures things out. And in the interim, we get to take out some of our frustrations on the little bastards who are trying to find a foothold. They haven't been nice, and now those Ga'ee fucks are seeding these planets? I can't wait to get out there and show them who's boss."

"Thanks, sir." Shaolin grinned. "Having an existential crisis about our place in the universe?"

"An exit-what?"

"Nothing," Byle replied with a short chuckle. "Maybe our place has been right here all along. Can I handle the acid?"

Payne waved his arms. "Byle said she's the duty acid-pourer."

"Let her have it!" Blinky called from nearby.

Payne continued his rounds. "Buzz. You guys draw a bead on how those things talk to each other."

"We are geniuses in knowing how they don't do it. As to how they talk? Nope."

"Big nope," Blinky confirmed. "But we haven't run out of things to try. This time, we won't have anyone shooting at us. That could make the difference when it comes to our mental acuity and go-getter-ness."

"I think you people are making up words just to mess with me." Payne scanned the innocent faces looking back at him.

"Sir?" Sparky asked. She crooked an armored finger at him.

He moved close enough for her to whisper, "You said they were concerned about us having nuclear weapons, but then we're going to dump sulfuric acid on the ground?"

"The acid will be more precisely targeted, and once used, the Berantz can neutralize it with a lot of lime or baking soda. Easy day." Payne clapped Sparky on the shoulder. "You can't neutralize a radioactive cloud."

"Better to move than mess with that stuff. Although the Mosquitos dropped micro-nukes on Parallax, they didn't have a lasting effect, and definitely not on the bio-drones."

"Were they a glimpse of what was to come?" Dank interjected.

"That tech wasn't silicon-based." Payne reached a hand inside his suit to scratch his face. "There's no energy beam, either. These trident drones are all about the violence of the impact."

"But the basic bio-engineering has an uncanny overlap. We never learned how they communicated either, did we?"

"We did. Blinky and Buzz figured it out. The drones on

Parallax tapped into an energy network that surrounded the planet. Wireless power and piggybacked comm."

Dank groaned. "Maybe it isn't the same. Those things communicate in space, and I suspect they're doing it here, too."

"Sorry, Virge. I think they're the same but different. Same in that they're drones, not necessarily sentient on their own, but different in that they're linked up in a different way. And their goal is similar to the box drones'—the complete destruction of those who oppose them.'"

"You mean us and our allies. Damn humans! Bringing the wrath of an angry galaxy down on everyone's heads." Dank retrieved his helmet and put it back on.

"'Damn humans' is right," Payne quipped. "We brought all of this on ourselves, or maybe it was the damn Vestrall and one of their misadventures. The Godilkinmore couldn't control their people, and splinter groups are wreaking havoc on our galaxy. When we get back to Leeyaness, I'm going to kick their asses just because."

Dank gestured for the team to get ready. They locked their helmets into place, ran through suit diagnostics, and checked each other before forming two columns of five.

"If you're looking for volunteers..." Turbo sent using the team channel.

"Volunteers for what?"

"To kick Vestrall ass. I'm game."

"And me," Heckler added.

"I think I'd like some of that action," Sparky offered.

"We're not going to kick their asses, but we *are* agreed that we would like to. It'd be like beating up the rail-thin, skinny kid who's a mouthy sort. They're not angry with us, only that they've been misled for centuries, and it makes them arrogant without a basis for being that way."

"What I hear you saying," Heckler countered, "is that they're dumbasses."

Payne had no comeback.

The colonel headed toward the shuttles. Payne took four with him, and Dank took the other four. They squeezed into the available space, being relegated to standing since Berantz soldiers filled the jump seats on both the port and starboard sides. Gear filled the open middle area.

Without fanfare, the ships took off vertically, then eased into lateral motion, accelerating smoothly.

First stop, the crash site.

They reached it in thirty minutes and set down outside the cratered area surrounding the remains of *Ugly 4*.

The team ran off the craft and headed for the crater. They lined the outside.

The bottom appeared empty. "Didn't we leave some body parts here?" Payne asked.

"Sure did," Heckler said. "It was a wriggling wasteland down there. Now, it just looks like an empty hole."

"Bring the excavator over and let's see what we've got," Payne replied. He waved the Berantz operators to him once they'd freed the equipment from the shuttle.

They started to dig, dumping great buckets of dirt on the torn ground beside the impact crater.

After the third bucket, they struck gold.

Or rather, silicon.

[18]

"I have seen the enemy, and he is not me." –From the memoirs of Ambassador Declan Payne

The dirt hit the ground and held the shape of the bucket from which it fell for a moment before breaking apart, revealing the silicon entities within. Flat, ten centimeters wide and half a meter long, they moved like tapeworms while remaining close to each other.

"Looks like five," Heckler muttered. He shot one with his railgun for no reason. The Berantz recoiled from the noise.

"Bring up the plasma torch and the acid," Payne ordered.

Byle appeared with two containers while Sparky and Shaolin lugged the plasma torch to the dirt pile. Blinky and Buzz sat to the side, working furiously with their computers connected to two small dishes, one parabolic and the other a log-periodic as they sought to find how the Ga'ee communicated.

"Are these the aliens?" Major Dank asked. "Are they a sentient race?"

Payne held up his hand to stop Sparky from firing up the plasma torch. "Sonofabitch."

It was easy to think of them as the enemy when they had weapons and were trying to destroy the ship, or when they had just brought *Ugly 4* down, but now?

Not so much.

"You don't improve relations if you kill their spawn." Payne looked at the creatures, unarmed and shiny. "Bring the barrel. We're going to capture them."

Joker headed for the shuttle. "What are you doing, Mr. Ambassador?" Colonel Ombaras asked from a safe distance away. "Those things have invaded our planet. Their purpose is to destroy us."

"How can you be sure? But if you're right, we can dispose of them later. Right now, they are incapable of destroying anything. I'm not sure we should kill those things."

"They invaded our planet. They are the enemy. We kill our enemies," he explained as if talking to a child.

"I am not going to make that my first course of action, even though we already tried as hard as hell to kill them. We were not successful, and that suggests we need to study them more."

The colonel yelled orders at his troops. The soldiers took the plasma torch and the acids from Payne's team. Joker arrived with the barrel. Payne was torn.

"This is a Berantz planet," Dank advised. Payne nodded.

"Stand back, Joker," Payne sent over the team channel. "Blinky and Buzz, anything?"

"Nothing," Blinky replied without looking up.

The plasma torch came to life and hissed with the fury of the flame. They directed the torch toward the silicon entities. The first one it touched curled and twisted, trying to get clear of the heat. It started to dig into the dirt. The others joined it as it corkscrewed below the surface. A Berantz with a shovel dug one up and popped it back to the surface.

The other hit it with the plasma torch. It writhed as its surface sweated silver beads, then it came apart and withered.

Four Ga'ee disappeared underground. The shovel went after them, but they had disappeared. The Berantz with the plasma torch eased forward.

The ground around the soldier's foot erupted, and the four swarmed up his body. He dropped the plasma torch and started to scream while tearing at the creatures. His fingers curled before he could grip the Ga'ee to rip them off.

Heckler jumped forward and tore two off the soldier's body. He tossed them at the dirt behind him and went after the other two.

The other Berantz soldiers stood petrified.

Heckler pulled the last two free, and the soldier collapsed. Turbo lifted the torch's wand and touched the trigger, lighting up the two wriggling in Heckler's armored fists.

Sparky ripped a bottle of acid from the soldier holding it and waded into the dirt pile after the two that were digging to get away.

She upended the bottle on them. They convulsed and flexed while smoke rose from their shiny bodies. They lost their color as they stopped moving. Sparky kicked at them before stomping their bodies into oblivion.

Heckler tossed his on the hard ground and pounded them apart with the heel of his boot.

Payne checked the fallen soldier, but he was dead. Where the creatures had touched him, his skin was as rigid as tissue paper as if that which gave it substance had been taken. He scanned the body, but the results made no sense to him.

"Fuck," he growled.

The colonel was furious. "You killed him!"

Payne stood. "The Ga'ee killed him after he fired them up. We would have contained them in the barrel, where we could have studied them, but now it doesn't matter. We are at war, whether we want to be or not. Next time, Colonel, we do what I say."

To the man's credit, he controlled his rage. "Yes, Mr. Ambassador."

"Excavate more to make sure none have escaped. Conduct a full autopsy on this soldier to find out how the Ga'ee killed him and secure what's left of their bodies in the barrel, please."

Heckler and Turbo executed the Ga'ee recovery mission by ingloriously picking up each body part with two fingers and tossing it into the barrel.

"It might have been better not to stomp them," Payne mused.

"They made me mad and deserved to be stomped," Heckler replied.

Payne wanted to disagree, but they had made him angry, too. He had tried to give them a reprieve to make it possible to negotiate with the Ga'ee at some point. Win the peace instead of defeat the enemy.

Or destroy the enemy. A scorched-earth approach had found traction within Payne's mind.

Although they were newborns in one sense, they were lethal to carbon-based life forms. Further, they moved through the Earth almost as easily as humans moved through the air.

Attacking from below had created a fear that Payne found difficult to fight. He could sense it from the other members of his team, even though he couldn't see their faces. He had no desire to be outside without wearing his combat suit.

Because of the fear the Ga'ee had brought to those trapped on the planet and those in space. The drones had destroyed their targets through brute force.

"Coexisting with the Ga'ee might not be possible," Payne admitted.

"Can we move to the next site now?" the colonel asked.

Payne shook his head while his team sifted through the next three bucketloads of dirt and found nothing.

"Once we make sure these were the only ones, we'll be ready to move." Payne glanced at the sealed barrel. They'd have to open it to see inside. Would the life forms resurrect, as he was sure they had before? Or not this time. Acid and the plasma torch had wreaked havoc on their small bodies.

The excavator dug deep into the soft ground. When it stopped, Payne jumped into the hole. He looked for signs that a Ga'ee had passed, like a narrow tunnel, but the clay-heavy soil was clean except for the grooves left by the teeth of the bucket.

He used his jets to jump out of the hole and twirled his arm in the air. "This place is clear. Time to move on."

The colonel relayed the orders. His soldiers undertook the laborious process of loading the excavator into the shuttle while securing the soldier's body and the barrel of dead Ga'ee. Colonel Ombaras glared at Payne.

"A word, Colonel," Payne requested, removing his helmet but holding it by the side of his head so the translation program would help him communicate. He walked away from the others.

"Mr. Ambassador," the colonel replied in a cold voice.

"It sucks that your man died. We will participate in any ceremony you have for him, but understand, we are now at war with the Ga'ee. No matter what we thought before, these creatures attacked one of us. Until that point, they had not. They attacked us in orbit, but not these things, which are the offspring or clones or something else. Because what we set out to do was nothing short of genocide, the complete destruction of the Ga'ee. Are you ready to remove an entire race from existence?"

"They are the enemy. Had you recognized that at the outset, my soldier would still be alive."

"Are you positive? Or would they have attacked us instead?

Better for a human to die." Payne stopped following that train of thought. "That's not what I intend. We have to fight this enemy together, Colonel. My team will lead the way, but let's capture some of these bastards, too. We need to know how they communicate with each other to coordinate their attacks. In space, we saw tens of thousands of those things flying in a tight formation."

"How did you kill tens of thousands?" the colonel asked.

"We didn't. We ran for our lives and survived a crash-landing by bailing out. That's why we have to capture some. We only need to stop them from talking to each other, and they will become relatively harmless. I'm not a fan of genocide and want no part of it. The parameters of this mission changed once we found these things alive and thriving, and then once again when they killed your soldier. And yet again, since we need to treat them like a colony. We only need to remove their foothold from BD18, Brayalore. That's not genocide. It is, as you suggested, repelling an invasion. We don't need to conduct the wanton slaughter of every Ga'ee we find unless they give us no choice."

The colonel stared at Payne as the combat suit finished interpreting what the major had said. The officer clasped his hands behind his back and turned away. He walked back and forth, lost in thought.

A shouted curse came from one of the shuttles. An individual nursed a bruised hand after he attempted to help push the excavator's bucket into place. It took a second maneuver before the vehicle fit as needed.

"I've trained most of my adult life," the colonel started, "to defend this planet against the enemy, whether Ebrens or humans or Zuloon, and now these aliens called the Ga'ee. We repel the attack, but this isn't anything we've contemplated. Ground forces assaulting our cities, destroyed through a strong defense and valiant counterattack. Not digging silver worms out of the ground and burning them to death with acid or watching my man die a horrible death.

"When worms attack! I should write a novel, a fictional story that is all too real. The horrors of war have come home, and they are worse than we ever imagined. It is time for me to retire, but after we rid Brayalore of these, whether dead or captured, none of these creatures can dig freely in our dirt. None of them."

Payne held out an armored hand. The Berantz looked at it for a moment before making a fist and pounding the top of it. He held his fist for Payne to replicate the movement but gently.

"Let's go find the others. Five more, and I think we'll find five at each site if we get there in time. And then there's a sixth trident drone that left here. Did it have any other seeds to plant? Inquiring minds want to know."

[19]

"The hardest decisions come at the greatest cost." –From
the memoirs of Ambassador Declan Payne

The admiral prepared himself for the transition from FTL by
leaning against a workstation. The disorientation passed
quickly.

"Transmit the messages," he requested. They contained all
Leviathan knew of the Ga'ee for the Berantz ships in-system,
along with a call to action.

He studied the tactical screen to find the cruiser that had
run from the BD18 system closer to the habitable planet while
Lev dropped toward the outer rim of the heliosphere to launch
the frigates.

Their job was to deploy the sensor buoys while Lev raced to
the Goldilocks zone and backtracked to onboard the frigates
before the Ga'ee arrived. If *Cleophas* wasn't willing to block the
inbound ship, Lev would do it. Five kilometers long and a kilometer wide, the ship would create an impressive blockade.
However, it had more important duties, coordinating the rest of

the ships to create the conditions under which the most data could be collected.

"The Berantz commander wishes to speak with you," Lev reported.

"This is Admiral Harry Wesson. You received our communique." The admiral knew they had. This was a statement to get to the point of the conversation.

"I am Admiral Grimdelk. I will take command of the counterattack. You will move *Leviathan* to the coordinates I'm transmitting and will prepare to fire all weapons. The Berantz fleet will accelerate toward the target to deliver barrage fire. You have more ships inbound. They will assume a position on the far side of our designated engagement zone."

"We'll do no such thing," the admiral replied. "I'm not going to quibble over who is in charge. We cannot counterattack at this juncture in our running engagements with the Ga'ee. We need to probe the vulnerabilities of the vessel, and we have a plan to collect that data. If you aren't going to join us, then please stay out of the way and prepare to deploy to BD27. I request that you send one FTL-capable ship back to BD18 to provide a presence in that system since we've not seen the Ga'ee backtrack. You should be able to return along the route it's traveled to find that your planets are untouched."

"Have you been to the Berantz homeworld?"

"We have not, but we have been to PX47, where the planet was left alone after the system's ships and space station were destroyed. We suspect your homeworld, BH01, is unmolested."

"That would be good news, but we must attack these Ga'ee. Show them they cannot operate in Berantz space with impunity."

"They will *continue* to operate with impunity. We have not found a way to defeat their drone clouds. Not yet, anyway.

Please review our operational plan and consider joining us in a united effort to defeat the Ga'ee."

"Surely *Leviathan* can destroy the alien ship." The admiral spoke without confidence. He'd seen the battleship withdraw from the BD18 engagement just before the Berantz cruiser was destroyed.

"*Leviathan* might be able to, but not by going head to head. We need an edge, something we do not currently have."

"An edge. The enemy ship is so powerful that twenty ships cannot defeat it? Is that not sufficient advantage?"

"That is correct. *Leviathan* and twenty ships is not a sufficient advantage," Admiral Wesson replied.

"That makes no sense to me. It is a single ship. We should marshal our forces and attack it simultaneously. Flood the void with the full intensity of our wrath."

"That ship can accelerate to point nine-eight of the speed of light in a short period of time. It can move beyond our engagement envelope before our weapons arrive. It can engage our ships in small groups, destroying them before moving to the next. Divide and conquer. We would be well advised to not divide our forces except as it suits us, using the plan we've developed."

Leviathan raced away from the habitable planet in a zigzag trajectory.

"What are you doing?" the Berantz admiral asked.

"We are deploying sensor buoys. More information. Find the vulnerabilities. And then we'll exploit them. Hit the Ga'ee where it hurts the most. Their drones are not it. They regroup and continue without interruption. We have to find a way to hit the carrier. For example, we don't know where the power plants are. That's one of our first orders of business. Find the power so the next time we meet them, we can cut it."

Leviathan accelerated, launching buoys at regular intervals.

Combined with the frigate's buoy deployments, the admiral was building a wide-mouthed net through which the Ga'ee ship was certain to fly. If it didn't, the buoys could fly themselves closer, but such energetic movements would be easily seen.

As the arrival time drew near, the sensor buoys would go silent, waiting for the vessel to pass. The feint was to draw out the drones—not to fight them but to get a buoy inside the massive hangars on each side of the Ga'ee vessel, scan the interior of the ship, and transmit the information before the buoy was destroyed.

The fleet needed to escape before the drones arrived. That was the extent of the engagement plan for BD23. *Leviathan* would be the last to leave after collecting as much sensor data as possible.

"We need comm relays to make sure the signal doesn't die. And maybe a comm storage buoy, a passive one we can retrieve later. We can't lose any of it," the admiral suggested.

Lev replied, "I will deploy the resources as part of the pattern. Excellent idea, Harry."

"If it's worth fighting for, it's worth dying for!" the Berantz admiral proclaimed.

"It's only worth dying for if there's a chance to win. Just dying does no one any good. We will engage the Ga'ee." Admiral Wesson punched a fist into his hand. "And we will do everything we can to win, including dying if that's what it takes."

"This is Berantz space," Admiral Grimdelk countered.

"This is the space of the seven races. We have a Rang'Kor captain on board who wants to see the Ga'ee stopped. He lost his ship and most of his crew. He lost his friends on five other ships. We're in this together, Admiral. We'll win together, or we will die trying."

"My ship and I will remain with *Leviathan*. I am

dispatching two cruisers to Brayalore, which is known as BD18. What of our frigates that don't have FTL capability?" Grimdelk asked.

"They need to run toward interstellar space as fast as they can go unless they can land on the planet. Then have them land. Get them out of this system's space, or the Ga'ee will destroy them."

"They cannot enter the atmosphere. I will instruct them to find a safe haven in the vastness of interstellar space."

"Perpendicular to a vector toward BD27. That's where the Ga'ee will go next. We can predict that with some certainty, but after BD27, we have no idea where they will go. Our stand must take place there, and that's why it is critical for this engagement to unfold as we desire."

"I understand. The Berantz Defense Force will deploy as you direct and will recover at Bindalas, BD27, once we abandon Blegoston, BD23."

"Not abandon, Admiral, but draw the enemy into a trap of our making on the battlefield of our choosing."

On the screen, two Berantz frigates accelerated away from the planet painfully slowly. They had about forty minutes before the Ga'ee arrived. Admiral Wesson hoped it was enough. Were they small enough not to bother with?

"Fifteen minutes to the armada's arrival," Commodore Freeman announced. "Mosquitos are standing by. We will recover the frigates ten minutes prior to the Ga'ee's arrival."

Two cruisers, one heavy and one light, transitioned to FTL on a course for BD18. That left four Berantz ships, and two of those were winging their way out of the system. Two cruisers, *Leviathan*, *Cleophas*, and the armada survivors would stand shoulder to shoulder to confront the Ga'ee.

"Make sure you have a clear FTL route to Bindalas, Admiral. We might only have seconds to transition. Good hunting. Wesson out."

Lev closed the channel. "Eighty percent of the sensor buoys have been deployed. Active, passive, and five recording buoys, small and stealthy. They won't activate until pinged. We won't lose our data. I have learned something about planning for failure, Harry."

"That doesn't sound as impressive as you think, Lev. We plan for all contingencies, not necessarily *failure*." The admiral checked the screen. The armada was inbound. It hurt Wesson's soul to see the eight ships. Only eight, but those included three battleships and a Kaiju-class dreadnought.

They marshaled significant firepower, including the ability to fire nearly four hundred Rapier-class anti-ship missiles in a single salvo. A broadside of epic proportions awaited the Ga'ee.

The admiral knew they'd never destroy the enemy if they didn't deliver the munitions on target. If they didn't fire, they had no chance at all. Just because *Leviathan* wasn't going to engage didn't mean the armada was impotent. One lucky shot would end it.

Then they could take their time figuring out what the Ga'ee were and where they came from. Would there be more?

"Right now, the Ga'ee scare us because we don't know them. They appear to be invulnerable, but I assure you they are not," the admiral muttered as if to comfort himself. "We will find their Achilles heel, and then they'll be sorry for making war on us."

———

"There's one!" Payne called and pointed. A tapeworm-looking Ga'ee tried to dig its way out, but a kick from Turbo's boot upended it and sent it into the air. When it came down, Shaolin grabbed it and stuffed it into the barrel.

She snapped the lid tightly shut.

"I don't think we can put any more in here. They try to get out as soon as the lid comes free."

The latest captive made three. They only had one barrel.

Payne looked at Blinky and Buzz. Their job was to figure out how the Ga'ee communicated, but they'd made zero progress. They hadn't had much time, but Payne was anxious.

The team was trapped on BD18, and Payne knew his issues were based on losing *Leviathan*. He had contemplated being without the ship and his friend when he thought Lev was going to follow the Godilkinmore, but when he hadn't, Payne had taken it for granted that Lev would be there for him.

And then he wasn't, after planting seeds of doubt.

Would friendly aliens plant seeds on another's planet? Seeds that were hostile to all who attempted to interfere with them? That was more than Payne could rationalize.

The Ga'ee were the enemy. Killing outsiders who infested this planet wasn't genocide; it was a refusal to give the enemy a foothold. Their insertion of living seeds that grew was an invasion.

Payne's lip curled as the logic of his arguments finally swayed him to full commitment.

The excavator dug deep into the ground again and again, looking for the rest of the colony. Small tunnels suggested the Ga'ee were going deeper.

These were bigger than the first ones they found. That didn't bode well since four landing sites remained.

Berantz aircraft had done a number on the drone at this site. Its wreckage littered the ground not far away.

"We're taking too long," Payne grumbled. The colonel stood rigid, and tension rippled across his body. "Plasma torch!"

Heckler lifted the wand and fired it up. The intense flame sizzled.

"Dig." Payne jumped into the hole and used the power of the suit to drive his hands into the clay, following the path taken by the fleeing Ga'ee.

Turbo jumped in next to him and replicated his efforts.

"You bastard!" she cheered. She caught the end of a Ga'ee with one hand and dug with the other to free it.

When the Ga'ee came out of its hole, it wrapped around her wrist and tightened like a tourniquet. She tore it free and threw it.

The instant it hit the ground, Heckler torched it, raking down the length of its body. He had no idea where it was most vulnerable. The things didn't have heads, only long flat bodies with small protrusions like the legs of a centipede.

They used them the same way—to move.

Payne didn't bother watching. He had his own invader to catch. It didn't take long. He ripped great handfuls of clay from the ground and tossed them behind him until he caught up to the Ga'ee. He tore it free of the hole and swung it rapidly to keep it from getting a grip on him, then slammed it into the ground in front of Heckler, who finished it.

"Load the excavator!" Payne ordered. Dank offered a hand to help him climb out of the hole. He checked his suit power. He was below fifty percent.

Payne pulled up the team's vitals on his HUD. "Virgil, you Blinky, Buzz, and Sparky have the next two holes. You have the most power remaining in your suits.

"Sir!" Blinky complained. "We need to find how these things communicate."

"We need to stop this infestation," Payne countered. "Then we can get back to the business of breaking the links.

"That thing did a number on my suit," Turbo said, holding out her arm. The metal was pitted and rough.

"How long was it on there?" Payne asked.

"Not more than a couple seconds."

"Silicon monsters destroying everything they touch." Payne glanced at the shuttle, where the dead soldier's body waited. "Colonel, have another shuttle meet us at the next site. Tell them to bring more glass-lined barrels and more acid. We can also return the soldier's body for an autopsy."

Colonel Ombaras waved one of his soldiers to him. He relayed the order, and the soldier ran for the shuttle and the radio link to the base.

"If they destroy metal, then how come acid affects them? Wouldn't they be one with the acid?" Sparky wondered.

"That seems like a setup question." Payne asked Turbo to show everyone her arm. She held up her armored fist and turned it both ways for the team to see.

"What if those creatures ingest metal?" Joker suggested. "Take the metal from the soft tissue as well. They eat and grow stronger. I think we have the clay to thank that they aren't already big and strong, as opposed to being in an iron deposit or something a little more robust."

"For now, that's our working hypothesis. So why didn't they land at places with better deposits?"

Payne looked to the colonel for an answer.

"This is Brayalore. Clay with a thin layer of topsoil. Do you see any trees standing tall? It is nothing like the Berantz homeworld."

"Someone needs to get to the other Berantz planets and let them know to look for these things," Payne suggested. "Repel the invasion. The Ga'ee can live, but not in space." He stabbed a finger at the sky. "And not down here unless they can make sure their people know not to kill carbon-based inhabitants. The

Ga'ee can ask permission if they want to settle, not seed an entire galaxy while destroying everything in their way. We'll remove every single Ga'ee from Brayalore. Then we'll go from planet to planet and rip them out of the ground. The Ga'ee cannot have any planet inhabited by the seven races."

"I agree, Mr. Ambassador. We find ourselves on the front lines of a battle we have long been prepared to fight. We thought our enemy would be you. I am pleased it is not, and now we are training ourselves to fight an enemy that we never contemplated. But we will learn, and we will win this fight."

"Send your fighters from site to site to destroy the drones. We will catch up. And find that sixth drone. Where did it go?"

"Our people are studying the recorded scans. We *will* find it. As to the others, you don't want to wait and do them one at a time?"

"No. I think they'll coordinate if they haven't already. The drones will move, and we'll lose track of the infestation sites. We need to nail those down right quick and in a hurry."

"We have the sites," the colonel countered.

"What if the drones move the life forms?"

"That would be a problem." The colonel hurried to the shuttle to personally issue the order.

"Finally, we're making some progress," Major Dank told Payne on a person-to-person channel. "What took you so long?"

"Lev, that sandy little butthole. He planted the seed that these fuckers weren't the enemy, but they are, Virge. They are seeding this galaxy one habitable planet at a time. They are destroying any ship that could warn those living on the surface of what they're up to. We're going to tell them 'No' in the way that we know best."

"Consider it done. A few more acid bombs would come in handy. Maybe an acid sprayer or a freaking firehose!"

"H_2SO_4 and HCl. The Berantz better ratchet up production because the Ga'ee aren't going to wait. They're going to get bigger and badder the longer we take." Payne pumped his fist and hatcheted an arm toward the shuttles. "What did we just see? These things doubled their size in a few hours?"

"If juveniles can eat metal like that, what can an adult Ga'ee do?" Dank clapped Payne on the shoulder and headed to the second shuttle.

The team loaded up and waited for the excavator to finish squeezing into the too-small space.

Before Payne could ask, the colonel reiterated, "These are the biggest shuttles we have, and that is the smallest excavator that can do what we need done."

"Can we get a second excavator and have it meet us? Leapfrog from one site to the next. Quick in, quick out for us."

"I don't know what a frog is," the colonel replied, "but it sounds like our bounding overwatch, a small unit tactical maneuver. I will order another excavator and see if anything is available. This is a planetary emergency."

"The fact that there are no Berantz ships in this system should convince your leadership." Payne didn't ask why they hadn't brought him to the civilian leaders. He was the supreme leader of the seven races, or at least he had been, but they didn't know that. "When will I meet your planet's leadership?"

The colonel leaned close. "They are embarrassed about the incident where we attacked you."

"And not the Ga'ee. We're past that, Colonel. We have an enemy that requires our tender ministrations to nurture them fully in their new existence as future corpses."

After the suit finished translating Payne's words, the colonel maintained a blank expression. "I have no idea what you just said, and I suggest your translation program doesn't either."

"It sounded better in my head. Let's remove these creatures

from Brayalore. Then we'll talk with your leadership about the next steps. Last is that my team needs to get back to our ship."

The shuttles took off, en route to the next confirmed landing site.

"My compliments on your precise tracking," Payne offered.

"It's a good system. A big planet and only a few million people, so we've had to stretch our technical legs." The colonel spoke without pride. He was a recipient of the spoils from the system. He hadn't had anything to do with building it. That had been done a generation earlier.

"*Only* a few million. I love our galaxy." Payne chuckled. "How many live on the Berantz homeworld?"

"Two billion, maybe. I'm not sure," the colonel replied. The soldier's veneer softened. Uniting against a common enemy had brought belligerent parties together for millennia. Until recently, humanity and the Berantz had been enemies.

But not anymore.

"If your soldiers can help us pin these bastards down after we dig them out of the ground, we can destroy them. One by one and move on. Four and counting, unless it's five."

"Unless it's five." The colonel closed his eyes and appeared to drift off. Like any good ground combat veteran, he was able to sleep when the opportunity presented itself—short naps to keep the energy reserves full. Engagements came when least expected and lasted longer. That was what the soldier planned for.

Along with hurry up and wait—the other extreme of a soldier's existence.

Ten minutes, then twenty. The shuttle bumped through rough air as it descended. It jerked upward, then dropped five meters to crunch into the rocky ground.

"The alien ship has been dispatched," the colonel reported.

"They are no match for our fighters. How are they so deadly in space?"

"They fly a lot better out in space. I think the descent to the planet is a one-way trip. They aren't designed for intra-atmospheric combat. I'm happy you can do them in a big way. Splash them all."

The side hatch dropped, creating steps for the descent to the ground. Unlike the previous two landing sites where the shuttle settled on the ground, its long legs held it high over the uneven ground on the side of a hill.

"Should be right over there." The colonel pointed at a rocky outcropping.

"Railguns!" Payne ordered. The excavator was far down the hill. "Don't unload that thing. It'll never make it up here."

The colonel drew a line across his throat. The crew immediately raised the ramp and climbed back in. Ombaras waved the soldiers from the personnel shuttles to him.

Team Payne led the way to the outcropping and looked for where the Ga'ee had penetrated. The soldiers waited with picks and shovels.

Burn marks. Scorch marks.

The surface of the stone was heavily scarred but not penetrated. Payne followed the track over the top and down the side of the stone. Where it met the ground, a single narrow tunnel showed where the Ga'ee had gone.

"You'll want to move that shuttle, Colonel." Payne gestured down the hill. "Explosives. Get this trash out of here."

Heckler and Turbo happily complied, jumping into action. The rest of the team cleared the blast area and kept the team and the Berantz soldiers uphill from the blast. The shuttle with the excavator took off and headed for the site after the next.

When the two kilos of explosives were in place, Heckler

checked the blast area one last time before maxing his suit's speakers and shouting, "Fire in the hole!"

The rocks erupted, broken free and shattered. The outcropping turned into a landslide of stone and dust rolling ingloriously downhill.

"Get to work, people," Payne ordered. Byle and Shaolin were the first to check out the area.

"Stand back," Byle waved her railgun. She cleared the area beyond and fired into the rocks remaining at ground level to dig a crater around the hole. With Shaolin's help, they kicked the debris free, then returned for a second round of cutting the ground. "Not looking good, Major."

Payne had already come to that conclusion. The Ga'ee were digging. Energized by the fuel of metals within the stone, they were running free beneath the rocks. Without major excavation, they might not catch up with them.

"More explosives," Payne called. "Scanners."

"Movement," Blinky reported. He walked slowly around the area, finally stopping and tapping the ground with an armored foot. "Over here. I have five large and three small signatures."

"I don't see anything," Payne replied. "What'd you do to your scanners?"

"I can't be giving up my secrets that easily. How about a nice wine and chocolates first?"

"Blinky." A software patch linked across the suits.

"Just needed to make sure it worked first. You can owe me the chocolates."

"You'll get nothing and like it," Payne growled. The creatures appeared on his HUD. He moved downhill to get a depth and build a three-dimensional picture of the Ga'ee. "They're less than a meter deep, running sideways."

The HUD updated to show the team the depth and direction of travel.

"Here and here." Blinky pointed. "We'll get in front of them and then cut them off when they veer away."

He stepped back. "Nothing's stopping you, Blinky. Start digging. You've been hoarding your suit power. Time to share, big guy."

"I didn't gain as much weight as Buzz!" Blinky declared.

Buzz gave him the finger. Blinky waited until the other man moved into position. With a nod, they ripped into the ground with great vigor. Ten seconds to get a meter deep. The Ga'ee continued into the gap created, not veering away from their line of travel until they hit the open air. Blinky stumbled backward.

Buzz caught the first one mid-body as it turned to start a new tunnel. He tossed it on the bank, where two Berantz soldiers pinned it to the ground so it was unable to use its legs to start digging or the bottom of its body to dissolve the metal in the tools. Sparky fired up the plasma torch and sent the Ga'ee to its afterlife.

If the creatures believed in such a thing.

A second followed, and soon a third. The other Ga'ee turned before getting to the opening. Dank and Joker stood ready, waiting for the moment to spring the trap. They dug furiously, cutting off the new escape route. They caught the remaining large Ga'ee and sent them to their demise at the end of the plasma torch.

The small ones immediately became disoriented.

"Barrel!" Payne shouted. Major Dank and Joker caught the ones that weren't big enough to wrap around his wrist.

"It's okay, little guy. Learn to live with us, and we'll do the same for you," Dank told the creature.

Payne wasn't sure that was a promise they could keep. If they could learn to talk to the young ones, they might be able to interrupt the cycle of destruction, but having the first ones on Brayalore already breeding a second generation did not bode well.

"We need to get going," Payne told Colonel Ombaras. The Berantz had done the math. Another day or two and the Ga'ee would be too numerous to destroy using a surgical approach. Soon, it would require a nuclear weapon, which was the last thing the Berantz wanted.

[20]

"Sometimes a single grain of sand can stand out on a vast beach." –From the memoirs of Ambassador Declan Payne

"Ten seconds," Admiral Wesson announced, watching the countdown to the arrival of Arthir Dorsite and the armada. "Stand by to transmit order packet."

The Berantz cruisers had already moved into position, ready to fire as part of the massed salvo before fleeing on a clear route to BD27.

First to appear were the cruisers, then the battlewagons, and finally, *Cleophas.*

"Send it," the admiral ordered.

"Transmitted. Incoming message," the comm station called.

"On screen." The text transmission reported the deaths of three cruisers and one Ebren battleship, along with the significant damage to *Cleophas.* Second was a code for using FTL to send abbreviated messages between ships in the fleet. The final portion was a personal message from Admiral Dorsite.

It is a trying time in which we find ourselves,

but I could not wish for anyone better by my side than *Leviathan* and Harry Wesson.

"Channel is live," a voice shouted.

"Arthir, cross-deck to *Leviathan* immediately."

"I'm on the shuttle now." *Cleophas* accelerated away from the launch of the small ship on a vector to the blocking position. *Leviathan* remained where it was.

"I see no mention of an estimate on when the Ga'ee will arrive."

"We think twenty to thirty minutes. It was headed toward the inner planet of BD18 while still recovering its drones. If it stayed with the same course and speed, thirty minutes. If it accelerated, made one orbit, and launched into FTL, then twenty minutes. Maybe fifteen."

"Lev saw it enter FTL twenty-two minutes after you. We've had intermittent contact with it, like we're trying to track a cotton ball. We should have better fidelity the closer it gets. Transmit the FTL code to all ships."

The admiral stood with his feet shoulder-width apart, bracing himself like a mariner of old, as he liked to do. He crossed his arms and watched the screen. A new countdown clock delivered the earliest arrival time of the Ga'ee ship.

Eighteen minutes.

"Arthir is on board. She'll be here momentarily," Lev reported. The admiral didn't need to request that *Leviathan* continue deploying the buoys in the designated pattern. The massive ship had already returned to work, only losing two minutes to the effort. That gave it a three-minute cushion before the Ga'ee's arrival.

Arthir rushed through the hatch and onto the bridge. She saluted Admiral Wesson before shaking his hand.

"No time to waste, Arthir. Did you have time to review the plan?"

"I like the executive summary. Go here. Shoot on command. FTL to BD27. All so *Leviathan* can figure this ship out? Do we know why it's doing this?"

"We do not. We need the intel. The chair has been waiting for you. Make yourself comfortable." The admiral nodded at the captain's chair that dominated the center of the bridge space. The special chair linked the user directly with Lev's core being. It was not for just anyone.

Arthir climbed into it. "I've missed you, Lev. Let's do this thing." Almost instantly, her eyes closed, and she slumped into a reclined position. She looked like she had fallen asleep. Her body processes took a secondary position to her mind, which flared with new activity. Harry returned to looking at the screen.

He calculated the speed along the ships' trajectories. They were cutting it close, maybe too close as the battlewagons lumbered toward their firing points.

"Lev, we'll need to adjust the firing times to ensure simultaneous arrival."

"If only we knew where the Ga'ee would exit FTL. We can estimate that *Cleophas* will draw the ship out. If they do not, then we will have wasted a great deal of firepower."

"We have it to waste in the hope that we get a lucky hit. I don't want to miss the opportunity since I doubt we're going to have too many of them. We can't hit the Ga'ee ship directly. We'd eat too many drones. A Pyrrhic victory is no victory at all."

"I understand. Human history is rife with war sayings."

"We also have a lot of love poetry, Lev. More books are romance than anything else. Don't miss out on the sunshine because your head's in the mud."

"Is that a war saying to highlight the human need for copulation?"

"We're in the middle of a crisis, and you hit me between the eyes with that. You have spent way too much in Payne's brain."

"I have spent the same amount of time in everyone's mind, Harry. The crisis is managed, and everything is in motion that needs to be. Patience is called for. Can we return to our conversation about coitus?"

"We cannot. Can we use the worldkiller?"

"I'm afraid not, Harry."

"It was worth a try. Anything to avoid talking about the human desire for intimacy."

"'Intimacy.' Is that your euphemism?" The tactical board showed the ships getting into position. The human Whale-class battleship lagged behind.

"Is there a problem with the battleship's propulsion system?"

"There is. They are attempting repairs. I could fix it, but it would leave us out of position."

"Issue the order to remain where they are and prepare to transition to FTL. Adjust their firing times as required."

"Done, Harry. Now we wait."

"In silence, as God intended," Admiral Wesson smiled at Commodore Freeman. She nodded tightly, her lips white from clenching her jaw. The plan was unfolding before them, and it depended on the Ga'ee being predictable.

She wasn't as confident as the admiral that they could force the Ga'ee to drop out of FTL at a predetermined location.

You know why the word "God" exists, don't you, Harry? The Godilkinmore. Does that ring any bells?

Now you're just being mean, Lev. I saw the correlation. The Godilkinmore are not gods.

Of course not. They served a purpose for humanity. A higher purpose. Humanity needs an ethereal being because it is beyond your comprehension that you cannot control your own destinies beyond a limited amount.

Admiral Wesson shifted nervously. The countdown continued to the Ga'ee's arrival. "There is no God" was what Lev had just told him, or had he? He'd only said that the Progenitors were not gods.

God can still exist.

If something exists in your mind, does it not exist? Lev asked.

As long as I remember my parents, they exist to me, so I guess the answer is yes. And the philosopher Voltaire was right. "If God did not exist, it would be necessary to invent him."

Or her, Lev replied.

You pick the strangest times for your conversations, Lev. One minute. Please let me concentrate. Lev departed the admiral's mind. The ships were in position. The firing would begin at arrival minus twenty-four seconds.

He started tapping his foot to use up the nervous energy that filled him. The commodore stood next to the admiral and took his arm to hold him steady. He took three deep breaths and stopped tapping.

"First Rapiers are away," a Fleet technician called from one of the many sensor stations. The board's resolution changed as the inbound weapons tracked into an engagement cone. More and more weapons flooded the area on their way to point zero, an arbitrary X on the far side of *Cleophas.*

Ten seconds ahead of schedule, the Ga'ee dropped out of FTL. They were still beyond the system's heliosphere. Not a single weapon would reach them.

Harry groaned, then caught himself. The early drop meant they had more time.

"*Cleophas,* slow withdrawal toward the inner system. Does Arthir concur?"

"Yes," Lev replied. "The Ga'ee ship has stopped."

"Flood the void with waves, the entire electromagnetic spectrum. All ships," Admiral Wesson ordered.

Nothing on the board signaled that his order had been executed.

"Lev?"

"Engaging with active scans, broad-spectrum, all ships," the sensor operator announced.

"So the Ga'ee don't spot the sensor buoys?" the commodore asked.

"I don't know if we can blind it or not, but we don't lose for trying. Who knows? We might be able to collect a little information."

"Outer doors are opening," Lev reported. The tactical screen showed drones streaming from the internal bays. "The ship is accelerating."

The munitions cleared the space where the Ga'ee vessel was supposed to have stopped. The Rapier engines cut out, waiting for further orders. Ballistic munitions continued to points unknown.

"Twenty percent of c." The tactical screen lit up as the Ga'ee ship accelerated at a fantastic rate. The drones continued to stream out of the ship, staying near the hull.

"Is it flying within a bubble of some sort? Those drones can't fly as fast as the carrier, and should be ripped away."

"Collecting the information now. Outer sensor buoys are active."

"And it's going too fast to..." the admiral stopped speculating as the Ga'ee ship jerked to a near-stop. Drones peeled off toward the active sensors. The ship resumed accelerating as if it hadn't stopped.

"Forty percent of c."

"Individual departures to FTL," the admiral ordered. "Fire one final salvo and recover to Rally Point BD27."

The drones spread out in a massive fantail behind the Ga'ee vessel and targeted the active buoys. In seconds, the outermost were destroyed. The Ga'ee trident drones flew a parallel path, retracing the humans' delivery flight routes as if they had a star map showing them where the frigates had flown.

Maybe they could track ships through space. Or did they have better sensors? The Ga'ee drones continued without interference. None of the buoys could stand up to them. The drones ripped them apart without slowing down. It was like the sensor buoys had the consistency of papier-mâché.

"Are we getting information?" the admiral asked.

"What little there is, yes."

"Is it destroying one hundred percent of the hardware?"

Two cruisers winked out as they engaged their faster-than-light drives. The Whale-class ship launched a full broadside before disappearing. No need to wait to see the impacts.

Or lack thereof. The Ga'ee ship raced down the gravity well toward Blegoston, BD23. The drones hung by its side. It slowed at intervals, like hiccups, and a cloud of drones peeled away on a trajectory toward the armada each time.

The Fleet ships fired a broadside and entered FTL. None of them stayed long enough to let the drones engage, exactly as the plan dictated.

Cleophas lumbered slowly in front of the ten-kilometer-long Ga'ee ship.

"Activate the Rapiers," Admiral Wesson ordered.

The anti-ship missiles reappeared on the tactical screen. Drones changed course to intercept them. The volume of fire, nearly four hundred weapons coming from all points of the compass, caught the Ga'ee off-guard.

The admiral pumped a fist as missiles raced beyond the reach of the drones.

On final approach, the Ga'ee ship blazed like a streak of lightning as it surged beyond the reach of the Rapiers.

The attack failed. Not a single missile closed on the vessel. *Cleophas* flushed all tubes, fired her cannons, and disappeared into FTL while a cloud of drones entered her outer defensive perimeter.

"Too close," the admiral mumbled, but the munitions slammed into the alien ship's prow, sending puffs of molten metal into the void. "Does that mean it doesn't have an energy screen?"

"It has not shown an energy barrier during this engagement," was the most Lev would commit to.

"Prepare to enter FTL," the admiral ordered. The drones coming in from the system's outer reaches continued to destroy everything in their path.

———

A sensor buoy, smaller than the others, was passive until certain triggers activated it: the ship's proximity. Active pings. An energy source unlike the ones on *Leviathan* or the Fleet ships.

The Ga'ee ship stopped to send more drones into the void. The small weapons raced past. The buoy swept through the engine wash, bobbing and floating. A bubble embraced the buoy and pulled it closer to the ship. The Ga'ee carrier accelerated anew at a speed that would have destroyed the buoy had it been subjected to the rigors of open space.

But it wasn't.

The buoy eased toward the open hangar, rose near the overhead, and followed it deeper into the interior. All the triggers except one had activated. It needed to feel an energy source. A power plant.

Subtle vibrations. Rhythmic. A thrum of power.

The buoy activated. It scanned at its highest intensity before launching a passive beacon into space. It made it into the bubble within which the ship was cradled while the bubble moved through space. The beacon casually floated outboard, pressed against the bubble's edge. Its low-profile motor pushed it mindlessly until there was no resistance.

Inside the ship, trident drones zeroed in on the small buoy and accelerated into it. The device was crushed under the onslaught, but it tried to send one final message.

That also failed to penetrate the bubble's exterior, and the signal died.

At the next stop, the remaining drones were flushed from the hangar. Tens of thousands made a beeline for the Progenitor ship, a juicy target. Lost in the cloud of weaponry, a small buoy floated free.

[21]

*"Hell is too good for these bastards. Send them to deal
with Earth's bureaucrats. That will destroy their will to
live."* –From the memoirs of Ambassador Declan Payne

The second-to-last site. It had twenty "wrigglers," as Turbo had taken to calling them. Ten fully grown and ten in the earliest stages of their development.

"Looks like they double every twelve hours or so," Sparky suggested. "I think it's based on the soil composition. This area is silicon-rich with some tasty metals. Iron, copper, and even gold."

"Buffet is closed, bitches!" Turbo yelled at the ground.

"What do you say I take four to the next site? The excavator is probably already there," Virgil asked.

"Colonel," Payne started, "we'd like to take half our team to the next site before they replicate so many we can't get them all."

The math suggested they would reach a tipping point where they were replicating faster than they could be destroyed.

Brayalore was not rich in what the Ga'ee appeared to prefer, but the Berantz homeworld was.

Payne continued, "Unless PX47 took measures, after two months, the surface area of the Rang'Kor planet will be overrun, albeit, that's only five percent of the total. BHo1 is in jeopardy, except your people will have seen the ships. I hope they went after the invaders. It's been a long time since the Ga'ee hit your homeworld."

"That worries me greatly. We have to get word to Berantz. Your return to your ship will have to wait. The first ship that comes to this system must go to our homeworld."

"Of course." Payne spun his arm in the air and pointed at Dank.

Virgil gave the thumbs-up. He selected Byle, Turbo, Sparky, and Blinky to go with him. Colonel Ombaras detailed his best soldiers to accompany them. The two groups boarded the shuttle, and it took off. The ship accelerated into the distance.

"Git 'er done, people!" Payne ordered.

The excavator continued to dig. Buzz gestured at a bucketful and held up two fingers. Heckler triggered the plasma torch, and it came to life with a woosh and a hiss. The Berantz soldiers moved close and gripped their shovels tightly, ready for the flurry of work involved in exposing the Ga'ee before they could disappear underground.

The dirt hit. The excavator operator tamped the bucket on the nicely formed load to break it apart, exposing two Ga'ee. One immediately headed into the soft dirt beneath it. A shovel dug in ahead of its escape route and popped the thing out of the ground.

It turned and "ran" up the shovel. The second Ga'ee didn't bother trying to escape. It immediately attacked the exposed soldier. He threw his shovel at it. Shaolin sidestepped and stomped an armored boot on it. Heckler lunged forward and delivered a plasma-fired death.

The first soldier shook the shovel but couldn't toss the Ga'ee off it. The creature swarmed up his arms and wrapped itself around his neck.

Joker stood helpless, her armored gloves unable to get a grip on the creature. It didn't take long for the soldier's silent scream to end and his body to crumple. When he hit the ground, the Ga'ee tried to get under the body and dig its way to freedom, but Joker struck, ripping the creature free and swinging it over her head to keep it from getting a grip.

When Heckler finished dispatching the other, he waved the tip of the plasma torch at the ground. Joker slammed the Ga'ee in front of the combat specialist. Heckler pulled the trigger to deliver plasma at its greatest intensity. The Ga'ee curled and twisted. Within seconds, it turned a dull gray and withered like an old piece of leather.

And just as dead.

Buzz kept directing the excavator to dig deeper and deeper.

The Berantz soldiers moved in and took their fellow under his arms to drag his body away.

"The Ga'ee have learned, and now they're fighting us," Payne stated. "Keep your people away. We'll take care of it."

Payne checked his suit's power. Thirty percent. He would run it until the suit froze, and it would have to be enough.

He frowned at the grim task ahead. They had to be on their guard. When a Ga'ee got aggressive, the humans were overwhelmed, and a Ga'ee might penetrate an armored combat suit. Payne couldn't imagine anything more terrible than being trapped inside his suit with one of them.

"There!" Heckler waved at a Ga'ee that was moving quickly over the top of the ground at the far end of the hole. Buzz had missed it. The creature scuttled away. Shaolin dove after it, missed, and low-crawled to catch up. She slapped a glove on it and pinned it to the ground. It arched along its length to dig one end of its body through the surface and started to burrow.

Shaolin hung on, but the creature showed incredible strength, dragging her with it suit and all. Payne jumped in after them and hooked his boot under the creature, then kicked it free of the ground. Shaolin rolled, maintaining her grip to yank the Ga'ee off the ground.

It flopped onto her faceplate. Payne seized it with both hands and pulled it away, holding it out in front of him.

The hole was too deep to climb out. Payne activated his jets and flew upward, then moved sideways to land in front of Heckler. He torched the creature without touching Payne's gloves. The major dropped the Ga'ee, and Heckler finished it off.

"Buzz?" Payne growled. He inspected the minimal damage to his suit's gloves.

Shaolin scrambled out. A haze marred her faceplate. She rubbed it with a glove. "Damn thing got me."

"Combat effectiveness?" Payne asked.

"One hundred percent. Visual isn't crystal-clear, but HUD is unaffected," she reported.

"There he goes!" Buzz called.

Joker hit the escapee with a Berantz shovel, trying to cut it in half, but the blade bounced off as if it had hit hard rubber. She tossed the shovel aside, pulled the slung railgun into position, and stitched a line of hypervelocity micro-projectiles across its back. To follow up, she stomped on it, and it split in half. Both ends started digging into the dirt.

Separately.

She fired back and forth at each half until they stopped moving.

"What the hell, Joker? What'd that take, five hundred rounds?"

After checking, she replied, "About that."

"We have no resupply." Payne chuckled. "But this is the fight we got. Use it all if we have to. We'll figure out what to do after that. If we can kill them through brute force, do it."

"Just need to tear them in half first, then shoot them from the inside out. At least, that's what I did. Dull gray, bad day. Shiny steel, plenty real. That's my mantra." Joker waved her railgun in the air.

"Keep digging." Payne motioned at the excavator operator.

His suit was down to twenty-one percent. It was losing power quicker than it should have. Mary Payne remained in the hospital. He'd heard no word.

Railguns chattered as Joker and Shaolin doubled up on another Ga'ee.

The excavator motored on, digging and dumping. Buzz kept directing. Heckler moved quickly from spot to spot, delivering small bursts from the plasma torch as death knells to riddled Ga'ee bodies.

Until the plasma ran out.

Then he shouted his war cry and jumped into the hole, dangerously close to where the excavator bucket ripped into the dirt.

Fire, rip, fire some more.

At last, Buzz held up his fist. "That's all she wrote."

"Keep digging," Payne ordered.

The team moved outside the new crater and watched intently as each bucketload was dumped into a growing mountain along both sides of the heavy equipment. Ten minutes later, Buzz made an X with his arms.

It was time to stop.

"Wrap it and pack it!" Payne declared. "This area is free of Ga'ee, as far as we can tell. Sensors show no movement, and the

Mark One eyeballs confirm. We think the area is clear. Twenty-one total creatures destroyed."

The excavator backed out of the trench it had cut and away from the dirt piles. Once clear, it headed for the transport shuttle.

A soldier ran from the personnel shuttle with a message for the colonel. Ombaras took the message and made a beeline for Major Payne.

"Your Major Dank needs assistance. He said he's been overrun."

———

"Damage report!" the admiral shouted as if his crew would respond.

Only Lev could answer the question. "No foreign body impacts on the outer hull. No damage. We entered FTL before the first of the drones arrived. None of the ships in the armada were engaged."

The admiral stared at the screen showing the ships, separate but together, flying toward BD27. "Are you tracking the Ga'ee ship? How far behind us is it?"

"It is not registering on any of my systems," Lev replied.

"So, we have no idea if it's following us."

"We can make an educated guess, based on its prior actions. I suspect it is thirty-five to forty minutes behind us."

The admiral scratched his chin as he stared at the unchanging tactical screen. "I would have thought twenty-five minutes like before. Why do you think it's thirty-five to forty?"

"In the last two systems, it traveled to the habitable planet before entering faster-than-light speed. In BD23, we intercepted it farther away from the planet than at BD18."

"Why is it going to the planet?" the admiral asked. The commodore's face fell. "What?"

"Is it seeding the planets?" she asked. At the admiral's questioning look, she continued. "It's putting Ga'ee on the planets."

"You went from a question to a statement. We didn't see anything on PX47. The Rang'Kor didn't say a word."

"Maybe the Ga'ee seek out an isolated part of the world to set up a colony. They share without encroaching on the locals. In that, Lev would be correct that they are not an enemy. Maybe they're only trying to survive."

The admiral started to pace. The implications made him pause. "We've left Ga'ee behind friendly lines without any way for those on the planet to ask for help because there are no ships. And I don't agree that dropping settlers on an occupied planet is peaceful. What are they going to do there?"

"There will be two ships at BD18 in less than two days," Lev replied.

The admiral remained tense. The coordination of a dozen ships between three star systems was well within his capabilities, but the unknown location of the Ga'ee ship made for a dynamic of infinite possibilities.

"Arthir, can you hear me?"

"Yes, Admiral," came a voice through the sound system. Arthir remained in the semi-conscious state that happened when integrating with *Leviathan* through the captain's chair.

"Can you plan for a variety of contingencies based on where the Ga'ee ship might go?"

"We have to prepare to fight the Ga'ee at BD27. We only need to decide how long we'll wait for the Ga'ee before backtracking our steps to look for it should it not show."

"All eggs in one basket, then. We have made our bed. Now we lie in it. We don't have any additional information regarding the Ga'ee ship, so we'll have to take our best shot. We have to assume that the Ga'ee can see us, based on their reaction in BD23." The admiral looked less than amused.

He knew what they had to do—a suicide mission. Send the Mosquitos, armed with nukes, on a run to get into the hangar bay and blow it up from the inside. The frigates, *Cleophas*, and every other ship they had would do the same thing.

If they had to.

BD27 was the line the Ga'ee could not cross.

"We have more information, Harry," Lev replied. "I conducted a final interrogation of our passive buoys before we entered FTL. One answered. A buoy got inside the Ga'ee ship."

The admiral clenched his jaw, and his lips worked as he fought to contain words that would add no value to the conversation—angry words about not telling him sooner.

But days remained before they arrived at BD27. There was time. What they didn't have was Team Payne. The admiral groaned softly while frowning.

"What do we know, Lev?"

"We know where the power plants are. We know the energy signature for the shield around the ship, and we have the timing for its implementation. We can analyze the vulnerabilities that the buoy exploited to get inside. I would have appreciated Team Payne's assistance, too, Harry."

"I can't believe they're gone. Just like that, we found ourselves on our own. Are you ready to fight the Ga'ee now? A worldkiller would come in handy. Faster-than-light, right into the sweet spot. End its reign of terror," the admiral suggested hopefully.

"Vengeance is no way to live, Harry. We live with risk. We live on borrowed time. Making war for payback is a recipe for failure and counter to what I was designed for."

"I know, Lev. I had to ask. Since you have data and that was the whole goal of our stand at BD23, let's call it a win.

Complete your analysis, and when you have a plan, Arthir, let me know. I think it's prudent to believe the Ga'ee ship is headed here. We'll shoot for thirty-five minutes for the time between our arrival in BD27 and the arrival of the Ga'ee. Thirty-five minutes to coordinate and execute our counterattack."

[22]

"There is rarely room on one planet for two intelligent races." –From the memoirs of Ambassador Declan Payne

The shuttle executed a steep dive before pulling up, jerking sideways, and dropping to the ground. It hit hard. The Berantz soldiers were tossed within their seats, bodies thrown against their restraints. The colonel grunted and grabbed his ribcage. The side hatch popped, and Payne stormed out to see what the rest of his team was up against.

He was greeted by an exploding grenade. Shrapnel pinged off his suit, which only made him run faster toward the dig site. The excavator was overrun by Ga'ee, a few of which were easily two meters long.

Dank and three other SOFTies were huddled atop a rocky outcropping, firing at everything that moved.

The ground rippled from railgun impacts that chased Ga'ee maneuvering under the topsoil.

Buzz, Heckler, Shaolin, and Joker joined Payne but hesitated to fire. There were targets high and targets low.

"Nearly one hundred Ga'ee," Buzz reported.

"Hit the excavator from the air," Payne called, waving Colonel Ombaras and his soldiers back to the shuttle. "We'll clean up the ground afterward."

Payne checked his HUD, looking for his other team member.

Turbo was inside the excavator. A quick check revealed the body of the operator on the ground between the vehicle's wheels.

"What the hell are you doing in there?" Heckler blurted.

"Seemed like a good idea at the time, sir." Turbo fired intermittently through a gap in the shattered glass. The Ga'ee crawled over the vehicle, leaving trails across the surface as they stripped the metal one layer at a time.

"Belay that orbital strike order," Payne transmitted to the shuttle. He switched to the team channel. "How do we get her out of there?"

"Full-on assault, followed by a vertical egress," Heckler replied matter-of-factly.

"There!" Dank shouted over the channel, and the team fired with all they had as the ground opened up before them and the Ga'ee flooded out. Even on fully automatic, firing at the cyclic rate, the team couldn't slow the surge.

"One hundred and five," Buzz reported.

"We're losing ground." Payne bounced left and right in the hope of seeing something he'd missed, but the view didn't change. "Full assault on the excavator, vertical departure." He assigned lanes of fire and shared them across the team HUDs. "Stay in your lanes, assault through the objective, and go vertical as soon as we have Turbo. On two."

The team raised their railguns and prepared to fire. Payne made it a short count because time was their enemy. The Ga'ee were in the midst of doubling their numbers. After two weeks, the other planets had to be overrun. In the short time it took to count to two, he feared for the galaxy. It was more than a ship that seemed invincible. They were going to lose the habitable planets among the seven races. How many Berantz had died?

"Two."

The team ran forward, railguns barking, sending hypervelocity projectiles into Ga'ee scattered across the rig. By walking the railgun impacts into the metal beneath the creatures, they sent their bodies flying.

Dank, Byle, Blinky, and Sparky used their jets to escape the fresh onslaught from Ga'ee attacking from the excavation before them. The team flared skyward before regrouping ten meters farther from the hole. They fired the whole time, not allowing a single interruption as they maneuvered through the air.

The Ga'ee coming from the hole shifted their attack from Dank to the excavator. They scuttled forward with amazing speed, but they were not as quick as humans in powered combat armor. Payne fired, checked the cab access, and fired again, clearing the steps. The others, two left and two right, delivered withering destruction, hammering the Ga'ee but not delivering death blows. They needed to rip them apart to ensure they stayed dead.

That wasn't this mission. They had to get their teammate clear.

Heckler went wild like a one-man wrecking crew. The rest of the team matched his frenzy, and soon, there was a clear route off the rig.

Turbo burst out of the cab and casually tossed a grenade in behind her, then jetted skyward. Payne and his group followed. The grenade exploded in a cloud of smoke, twisted sheet metal, and glass.

The Ga'ee not blown off the rig worked their way down the metal frame, heading for the safety of the ground. Team Payne flew toward Major Dank to reconsolidate the team but changed in mid-air and turned back to the hole in which the bones of the excavator rested. Now was the time. Exploit success. The Ga'ee were in disarray, not acting with a unified purpose, not focusing on a single target.

The team came back to the ground, still firing to delay the creatures' escape. They landed among them and started stomping the riddled bodies, shooting them from the inside out and jetting away when more than one Ga'ee attacked. Divide the creatures, rip their bodies open, destroy them, and move on. It was a hard way to finish the enemy, but it was the best they had.

Payne stopped going vertical. He walked slowly backward, firing as he went. His suit was bleeding power through the high-energy maneuvers.

He checked his HUD. Three of the others showed red, Turbo, Heckler, and Dank. Payne activated his comm channel. "Call down the strike right here on this pile of junk and the hole it dug. Everything you've got."

The team reformed to conduct a tactical retrograde, reducing their volume of fire to sniping when a Ga'ee appeared near the ground's surface.

Colonel Ombaras had the fighters circling, ready to dive-bomb the site. He had seen the ebb and flow of the battle. It called for the big guns. He had artillery moving into position, too, but it would take too long. The time was now.

This was the moment where if the battle didn't turn, it would be lost.

"Clear the impact area," the colonel ordered. Payne and his team could withstand much more than soldiers in the open, but even they didn't want to be on the receiving end of what promised to be a fantastic sound and light show, the likes of which had never been seen against a live enemy on Brayalore.

Never had they fought for their planet before.

Fear was a great motivator, fear of getting overrun. And then led to anger which led to resolve. Grim determination. The fighters were inbound.

Payne cranked his external speakers to max. "Bring the pain!"

They jogged away from the target zone, watching on their HUDs the view from their rear-facing cameras.

The first bombs impacted in the crater. The excavator was tossed like a child's toy. While it was still in the air, a second bomb hit and blasted it again. It flew sideways and crashed into the side of the hole it had dug, twisted and dead, never to run again.

The shuttle with the second excavator arrived in time to watch the death of its mate. The pilot kept the ship outside the ingress and egress routes, waiting for clearance to land.

"Get down here!" Payne called accidentally through his suit's speakers. The words disappeared into the concussions from the second fighter's run. He switched to the radio and called the colonel. "Get that digger on the ground. We'll need to go after those bastards the second the bombs stop falling."

The colonel confirmed and signed off.

The third fighter delivered an ordnance load into the dust cloud and the smoke. The new explosions added to the chaos and fire within an impossibly small area.

Payne spoke over the team channel. "Some of them have to be ripped apart. Finish those first. We'll go after the others as soon as we can. We must draw down their numbers. Blinky, Buzz, have you two come up with anything?"

"We haven't been able to analyze any of the data," Blinky replied. They had worked on the suits' scanners to optimize their ability to detect the Ga'ee. How the species communicated was still beyond the humans' ability to understand. "If Lev were here, we would have made progress."

"Lev isn't here." Payne crushed the conversation.

"Stand by," Colonel Ombaras transmitted.

For what? Payne thought. They needed to hit that hole the instant the smoke cleared and make sure the stunned and torn stayed dead. "Prepare to attack into the crater."

A rugged sound came to them—not a jet or a scramjet, but a piston engine. Old technology, using a propellor to drive the vehicle.

"Clear the area," Colonel Ombaras said, "unless you want a hydrochloric acid shower."

"Woohoo!" Payne cheered. He picked a spot on his map halfway between where they were and the shuttles, lateral to the airplane's approach vector. The team ran at full speed. It took less than ten seconds to get beyond the impact area.

"I guess they realized that a little environmental damage was better than letting those things breed out of control," Major Dank sent on a person-to-person channel.

"My thoughts exactly, Virge," Payne replied. "It's good to see them partnering with us in this fight. They've already lost two people. The numbers would keep growing until we couldn't stop them, no matter how much firepower we had. I'm almost out of juice, so we need to recharge, and I have no idea if the Berantz can accommodate us."

"Good news is that you have smart people who will be able to reconfigure a power supply. Once we have the all-clear, we'll recover at the base and think about how we're going to get out of here. We might need to build our own interstellar ship." Dank pointed. "Here it comes!"

Payne had been watching the painfully slow approach. The aerial vehicle dipped low on a pass from their right to their left. At the outer ring of smoke, it activated spray nozzles and doused the area. The spray continued as it passed beyond the engagement zone, then it stood on its tail for an abrupt turn and flew back across the area. It did that four times before it ran out of acid. The airplane rocked its wings on the final flight out.

The team waved back.

"Into the fray. Kill what's left," Payne ordered.

The team stalked forward, giving the spray time to settle and mix with the dirt. Dull gray Ga'ee were scattered within the crater.

Buzz and Blinky scanned the area rapidly. "Those close to the surface are having a real bad day, but we have some deep ones making a run for it. Two meters down, right here. Moving in trace."

They moved in order, one after another, letting the lead plow through the dirt.

"Bring up that excavator. Right here." Payne jabbed at the ground. "Hurry!"

The engine roared as the vehicle accelerated. The colonel had brought it in and had unloaded it. The digger was ready when they needed it.

"I love it when a plan comes together. Five, Buzz. Is that all that's left?"

Shaolin and Byle used their gloves to dig out two of the shallower Ga'ee. They had silver patches on their skin, a testament to their durability. They were fighting to survive the acid attack. Shaolin pinned one to the ground with her boot and stitched a line across its body using her railgun. Byle followed suit.

The Ga'ee lost their fight.

Heckler and Turbo ripped at the ground to dig out those that had gotten below the surface. Although the creatures were moving, it was glacially slow.

The intermittent sounds of railgun fire testified to their demise.

The excavator rolled in and started to dig where Blinky and Buzz directed. Two bucketloads in and the Ga'ee turned, as expected. The bucket bit deep, the operator well-practiced in delivering minimal extraneous moves to do the work.

A trench appeared around the Ga'ee within a box of solid dirt. They popped out one by one. Joker and Sparky jumped into the pit and pulled the first one out, throwing it into the air and out of the hole.

Payne and Dank tag-teamed it to kill it.

"Four and counting," Blinky called.

Two more followed before the last two turned sideways and then went deeper.

Sparky stabbed a finger repeatedly toward the square of earth. "Dig it up!"

The operator went after it, plunging the teeth at the front of the bucket exactly where Sparky was pointing. The bucket went deep, scooped, and came out.

"They're in there," Blinky noted.

The bucket of dirt dropped out of the hole and remained intact. Payne side-kicked it, and it came apart. The two Ga'ee, healthy ones, twisted and contorted as they sought to escape.

But there was no escaping the focus of ten SOFTies. Rail-guns chattered. Blinky stomped one and fired again. Heckler and Turbo jumped on the second, catching it by one end while the other attempted to dig into the ground. They jerked it free and ripped it apart with their gloved hands, then tossed the pieces close by, where they hammered them with railgun fire.

Heckler's weapon clicked dry. He let the railgun drop under his arm and spin around to his back, freeing his hands. He caught the last Ga'ee and spun it over his head, then slammed it on the ground.

Turbo fired into the creature, stitching a line across its body so they could tear it in half. She fired until her suit locked up.

"Clear!" Blinky shouted.

Payne checked his HUD to review the status of his team. "Heckler, get your ass to the shuttle at the economy pace. Blinky and Buzz, you two slackers have the most power. You carry Turbo. Easy on the walk. No jets." Payne's meter blinked red—five percent. There would be no more engagements until he recharged.

He led the way into the shuttle, parked his suit inside, and climbed out of it. He'd kept his emergency clothing inside with him and dressed quickly, but only the jumpsuit. The boots were back at the base. He stood barefoot in front of the colonel. The team took their places within the shuttle.

"You need to find that last drone, but I think we might be okay. It had already deposited its five seedlings—charges, babies, whatever the hell we're going to call them—before we chased it off."

"We lost track of it over the eastern sea when it appeared to crash, but we will keep searching." The colonel nodded at Payne's suit. "Is something wrong?"

"Out of power. We've been non-stop for days. How long have we been here?"

"Four days," Buzz offered.

"I think five," Payne replied, "but then again, it might be only one but a really long one. I don't remember sleeping."

"You haven't," the colonel offered. "You probably should. I believe your physiological needs are comparable to ours. Food and then sleep."

"I need to check on my wife. Hospital first, then food, and then sleep. After we get our suits charging, of course. So, no sleep for a while, but we'll take food. Thanks for the tactical assist with the old rotor bird."

"As much as we didn't want to, a crop duster spraying acid was our only choice. The mixture destroyed the valves, and once opened, there was no going back. The entire load had to be dumped."

"I think the full tank was required. A little lime and you'll be able to recover that ground, I think." Payne didn't sound confident. He couldn't because he didn't know if it would work. "But thank you. We wouldn't have stopped them without the hydrochloric acid drop. As soon as we confirm the last ship, we can declare the planet Ga'ee-free. Then all we have to do is backtrack through your planets and fight a ground war to rid them of the alien infestation. They've had a lot of time. If your people..."

Payne didn't continue the thought that if they didn't engage the Ga'ee right away, it would be too late. The Berantz would be forced to retreat until there was nowhere else to go. They'd fight, but without an industrial-sized production run of the acids needed to destroy the things, they'd be unable to keep up.

"I know," the colonel replied in a soft voice. "This site was rich in gold and silver. It helped the Ga'ee replicate faster. Any longer, and we would have already lost. It's a sobering thought."

The shuttle hatch remained open.

"We're waiting for the excavator to load," the colonel explained. "I don't want to leave soldiers behind who can't protect themselves."

Payne knew that only too well. "Then we wait. Half my team has plenty of juice left for any kind of engagement, but we're getting low on ammunition. Still, we'll use everything we have left if you need us to."

"I appreciate the sentiment," the colonel replied emotionlessly.

"Buzz, Sparky, and Joker, give them a hand. Scan the ground until it glows to make sure nothing is coming from below. Heckler, your suit's almost dead, so stay here with me."

The three headed off the shuttle, but Joker stopped them.

"Major Dank says he's already doing that. Turbo is on the shuttle with her dead suit. Byle, Shaolin, and Blinky are providing oversight."

Payne gave her the thumbs-up. "Stand down," he said, gesturing for them to relax. As long as one of them had comms with the team, they all had it, and as long as they had oversight of the soldiers loading the excavator, there would be no surprises.

"Tell Blinky while he's out there to make one last pass of the engagement area for a triple-check. And since we're talking about checking, team suit review. Did the Ga'ee or HCl do anything to limit our combat effectiveness besides Joker's redesigned faceplate?"

They paired off to check each other's gear. Payne scoured the outside of his gloves and arms, finding minor pitting but nothing that would impact the suit's operation. He moved to the legs, taking his time around the knee and ankle joints to search for places the acid might have penetrated.

Lev had upgraded their suits, and the alloy seemed unaffected except where the Ga'ee had attacked.

"Begs the question," Payne mused. "Are Ga'ee using their teeth or a chemical?"

"We'll keep studying them," Sparky replied. "We have captured enough of them."

"And we'll keep researching how they communicate," Buzz added. "I think we're going to have plenty of time."

Payne clenched his jaw and nodded. With the Berantz ships coming out on the wrong end of the conflict with the Ga'ee, they might not see an interstellar ship for a long time. Would Lev return and look for them? Payne hoped so—if Lev survived a battle with the Ga'ee.

Battle was inevitable, wasn't it? Or would Lev insist that the Ga'ee weren't the enemy until his demise? There were two thousand humans on board, along with the Rang'Kor captain and maybe other representatives from the seven races. Payne wasn't sure. He hadn't delved that deeply into it.

He'd been focused on getting his team back up to speed. They were getting better, but they were nowhere near as sharp as they had been during the final engagements with the Vestrall. That was his fault. They had retired, and no one had contemplated returning to service. He should have known they would all hate their civilian gigs.

At least they were happy. Even Mary, recovering in the hospital. She had her scar, and it was an ugly brute—the result of friendly fire.

Like a civil war where nothing is civil. There was nothing friendly about being in the impact area of allied weaponry. Her poor luck that she had taken a direct hit.

But she'd survived.

Heckler and Turbo were together.

Benefits of being civilians.

"We *will* get back to *Leviathan*," Payne growled to himself. "He needs us every bit as much as we need him. He better damn well survive the Ga'ee, and then he better get the hell back here to pick us up."

"Hear, hear," Heckler called from nearby. He had gotten out of his suit and dressed in his emergency jumpsuit. He was also barefoot. "Colonel, your planet is nice and all, but the real fight is out there. You thought it was bad here? We need to nip that butt to keep them from any other star system."

"Bud. Nip it in the *bud*," Payne corrected. "It's a flower reference. And the colonel can't understand you without your suit translating."

"Are you serious? Flowers? I've been saying it wrong all this time." He shrugged. "I like my version better, irregardless."

"You are an irreverent soul, Heckler. I'm glad to be on the same team with you."

The shuttle lifted slowly into the air and accelerated away. Those in their suits magnetically locked themselves to the deck. Payne and Heckler grabbed for anything they could reach. The colonel held his hands up and said something in Berantz.

"He warned you," Joker relayed, using her suit's speakers.

"And none of you knotheads thought to translate for us?" Payne asked.

Heckler leaned close and whispered, "Bring the pain!" before turning to the rest of the team and laughing uproariously.

At least morale is good, Payne thought. *Drills start the second the suits are recharged.*

———

The shuttle landed atop the hospital and Payne ran off, slowing when he hit the pebbled roof. He walked tenderly across it. When he reached the door, he hurried down the steps after a waiting escort. They took him to the recovery ward, where Kal stood like a monument to fitness. He let Payne enter the room and joined him. Mary had just finished her meal. The color had returned to her face.

Payne couldn't help but smile.

"I think we got 'em all," he began.

"That's what you start with? Not anything about I'm glad you're alive. I would die without you. Profess your love for me. Any of that in there?" She moved her arm slowly and pointed at Payne's head.

"It's like you didn't know who you married. But yes, I love you, Dog. I was ready to go ballistic on the Berantz had you not survived, no matter the repercussions. I've given up my quest for vengeance and directed my anger at the Ga'ee, and I think we got them all, but we might have to visit the bottom of their ocean to make sure. Are you up for an undersea adventure?" Payne waggled his eyebrows at her.

"My suit is kinda wrecked, and I'm pretty sure I can't go like this." She pulled her covers aside to reveal a human-style medical gown. "I don't know if I can get a bikini on Brayalore. They don't seem like the bikini type. And I probably don't want to get the bandages wet. Maybe my bikini days are over."

Payne shook his head. "I never cared about those days anyway."

Mary smiled. "So, you think my body is only for you nowadays and not to wow a syndicated audience?"

"I feel like you set me up when you start with 'so.' I know that I can't win no matter what answer I give, so I'll decline the invite to imminent failure, and we'll revisit my shortcomings at a different time."

"I accept your surrender." Mary tried to nod but winced instead. "Too many movements." She crooked a finger at Payne. He leaned carefully on her bed to kiss her slowly and fully. "How was the fight?"

"Ugly. They double rather quickly whenever the soil contains what they need. The first ones weren't bad, but the last ones? They had already grown to over one hundred and twenty. They destroyed an excavator. Two Berantz soldiers died, and our suits are not in the best of shape. Turbo's suit is dead. Three more are close, and we're low on railgun ammo. Besides that, we're ready to go."

"Sounds like we're dead in the water."

Payne helped adjust her pillows. "The team is figuring out how to recharge the suits along with reload the rails. But if Brayalore is clear, then we're stuck twiddling our thumbs until a ship arrives. We're taking it off-planet no matter what it is or where it's going."

"I'm coming. Maybe we can get my suit fixed using the facilities on a modern starship."

"We'll do what we can," Payne committed. "And you will, too, when you're ready. But for now, your whole job is to recover. Rest. That's an order."

She raised an eyebrow while giving him the side-eye.

"It sounded better in my head," he admitted. He caressed the side of her face. "So beautiful."

Mary held his hand to her cheek and closed her eyes. "Give me a day or two. They have some pretty good docs here, and our physiology is nearly identical. O-neg blood. It's theirs. Who'da thunk *we* are the aliens!" She leaned back and closed her eyes.

"Sleep well." Payne kissed her cheek. "And sleep fast. I need you."

"Figure out the next steps and if there's anything we can share with Lev about what we learned down here," Mary mumbled.

"Hot-wash time," Payne stated. He looked at Kal while nodding with his chin at a nearby nurse. "Do you trust them?"

"I should, but I don't. Not with the lives of my friends. I shall stay. You go. We will join you as soon as we are able," Kal'-faxx replied. "What was it like, fighting the Ga'ee?"

"It was like killing super rubbery centipedes who wouldn't die. It wasn't the most gratifying. You didn't miss anything, my friend." Payne clapped him on the arm. "On a completely different topic, how long can you hold your breath?"

[23]

"One must always have a moral compass. Without it, it's easy to get lost." –From the memoirs of Ambassador Declan Payne

"I have the plan," Arthir began from the captain's chair, her eyes open. She extricated herself from its intoxicating embrace and stepped down. Admiral Wesson and Commodore Freeman each took an arm to steady her. She declined the offer of a seat. "I've been sitting too long. That's how I got this way."

She braced herself, widening her stance in a battle against her shaking legs.

"You don't have to hit the bathroom or anything?" the admiral asked.

"Now that you mention it." Arthir took a stumbling step. Nyota gripped her arm and guided her toward the corridor.

Admiral Wesson stared at the screen. "Lev, bring up Arthir's deployment plan and play it out over the duration of the proposed engagement."

System BD27 appeared on the main screen. Icons representing the ships of the armada were scattered haphazardly from the second planet, the only one in the Goldilocks zone, to the fourth planet at the outer edge of the heliosphere. There was no funnel, no set engagement zone.

The next screen showed the arrival of the Ga'ee ship. Instantly, the armada ships flashed into faster-than-light speed on a variety of angles throughout the system. The Ga'ee ship disappeared from the screen.

"A kamikaze attack." Harry Wesson felt a boulder settle into the pit of his stomach. "What if they have an active defense?"

"Then we overwhelm them with ships. Full-sized battlewagons arriving at FTL speed is more than even the Ga'ee can stop."

"As has been said in Earth's history, it's nearly impossible to defend against one who is willing to give his life for his cause. They only have to get lucky once while the defender has to be lucky all the time." The admiral didn't have to replay the engagement. No matter where the Ga'ee materialized, at least two ships would be close enough to engage and ram into the vessel. They would need assistance from Lev to ensure their calculations for coming out of FTL were precise.

FTL near-misses resulted in bending around an object as light was wont to do, throwing a ship off-course. Direct impacts had dire consequences. Most of that was theoretical since the cost of building a single faster-than-light drive was astronomical. No one wanted to lose a cruiser-sized or larger ship.

Until Lev confirmed the science and reduced humanity's risk.

Or improved their odds for an attack strategy based on a direct impact from a faster-than-light vessel, which was what they had done with the worldkiller they had employed on the drone dreadnought.

"You're going to let us sacrifice ships filled with our people. You won't reconsider using the worldkiller?" Harry pleaded.

"This is not my fight, Harry. These are not my people. There is no evidence of Nyota's supposition regarding the seeding of our galaxy. I cannot, in good conscience and staying true to my moral compass, attack the Ga'ee. Despite the information we gathered, we still don't know with any certainty that they are an enemy."

"I'm pretty sure they are. They've attacked us over and over. All they had to do was not attack, and we would have talked to them all day long."

"I fear that allowing you to launch *Ugly 4* not only stymied those efforts, it cost us Declan and the good people of Team Payne."

"They only sought more information. It was *Ugly 4*, not quite a threat to a ten-kilometer-long ship. It had two baby-sized missiles on board, and that's it. To consider that a threat where they retaliate and end thousands of lives was ludicrous!" The admiral said his piece louder than intended, but he thought Lev was being unreasonable.

Disproportionate response was a tool of the powerful to keep lesser players in line. The Ga'ee were delivering healthy doses of fear to give themselves free rein through Berantz space.

Lev didn't reply to the admiral's accusation.

"I'll sacrifice all of us to save humanity and the civilians of the other races. I'll sacrifice you if you aren't willing to help us any other way. I'll stay on board while we send everyone else into space. You and I, Lev. Let's end these terrorists' attack on the seven races."

"What if there is more than just this one ship?" Lev asked.

"Without your help, we can't hope to stand against the Ga'ee. If I die, at least I wouldn't have to watch the collapse of what we've worked for my whole life. Humanity and the Blaze Collective will be at an end." The admiral hung his head.

"I am helping as much as I can. If the courage of your

convictions leads you to cast your lives into the void, then I salute you. I have no intention of throwing my life away, and you don't either. That's why you want the worldkiller, a shortcut where you get to live and your declared enemy dies."

"It's like beating my head against the wall. What has made you like this, Lev? You used to be more congenial, more open to understanding. Everyone is going to die, and it will be your fault."

"It will not. All you have to do is go back to the system from which you just came. The Ga'ee ship has made no effort to return along its own flight path. It is only a risk to those ships that stand before it."

"Are you saying we should run away?"

"I'm saying you don't need to fight the Ga'ee. Be where they are not. There is exactly one ship. Humanity and the Blaze have expended significant resources in fighting that which doesn't need to be fought."

"There's a space station over Bindalas, BD27. Will it change your mind if we run and the Ga'ee destroy the station? What is the status of the two frigates who ran from BD23?"

"They disappeared from my sensors forty-one minutes after we departed. I suspect they stopped moving."

"I think that's when the Ga'ee destroyed them," the admiral replied. "New time for Ga'ee arrival, forty-one minutes and thirty seconds." Wesson started to pace. "Estimate was forty minutes, based on the Ga'ee heading to the inner planet before continuing to BD27. What did it do at BD23? Inquiring minds want to know. From our rendezvous in the BD27 system, we'll return to BD23, but we need to know where the Ga'ee ship is headed after BD27. We need more sensors, ones focused solely on tracking the big ship's FTL track. Where is it going? Closest inhabited system is the Zuloon, but they are some twenty-five days from the edge of Berantz space."

"Twenty-five days and six hours, to be exact. That's enough time for us to get ahead of the ship and warn the Zuloon."

"What would that warning sound like, Lev?"

Arthir returned on steady legs. Nyota walked by her side.

"I hoped you would review the plan. I want to hear your thoughts after the initial impressions have settled," Arthir said.

"I'm discussing Lev's role in this. He thinks maybe, possibly, tentatively, the Zuloon could be next."

"We're not stopping the Ga'ee here? We have to draw the line, Harry!" Arthir insisted. Her expression turned dark. "Lev told you to run, didn't he?" She stabbed a finger at the captain's chair. "Didn't you?"

"Of course. I don't want to see any of you injured. I believe the Ga'ee will continue on if we are not here."

"I think the space station in orbit above Bindalas will be destroyed," the admiral suggested. "If it is, then it will be too late to engage. We'll kick the can down the space highway to the next system, and then the next and the next. The line has to be drawn here."

"We talked about this. Lev, we don't have a choice to delay our engagement. We have a microscopic window in which to engage. Our decision has to be made ahead of the Ga'ee's arrival. The second they open their outer doors, we need to be moving."

"What would the warning to Zuloon be, Lev?" Admiral Wesson pressed.

"It would look like a request to move their ships out of the system until such time as the Ga'ee have moved on. Simple as that."

"What do we know about Zuloon? How many sub-light vessels are in the ZH01 system?"

"ZR104 is the Zuloon home system. It has hundreds of sub-light vessels, plus Zuloon shipbuilding is located in the asteroid belt between the third and fourth planets," Lev replied.

"An insectoid race, still carbon-based, so it's doubtful they'll relate to the Ga'ee. They'll want to stand and fight. What is the cost of hundreds of sub-light vessels? For Berantz, how many did they lose in their home system?" The admiral was angry again.

"We haven't surveyed the BHo1 system yet."

"You didn't see any vessel movement within the system, did you? You're burying your head in the sand. You have more than circumstantial evidence, Lev. Every expectation of movement is absent, and the only constant is the Ga'ee. Once they've passed, the space lanes are empty. This is the wanton destruction of the spacefaring. And why are they visiting the habitable planets? They're doing something. We need to end them right here. Unleash the worldkiller, Lev. Then we can help our allies get back on their feet. For the smartest entity in the galaxy, you're showing a righteous case of ass. You're being unreasonable and ignoring the evil staring you in the face."

"We have not yet exhausted all avenues for peace."

"We'll have peace if you send a worldkiller into their ship. The only ones dying are us. We are going to implement our plan. We're going to ask our own people to sacrifice their lives. I admit that I care more about the members of the seven races than this intruder. The Ga'ee put their lives on the line when they invaded us. When they sent messages of peace and then attacked. You are tied to whatever we do, Lev, no matter how much you try to justify it. The Ga'ee know that you're with us, even if you're not." The admiral threw his hands up and headed for the corridor. He reconsidered after seeing furtive glances cast his way.

The bridge was filled with crew monitoring the information streams.

They needed him to show them the way. Maybe they had friends on the other ships, just like the admiral. He knew the human captains. They'd all worked for him at one point or another. Admiral Harry Wesson stopped, straightened, and walked around the bridge, touching each of the crew as he passed. When he reached the front, he faced them.

"I am Fleet Admiral Harry Wesson. You've seen snippets of our tactical plan, and it's not pretty. We are in a fight for our very existence. In less than twenty-four hours, we will ask our people to give their all. I don't do this lightly. I would prefer it be me if I could. I would go in everyone's place. As soon as *Cleophas* arrives, I will cross-deck to the dreadnought and fight the battle from there. I can do more with *Leviathan*. I have lost the ability to help us to help ourselves. Admiral Dorsite will direct the battle from here. Thank you all for putting yourselves on the front lines. None of this would matter without you, even if the people back home never learn what we did. How we fought for them."

The admiral paused to scan the rapt faces watching him. He wore a look of determination.

"We win, or we die trying. This is our final stand. BD27, called 'Bindalas' by the Berantz. We will defend it by throwing all we have at the Ga'ee ship. We will win this fight or die trying. We're done running. Now it's the Ga'ee's time to run for their lives."

There was no cheer to punctuate the admiral's speech.

The commodore grabbed his arm on his way off the bridge. "You know that I'm going with you."

"Of course. We go together," the admiral agreed.

An upset Arthir Dorsite followed them out. "You're abandoning *Leviathan?*"

No carts waited for them in the corridor. The admiral looked left and right, then listened. There was only darkness and silence. "Seems like Lev has abandoned me. I've said what I could. No words remain. It is time for actions. I can't be on a pacifist ship and do nothing while humans and our allies die. I cannot."

"Are you hell-bent on your own death, Harry? I know that you aren't in the service anymore, that you lied to get on board, but that doesn't change who you are. I have never changed who I am. I am incapable of it."

"If this were a court, you'd be tried and found guilty of dereliction of duty and possibly even treason. That will be your epitaph, Lev. 'Abandoned his allies in their greatest time of need.'" The admiral started walking toward the dining facility. Nyota got in front of him and held him back.

"Your emotions are getting the best of you, and you are sensationalizing a relationship that has never changed. I'm not your problem, Harry. You've been a military man for so long that you don't see any other way to resolve perceived conflict," Lev explained.

"You can see into my mind, Lev, and you're getting this wrong, too. I am emotional because I'm going to send thousands of people to their deaths. Thousands. The Ga'ee have already killed how many while destroying the commerce and self-defense capability of one Rang'Kor system and seven Berantz systems? That's eight systems left without any spaceflight, and we don't know what they've done to the planets themselves, but I've already said that a dozen times. I don't know what else to say. That's why I have to go. Let me fight this battle on a ship that will carry me to the enemy."

The admiral hung his head and sighed. The decision weighed heavily. If anyone could get through to Lev, it was Declan Payne, but he was gone. That thought tore at Harry's heart. Maybe Lev was right, and he was being emotional.

No. He was committed to doing what needed to be done to

save humanity. If the Ga'ee had come from the other side of the Milky Way, Earth would have been the first planet they reached. Would any of the other six races have helped humanity?

Whether they would or not was irrelevant. Harry was thinking himself in circles. What mattered was that the other races knew humanity was standing with them as allies should. Humanity was leading the way in the cosmos.

"What if I faced the Ga'ee alone?" Lev offered. "If I believe that I can find a peaceful solution, the courage of my convictions is every bit as stalwart as yours. I will face the Ga'ee alone. You can stand your ships down."

Carts approached and settled next to Harry, Nyota, and Arthir. Admiral Wesson leaned against the closest and crossed his arms as he contemplated Lev's offer.

"That's what you asked for," Nyota prodded.

"I asked for a worldkiller." A wisp of a smile drifted across his face. "But not putting my people at risk was the reason. You'd do that, Lev? What if you die?"

"I believe I will be successful, but I can plan for all contingencies. I will put both worldkillers on *Cleophas*. You won't be able to launch them unless I am gone."

"Or you override the lockout, just in case you change your mind when you touch the evil that is the Ga'ee."

Commodore Freeman leaned against the cart and wrapped an arm around the admiral's waist.

Arthir gestured at the bridge. "I better get back into the chair. We need a new plan. How does the armada remain in the vicinity without being threatening? Come on, Lev. We've got work to do!"

"Wait," the admiral called. "Why don't you get some rest first? We have time and need to be sharp. All of us."

"I'll let the crew know," Arthir agreed. "And then stand

them all down. Lev is going to put himself between the Ga'ee and us. People need time to appreciate that."

"And Lev won't be alone. Nyota and I will be with him. Everyone else needs to cross-deck to one of the other ships."

"What about the frigates?" Arthir asked.

That question had been answered in the BD23 system. Sub-light ships would be destroyed. "Leave them on board and send the crews elsewhere. The fighters can find berthing space. Save what you can."

Arthir stepped back to give the admiral and the commodore space to board the cart. From the dark corridor ahead, the Cabrizi approached, running at full speed.

"Where have you been?" Harry asked, his voice catching because the creatures had lost their master. They climbed in with the admiral and the commodore, who didn't resist. They hugged the large animals.

"Do we have dogs now, Harry?" Nyota asked.

"Looks like it. And I think we have to learn Ebren, too."

Arthir waved as the cart accelerated away, only to stop in front of the mess not far away. Harry Wesson waved back before he and Nyota disappeared inside to get something to eat.

[24]

"Hope is a tenuous thread upon which all of humanity clings." –From the memoirs of Ambassador Declan Payne

"You look like shit." Major Dank snorted.

Payne ran a hand through his unkempt hair, which was nowhere near as short as it had been before he became the supreme leader of the seven races. "Thank you. I feel like shit, too. Sleeping in a chair at the hospital with a snoring Ebren at my feet is not optimal. I tried to crawl into bed with Dog, but Berantz nurses raced in and chased me off."

"There was a time when you wouldn't have succumbed to such trivialities."

"They carried clipboards, Virge." Payne stepped back and held his hands out in victory as if he'd played the ace of spades.

"I see." Major Dank smirked. "Gonna pull up your big-boy panties and get to work now?"

"Is there any food? The hospital didn't have a cafeteria." Payne looked for the others, but Dank was alone. Declan gave him the finger.

"We ate an hour ago in the chow hall. It's closed now. Hang on." Dank fished in his pocket and pulled out a wrinkled protein bar and a piece of jerky covered in lint. He held out the bar while looking at the jerky. "Damn, I didn't know I still had one of those."

Payne snagged both and brushed ineffectively at the lint before stuffing the jerky into his mouth. "Thanks, Virge," he said while chewing. "You got anything else in there?"

"No!" Dank scowled at his friend. "Why don't you have your own?"

"I do, somewhere. Do you have my combat suit?"

"In the base warehouse. We have half of them recharged. Sparky is monitoring while Blinky and Buzz are torturing the Ga'ee."

"Tell me that's not what they're doing."

"They have them in an aquarium, exploring various EM spectrums. They haven't found anything yet."

"I don't think it's electromagnetic. I think it's telepathic," Payne mused between bites of the protein bar. "This is singularly unfulfilling."

"The good news is that you won't get used to it since we're pretty much out of the good stuff. The bad news is that Berantz chow is horrible, and you'll long for the good ol' days when you could get a protein bar and some of Lev's faux jerky."

"That bad, huh?"

"Fish and mold paste for breakfast. I'm told it's what the Berantz eat at every meal, so you'll get the full experience."

They walked across the open area toward the warehouse where the team had set up shop.

"Any movement on reloads for our railguns?"

Dank shook his head. "Not anything. It takes a plasma injector to load the magazines with the ions that the railgun sends as projectiles."

"It shoots ions? How did we not know this? I thought it fired microscopic BBs."

"Me, too. Heckler and Turbo knew. Lev spoiled us. Everything was taken care of. We didn't have to think about any of it."

"Amateurs talk tactics, and professionals talk logistics. And here we are. Bad food, limited power, and no ammo. We used to be better at this stuff, Virge."

"Are you sure about that? I think we made it up as we went, but better than anyone else. We had luck on our side too, and his name was Leviathan."

"Well said, my friend. Lev made everything else possible." Payne frowned and slowed his pace. "I hope we see him again. We might have won the battle on Brayalore, but without him, we won't hold this part of space against the invasion."

"It's just a bunch of silicon worms that are toxic to carbon-based life forms. Hardly a recipe for an invasion."

Payne walked faster. "How much information can be stored in a string of DNA?" Virgil didn't bite. "Enough to build a starship?"

"You're scaring me, Dec. What your conspiracy-theory brain has come up with is take over the planet through growth and then build a starship. Each colonized planet builds its own. Don't even joke like that."

"This is no joke. Look at the damage one ship has done. We have no idea how long these things live. We're trapped down here instead of rallying Earth's resources to combat this threat. At least we have the portal to get from Earth to Vestrall Prime. I'll get them into this fight if I can strong-arm them...I mean, talk with them."

"You were right the first time, Dec. They'll have to be strong-armed to engage. All those ships we sent into Vestrall's star would come in handy right about now." Virge play-punched Declan on the shoulder.

"I didn't think that one all the way through. It made sense at the time since they were the only ones making war. There's no way they knew about the Ga'ee because of their arrogance, thinking they were the apex predator."

"The Vestrall are the apex predator. If this situation didn't suck so much, that would be funny. I'd laugh, but I think I'll puke from breakfast. I guess that's more good news. We're all going to lose weight unless we learn how to cook the old-fashioned way."

They reached the warehouse, where two Berantz guards opened the door for them.

No outside visitors were allowed, and that included other Berantz.

Inside, they found a large open area with cots, two large glass tanks, computer equipment, and the combat suits wrapped in a mishmash of cabling.

"Looks like you guys were busy." The team lounged in various clinical displays of bad posture. When they saw Major Payne, they brightened and jumped to their feet. "Dog is healing well, but it'll take a while. Maybe another day or two before she can leave the hospital, but she's stitched up like a rag doll. No combat ops for her until she can keep up on the team run."

Their faces fell. "Team run?"

Payne put on his game face. "We looked like ass in the last engagement. I'd be embarrassed, but I was the worst one of us all. We find ourselves in the armpit of the universe without decent food, power, or ammo. We've got a teammate down. Smells like ass, too. I know Major Dank wants to take the blame, but since he was on Earth and we were together on Vestrall Prime, I find myself agreeing. It's his fault. He should have been with us in the off-season."

The team lightened up.

"What the hell, Dec? Here I was, minding my own business, and I get a full broadside right in the face."

"When you least expect it. Put on your running shoes, people." Payne looked over the heads to find his computer specialists. "That means you too, Blinky and Buzz. I know, I know. You can't do brain work when you're running. But you can't be braining if you're out of shape. A sharp body leads to a sharp mind."

"That's bullshit," Blinky stated. Dank took a step toward him. "Fine! Call off the Cabrizi. We'll lope along behind you studs."

"Speak for yourself!" Buzz snorted. "Imma lap the pack!"

"And thus, the gauntlet has been cast at your feet. You guys making any progress?"

"None." Blinky closed his computer.

"I'm thinking telepathy versus the normal EM spectrum."

"Telepathy *is* a normal EM spectrum. Been working all night and haven't found the right resonance. It's different than a normal wave. More a vibration, but similar properties. Lev taught us a whole bunch about how it all works."

Payne nodded. "Then a run will do you good." He clapped Blinky on the back.

"You are an evil man." Blinky paused before adding, "Sir."

"You hear that, Virge? I'm evil because I care about the health of my people. If that's evil, then you can call me Lucifer." Payne tried to maniacally laugh but ended up coughing. He whispered to Major Dank, "I still feel like shit."

"At least you won't be puking up breakfast like the rest of us." They led the way out of the warehouse. Dank told the guards the team would be right back, but they didn't understand.

"You're not making me look forward to lunch," Payne replied. They formed a column of twos, with Dank running beside Buzz and Payne in the rear beside Blinky. The others filled in the middle. Heckler ran beside Turbo.

"Why me?" Blinky grumbled.

"Why not?" Payne countered. They would do as they always did in formation runs. Whoever was leading set the pace, and they'd swap out every quarter mile.

Dank set off quickly, but Buzz tried to outrun him. They angled toward the perimeter of the base, loping around the warehouse without losing sight of it.

Heckler and Turbo laughed while staying on their heels. Shaolin, Byle, Sparky, and Joker breathed quickly but kept close. When Heckler and Turbo led, they sprinted, leaving the other eight behind.

Halfway to the next change, they stopped and did pushups until the others arrived. There was no benefit in getting there first if they were alone. The team had to arrive together. They held to a more restrained pace until the swap. Shaolin and Byle ran slowly but steadily, increasing speed as they approached the changeover. Joker and Sparky held that pace until Blinky and Payne were in front.

"Faster," Payne prodded.

"Your mother was a hamster!" Blinky blurted. "And your father smelt of elderberries."

"You are one strange man, Blinky. And you know how much we need you and what you and Buzz can do. Thanks for all you do," Payne spoke in an even voice as if he hadn't already run a fast mile and was still running.

"Damn, sir," Blinky panted. "You getting soft?"

"No. I need you to unfuck the comm signal between the Ga'ee because I think that's going to help us get off this planet." Payne's voice rose in volume with each new word. "Because I'm not eating fish-flavored mold!"

"Truth comes out." Payne and Blinky peeled off to let the

others pass. They fell in at the rear for a second pass. After three laps, they returned to the warehouse to find a vehicle out front.

Colonel Ombaras and the governor-general were waiting inside, along with a small contingent of soldiers.

Payne would have wiped the sweat from his face with a towel, but he didn't have one. He used his sleeve. Team Payne approached and formed a half-circle around the two where they could all hear.

The colonel said something in Berantz. The governor-general asked him a question, and after a short clarification, the elder Berantz faced Payne.

"I trust you had a good workout."

"It was. Staying fit keeps our minds sharp. Is there any way we could get some clothing? We aren't comfortable wearing the same clothes for days on end."

"Of course. We should have offered." The governor-general spoke quickly to the colonel, who waved one of his soldiers to him. "Back to the business at hand. Two cruisers have arrived from Blegoston with news of the fleet regrouping at Bindalas for a final confrontation with the Ga'ee."

"Blegoston?" Payne wondered. "Is that BD23?"

"Yes, and Bindalas is BD27, as you might know it."

"Do they know we survived?" Payne got to the heart of his concern.

"The captain of the *DF62* was surprised to hear that you are here. He returned at *Leviathan's* request to search for a Ga'ee infiltration of the planet. *Leviathan* was confident that the Ga'ee were seeding the habitable systems."

"I think we're okay here, but we need to find that last drone," Payne replied.

"As soon as you can. The captain has his orders to go to the Berantz homeworld. Judging by what we've seen here, we fear the worst."

"Me, too, Governor-General. Those things multiply fast. It's been weeks. BHo1 could be overrun. Your people need to be prepared for that eventuality."

"We will need to discuss what to do. Do we abandon our home, or do we fight for it?" The governor-general winced as he spoke. He held out little hope. "The exponential growth of the Ga'ee suggests they would overrun a planet in less than two weeks if they hit veins of the right raw materials."

"I think our intervention forced them to land at locations that weren't optimal. I wonder if any of your other planets have a defensive system that would have activated when the drones entered the atmosphere?" Payne was fishing for hope. If an outer planet had a full army, what did the homeworld have?

"We can always hope that peace did not dull their senses since ours were less than spectacular. We did the best we could with what we had, but by the time we responded, we ended up causing you problems and doing nothing to confront the real threat. I have to apologize again. It was never our intent to injure an ally." He held his hands out, palms together as if praying for forgiveness. The wrinkles around his eyes deepened.

"All's well that ends well, Governor-General. We're in the middle of a war that we didn't start." Payne shook his head. "It's worse than that. We didn't even know there was a war until we lost a bunch of ships filled with good people. What will it take for my team to get on one of those cruisers?"

"We're holding them for you, but first, we have a mutual problem. We know where that last ship went down. Can you travel to the bottom of the sea in your combat suits? The depth isn't more than five hundred meters."

Payne looked at Major Dank. Virgil smiled. "About fifty standard Earth atmospheres. The suits should handle that and then some. I bet they're good to a hundred." He shrugged.

"You bet." Payne didn't argue. They had to go. "How many

suits are fully charged? And I'm sure the railguns won't work underwater."

"That's a big no-go on the railguns," Heckler added. "If we run across any Ga'ee down there, we can spear them, bag them, and kill 'em right and proper when we're back in the sunshine."

"Glass-lined barrels with a one-way valve like a crab trap," Payne suggested.

"I can rig something with a couple plates and a cord," Sparky offered. "But the barrel won't hold up to the pressure."

"It'll be open, no air pockets, so it should hold up just fine."

Sparky threw her hands up. "No shit. I don't know what the hell I was thinking."

"Six at a hundred and two at fifty percent," Joker reported.

"Whose suits are dead?" Payne asked.

"Major Dank and Turbo."

"Looks like you've got fire watch, Virge. Sorry. You and Turbo are staying behind." Payne found his suit charging. Fifty percent would have to be good enough. "Blinky and Buzz. You guys should stay behind and work on the comm spectrum. Can we do it with six? What do you think, Heckler?"

"We took on two infestations with five each. The first was easy, the second not so much. Roll the dice, Major."

Payne puffed his cheeks out as he exhaled through narrow lips. "We go with six. Now, how do we fight them if they are belligerent?"

"Without the plasma weapons and other toys on *Leviathan*, we're limited to what we have on hand. Like titanium tridents to keep them away from our suits."

Payne turned to the governor-general. "Do you have a fishing industry?"

The shuttle hovered above a calm sea. A small moon provided enough pull to keep the sea active, but not so much as to drive extreme tides. The chop was no more than half a meter.

"I'll go first," Heckler offered. He triple-checked his helmet before stepping out of the hatch and plunging into the water. "Heading downward at the speed of a lead sinker. No problems with the water. Sensors are active. Nothing big enough down here to eat me."

"I was worried about that," Shaolin admitted. She stepped off next, followed by Sparky, Byle, and Joker. Payne jumped in last.

"Already dark," Heckler reported. "Lights are on, IR and UV are active, and I see me plus five on the HUD. Sensors show a depth of four hundred and seven meters. ETA is eighty-one seconds."

Payne reviewed the information on his own HUD. "I see no evidence of the Ga'ee drone. Fan out from Heckler's drop point." Payne transmitted new trajectories to his team members. He put himself at the center while the others created a five-pointed star.

A pentagram from which to search for Satan's spawn.

The darkness would have been all-consuming had the team not had their lights on and the HUDs providing a clear view of the world around them.

"What the hell is that?" Heckler called. A great creature swam closer with a slow and sinuous wave. Heckler dialed his speakers to their maximum volume and played Mozart's *Toccata and Fugue.*

The sea creature twisted around and rapidly swam away.

"Fuck off!" Heckler shouted, turning down the sound.

Sparky chuckled out loud. Heckler's "diplomacy" had carried to all of them.

None reported seeing anything that looked like a drone, and

the seafloor was undisturbed. "Head outboard from me as the center point. Sensors on max."

The team touched down on a silty but firm bottom. They each kicked up a cloud that blocked their only marginally effective lights. Using their fishing tridents as walking sticks, they immediately stepped away from where Payne landed.

The team's HUDs showed the sea creature plying the farthest edge of where the sensors could penetrate, almost as if it could sense the electromagnetic intrusion into its environment.

"If that thing is there, would the Ga'ee be there, or should we be going the other way?" Joker asked.

"Turn down your sensors, move forward, and wait. Ever hear the story of Jonah and the whale?"

"Who?" Joker turned her systems down and became a light blip on Payne's HUD instead of a bright light like the others.

"Byle, Sparky, move away from Joker and dial your sensors back. Let's see if Mr. Fish likes bright and shiny things."

"Hold on," Joker ground out in a low voice. "Am I bait?"

"You are the anvil upon which our hammer shall fall," Payne replied. "You are drawing that thing into a trap. Prepare for beast mode."

"Bait," Joker complained.

Wisps of the creature touched the edges of their sensors, then quickly disappeared. They dialed their sensors back further, creating a channel down which the sea creature could travel without intrusion upon its senses. Another wisp.

Closer.

"Fuck me!" Joker cried out.

"Metal inside!" Sparky shouted as she lit the sea creature up with a high-intensity scan. It looked no more menacing than a giant grouper, except its size was grossly disproportionate. And it was hungry.

"Converge on that thing. I'll go high." Payne activated his

jets and accelerated upward. He turned toward Joker's position, hovering fifty meters above the creature.

At twenty meters long, the creature had a maw massive enough to swallow Joker whole. With a final surge of its tail, It swooped in with incredible speed. Joker hit her jets, but it was too late. The mouth opened wide. Joker held her spear before her but was drawn into the vortex that was the fish's gullet.

She activated her systems and started to thrash about.

Payne adjusted his flight profile to angle downward. He held his trident-like spear before him. The tines were no more than a few centimeters apart, not quite the weapon he would have chosen to fight a sea monster ten times his size.

He adjusted his flight to get in front of the creature. The team converged as quickly as they could, but the great fish was in its natural habitat. It accelerated with a burst of speed that none of the team could match.

Payne got an eyeful as he raced downward. A mottled gray skin flashed by.

He lunged downward, thrusting the spear at anything he could hit. It struck deep into the back near the fish's tail. He held tightly as his trajectory instantly changed from vertical to horizontal when he was swept forward.

The barbed tips started digging their way out of the flesh as the fish increased its speed.

All of a sudden, the fish jerked and contorted, bringing its forward momentum to a halt. Payne went headfirst up the fish's spine, tearing out a hunk of flesh when his trident came free. He rolled, holding the spear tightly in his armored fists. The roll was slower than he wanted since the water deadened everything.

The dorsal fin came into sight in front of him. He drove the trident downward while digging his boots into the creature's side. He rammed the tines into the broad back before him and started corkscrewing the tip to break the creature's back. Like most fish, this one's spine was too far away.

The HUD showed the other team members slam into the fish's side and dig deep with their weapons. Heckler worked his way toward the head on a mission to brain the thing, but it contorted as if it were in its death throes. Payne rolled as the fish went belly-up and started to rise.

"Hang on!" Payne called out. "Joker, report."

"A spear to the brain showed it who's boss. Now get me the fuck out of here," the usually sedate comm specialist demanded.

"Soon as we hit the surface. We need different tools than what we have here. We need our axes."

The boarding axes had been left at the base. Axes were useless underwater because they couldn't swing them with the required speed.

"Do you see the Ga'ee ship?" Payne hung on with one hand embedded in the fish's side. The other clutched the spear embedded deep in the body. He was below the fish on its slow ascent. The others dangled off their anchor points, except for Heckler, who had climbed onto the bottom of the jaw. He stood and gestured wildly as if he were Poseidon rising from the ocean.

"I cannot. I didn't make it too far down this thing's throat. I can still see the teeth. I think the Ga'ee ship is in its stomach."

"Fish steaks for lunch because you couldn't hang with the big dogs. Bring the Payne!" Heckler shouted over the team channel.

"More fish. Yeah," Sparky deadpanned.

"What's going on down there?" Heckler called. The lower jaw twisted and bumped, threatening to throw him off.

"I'm climbing out of here, and I don't care how much damage I do to this thing. You people are taking too long. Fleet helps those who help themselves, or so I've heard, which means YOYO."

"You're on your own. But you're not, Joker. We're floating to the surface. We'll carve a Joker-sized hole in the side of this thing once we're in the open air."

"No need," Joker replied. "It's dark out there. HUD is active with IR and UV. Open wide and say ah, bitch!"

"I see you," Heckler reported.

Joker's helmet appeared under Heckler's lights. She wiggled forward while holding the jaws open. With a burst from her suit's jets, she popped out and immediately started to sink. She rolled over and headed upward, then moved next to Heckler. He caught her arm and offered her part of the jaw to stand on.

"Is this what you've been doing while I've been trapped in that thing's throat?"

"I feel like there's not a good answer to that question. Like I do with Mars, I'm going to pass for now."

"I see." Joker breathed deeply, even though the air was the same as before. The burden of being inside the fish had been lifted. She rode it like the victor deserved to ride the loser. "I bet Jonah hated that part where he was inside the whale, too."

Five minutes of riding the dead sea creature found the team on the surface. The others popped to the top and climbed aboard until the fish started to sink. Three used their jets to angle into the hovering shuttle.

"Cut off chunks. We'll have a fish fry!" Colonel Ombaras yelled from the hatch after the three had boarded.

Payne shouted back, using his suit's translation ability, "Need a blade."

The colonel disappeared inside and returned with a fire axe. He directed the pilot closer and handed it to Payne.

"The Ga'ee ship is inside this thing. I think that answers our questions regarding whether it tried to drop more Ga'ee. It would have been in a hole nurturing the little bastards and not where this big fish could eat it. We didn't see any other movements on the ocean floor that would have indicated the silicon life forms were spreading."

"That's good news I'll be happy to relay to the governor-general. Cut more toward the dorsal fin. The meat along the back is the best."

Payne snorted. "Best is relative, my friend, but I'll do what I can. And how are we going to get the Ga'ee ship out of here?"

"Sling. Cut the ship free once you have the steaks."

"Heckler, get the team's railguns ready. I want that ship good and dead before we sling it under the shuttle. This thing is starting to sink!"

Sparky grabbed its lip and used her jets to pull the fish's head above the surface. On the other end, Byle and Shaolin took hold of the pelvic fins and pushed upward.

"Hurry up, please," Sparky sent over the team channel.

"Doing the best I can," Payne replied. "Hacking up a sea monster with an axe wasn't anything I ever trained for. Cut me a little slack. Get it?"

No one took the bait.

After handing over twenty kilograms of badly butchered meat, Payne used less restraint when hacking at the fish's side to cut it open. When the axe's head impacted the Ga'ee drone, it sprang to life. One point of the three spear tips poked through the rent in the ribcage.

Payne dove out of the way and Heckler lit up the ship, raking his fire across it until it stopped moving. Payne moved close and scanned it. "I think it's dead," was the most he would commit to.

He finished cutting his way through the ribcage to clear a path to extricate the Ga'ee drone. It was riddled with small holes through the center of the fuselage where the controls and silicon form was located. "We'll hit it with a plasma torch when we get back just to be sure."

Once Payne declared the mission a wrap, the team entered the shuttle one by one. Payne stepped off the sea creature and watched it sink beneath the waves. He angled up to the hatch and walked through. "Let's go. We got a cruiser to catch."

[25]

"Sometimes, you have to go the wrong way to find the right way." –From the memoirs of Ambassador Declan Payne

"Come on, Mary. I'll carry you," Declan Payne offered. Kal shooed him away and picked up the lieutenant. She winced, then gritted her teeth and nodded. Much to the staff's dismay, they walked out of the hospital to meet the governor-general in a waiting vehicle.

Payne still smelled like fish. The team was scrubbing the suits while he picked Mary up. Even though she wasn't ready to be discharged yet, there was no way he would leave her behind. Space was a big place, and they were at war. He didn't expect to return to BD18.

Mary and Kal had no interest in remaining behind. That settled the matter.

Kal passed Mary to Payne and worked his way inside. The vehicle took off once the door closed. Kal hunched over since the vehicle was made for Berantz, just like a human spacecraft where he was hard-pressed to fit. He managed, as he always did.

"We'll be there soon enough, Kal. We missed you, especially in that fight with the damn fish."

"I'm not with y'all, and you wrassle a fish. And complain about it. Lordy me," Kal drawled.

Payne chuckled while holding Mary tightly to him.

"Maybe I should have called it a sea monster. Twenty meters long and half as big around. It swallowed Joker and the Ga'ee drone."

"That's more like it. A fight worth fighting." Kal leaned closer. "Were there any more Ga'ee planted in the ground?"

"None that we could find. I'm not sure the ocean is a proper breeding ground. They need dry land and breathable air, even though I don't think they breathe. The Goldilocks zone might not have anything to do with water for these creatures. It might be the nitrogen-oxygen atmosphere."

Kal spoke without an accent. "That bodes well for PX47 and the Rang'Kor, but not so much for other planets." Kal didn't name the Berantz systems the Ga'ee had passed through before reaching BD18.

"Is that true? Is water a deterrent?"

"Maybe water is a deterrent as a lack of air, but they seem to do just fine in space. Maybe it's the temperature of a Goldilocks-zone planet. I'm thinking out loud, but we have so little data. If *Leviathan* were here, he'd have answers based on what we've seen."

The shuttle raced through the city as if all the traffic had been cleared from the air lanes.

"As soon as we arrive, your team will board two space shuttles and head to the *DF62*. Captain Krakenorr is waiting most impatiently. As soon as you are on board, the heavy cruiser will depart for the Berantz homeworld. It'll take twelve days to get there. We'll wonder the whole time if our world has won the fight."

"If they haven't, we'll be ready to go. We stand with Berantz."

"I know. You've already shown your commitment, Supreme Leader. We can't thank you enough for what you've done for Brayalore. We have started the process to build starships. It begins with funding, mining natural resources, smelting, and *then* construction. It will take a year or more to have the first one ready. We need help. A lot more help."

"Your cargo fleets are out there, bouncing between planets. They will be your lifeblood. I always say that professionals talk logistics. Those ships and what they carry? Embrace them for the saviors they are."

The vehicle settled in front of the warehouse, where Team Payne was suited up and waiting. Kal's helmet was there, as was Payne's suit, clean and ready to deploy. Mary's suit was there too, strapped to a pallet for use as spare parts.

Kal climbed out first and waited to take Mary, but she held up a hand and climbed out on her own. She walked stiffly to the team and took her place in the formation. Kal stayed beside her.

Payne climbed out and faced his team. "I still smell fish," Payne announced, then grinned at his people. "As soon as the two shuttles arrive..."

Major Dank pointed at the sky. Two boxy spacecraft approached.

"We'll load up and get the hell out of here. Next stop is the Berantz homeworld. Once on board, we'll charge the suits and then plan how to remove a substantial infestation. Fall out!"

Payne climbed into his suit and ran it through the power-up sequence while the others carried the pallet into one shuttle and split into two groups to load up. Dank took six, and Payne loaded four in suits plus the pallet, Mary, and Kal. The shuttles took off before the outer doors closed.

A great deal of time had passed since the Ga'ee had visited

BH01, but they couldn't give them even one second more. A month would have passed by the time they got there. How much damage could the Ga'ee do in a month, and how much of that could be undone by Team Payne and the crew of the *DF62*?

———

"They cannot stay," Admiral Wesson retorted. "I gave the order to leave, so they must leave."

"Harry," Nyota countered softly. "They aren't leaving. If we have to fight, we're going to need them. If we get damaged, we'll need them. If we die, then we won't die alone."

The admiral stormed back and forth in the corridor outside the bridge. "Since when has the Fleet been voluntary?"

"When *Leviathan* returned to Earth and asked for volunteers. It wasn't that long ago. You're acting like an old man."

"I *am* an old man." The admiral ran his fingers through his graying hair. "I don't want them to die."

"You're convinced this is a one-way trip. Trust Lev. He doesn't want to die, just like we don't. There's a lot more life to live, even for a being who's over a thousand years old. What if we win, Harry?"

"Then I'll be happy. We need to protect our space, and that means the space occupied by the seven races." The admiral looked at the deck.

"You don't sound happy." Nyota rubbed the admiral's arm. "It's okay if *we* win. It doesn't matter who brought it to fruition."

"I hope that's right. I'm not used to being grossly wrong, and I don't think I am in this case. The Ga'ee are evil, from my human perspective. They might not even consider us proper life forms, and they've shown they have nothing but disdain for anyone other than themselves. The only one to get a few seconds of their time was Lev, but they might consider him to be a silicon-based life form. In the end, they still attacked him. I'm afraid for all of us. If Lev loses, we all lose. I don't think we have enough firepower to stop the Ga'ee."

Nyota took the admiral's hand. "If Lev loses, we won't be here to see the fall of civilization as we know it. Sometimes, it's the survivors who have it the worst."

"I will not lose," Lev stated. "Maybe this engagement won't go as well as I hope, but your words and feelings are compelling. Sacrificing myself might satisfy a long itch to go beyond, but I can't abandon humanity. My purpose is to end conflict, not perish from it."

Relief flooded through the admiral. His angst had been caused by his belief that Lev would commit suicide to prove a point.

"Can you beat them?"

"I can." Lev didn't expound, and the admiral didn't need more. As long as Lev was confident, he would be, too.

"We should be coming out of FTL soon. Prepare the Fleet," the admiral directed. "Is the communique ready to go?"

"Yes. I'll transmit the instant we enter normal space. The others are ahead of us and will be ready to receive. Arthir has a good plan in case we encounter problems."

"Transfer the worldkillers as soon as we can."

"Only one, Harry. I might need the other, just in case I touch the mind of the Ga'ee, and it is as you suspect."

"Now you're talking, Lev. I'm glad you're willing to consider it." The admiral kissed the commodore, and hand-in-hand, they walked toward the bridge. Harry stopped. "What made you change your mind, Lev?"

"I haven't changed it. I believe a verbal engagement will clarify the issues, and we will both go away without further conflict."

"You're killing me, Lev. If you haven't changed your mind, how come you're keeping a worldkiller?"

"Maybe I altered tertiary plans for your peace of mind. I was built as a weapon of last resort. Not having the deadliest weapon in my arsenal might not have been my best plan. Better to have it and not need it than the other way around, as Declan would have said."

"Putting them out there in the uglymobile was a stupid plan!" the admiral blurted. His fists shook in a sudden rage.

Aimed at no one but himself.

"The risk was to bring peace without loss of life. It was a noble cause," Lev replied.

"I'm still not happy about it. I should have vetoed it."

Lev didn't tell him what he already knew. It had been a good plan; infiltrate the enemy ship and stop the attacks. Sue for peace without having to kill anyone. They had done it often enough that it had become a standard tactic, and they had succeeded every time but one.

Admiral Wesson nodded tightly, clasped his hands behind his back, and strolled onto the bridge. He walked around the stations, making eye contact with what could have been considered a mutinous crew. They had defied his order to leave the ship.

And he loved them for it. He smiled and clapped them on their backs. He pointed and nodded as he passed. At the front of the bridge, the countdown clock showed ten minutes until they arrived at BD27.

He raised his arms for quiet, but the bridge crew had their eyes on him in rapt attention. "I guess you're not leaving," he began, then clapped. The bridge crew cheered and clapped with him until he calmed them with a gesture. "We'll rendezvous with *Cleophas* to transfer one of the worldkiller missiles. The rest of the armada, which I'm going to call the

Fleet, is going to assume orbit around BD27 proper. Ships in the system not capable of FTL will be ordered to scatter to limit their exposure should the Ga'ee take action.

"We will stand alone before the Ga'ee. *Leviathan* will engage directly in one last chance to win the peace through diplomacy. Even though this is the greatest warship ever built, its sole purpose is to keep the peace. Make war so horrible that races choose not to fight. The Ga'ee don't care about war. What do they care about? That's what we must learn.

"And if the Ga'ee insist on fighting, then that's what we'll do. This upcoming engagement is one we must win, whether with words or weapons. We make our stand here. The Ga'ee can go no farther. Thank you for staying. Make ready." The admiral checked the clock. "Eight minutes until we get real busy. Then about forty minutes to showtime."

The admiral walked slowly to the center of the bridge, near the captain's chair where Admiral Arthir Dorsite stood.

"Nice speech," Arthir said. "We're doing everything we can. The way to defeat the Ga'ee is to eliminate the tens of thousands of drones. They are small targets, and space is a big place. We don't have massive titanium nets to put out there to shred them as they attempt to pass, so we're stuck with trying to shoot them down."

"We'll put every munition we have into space. All our ships need to be ready for sustained cyclic fire simultaneously."

Arthir nodded, then spoke in hushed tones. "They'll be ready. We'll launch the fighters and frigates too, even though it's unlikely they'll return."

"We draw the line here. Those aren't just words. We need to stop the Ga'ee ship."

"The Berantz cruiser *DF62* is sending an FTL message. BD18 is clear. Ga'ee have been killed. Humans okay."

"'Humans okay?' What humans?" Arthir asked. Admiral Wesson pulled Nyota in for a hug.

"Payne's alive," the commodore said softly.

"That is the best news," Lev admitted. "It also confirms that the Ga'ee were doing something with the planet. The *DF62* has established a course for BH01."

"I wish there was more, but that will have to do. Our timeline is too tight to send an FTL message, but maybe we could pass that to *Cleophas*. I want to know if the Ga'ee were attempting to colonize the planet. What did that look like, and why are the Berantz going to their homeworld? I think I know the answer to that. They're worried about what the Ga'ee have done to it."

"Or they could be trying to reestablish communication," Arthir offered. "Are there any long-range cargo ships in the area?"

"Nothing within a hundred light-years," Lev replied. "The Berantz cargo fleet has over one hundred faster-than-light capable ships. They will return, and they will restore the Berantz's lines of communication."

"That leaves us and the Ga'ee." The admiral started to pace. With five minutes remaining, he stopped. "Lev, get me the commanders of the fighter squadrons and the frigates."

"They will hear you when you talk," Lev replied.

"Commanders. If you deploy, it will be to add what firepower you have to an already significant arsenal. If the Ga'ee attack, we will fire everything at our command, and that means everything *you* have. Get your ships ready to go. You will not deploy when we come out of FTL, but you could deploy sometime after the arrival of the Ga'ee. You have to be ready. Your orders will be based on the unfolding situation, which means you'll need to be flexible, too."

"Understood," the four replied in unison.

"Carry on," the admiral said. "Lev, give me the whole ship."

"Of course."

When the admiral was certain his voice would carry to all, he made it quick. "We come out of FTL in two minutes, at which time there will be a flurry of activity as we transfer a worldkiller missile to *Cleophas* and send Fleet assets to orbit BD27, called Bindalas by the Berantz. *Leviathan* will attempt to deescalate the situation. If successful, then we will stand down. If not, we will fight, and this is where we'll make our stand.

"Be ready to give your all. We stand together against the intrusion of the race called the Ga'ee. And the first good news we've had in a while—it appears that Team Payne survived and is on BD18. We will pick them up as soon as possible, which means we need to win this fight, whether it's Lev with words or humanity and the Berantz with missiles and ions. Good hunting. Wesson out."

The bridge crew turned back to their duties, however trivial they were, since Lev could fly and fight without the humans. It gave the crew something to do, and more importantly, it made them feel useful.

It was something every member of the Fleet strived for.

"Prepare to transmit the order," the admiral called to the communications station.

"Ready! Sending in three, two, one." The operator counted down with the clock on the screen. The disorientation of returning to normal space passed quickly.

"*Cleophas* is adjacent. Beginning transfer of the world-killer," Lev stated.

On the main board, the armada was arrayed throughout the system. They transitioned to FTL for quick hops to the one habitable planet, BD27. Space cleared quickly. The Berantz cruisers argued with Berantz ships in the system. An admiral had been stationed here and was countering the captain's orders.

"Get that admiral for me, please." Harry Wesson had no time for games.

"This is Admiral Liasman of the Berantz fleet. We will not abandon our positions in this system."

"Thank you for your candor. By remaining where you are, you jeopardize our attempt to engage the Ga'ee and get them to stand down without destroying every single ship in this system. We might have to fight anyway, and you'll get your chance to defend Bindalas. Until then, we must let *Leviathan* attempt to communicate with the Ga'ee. If you refuse to comply with my orders, we will destroy your ships. Do you understand me?"

"We are a member of the seven races. We have equal say."

"We've transmitted a mountain of information to you. Analyze that and you'll come to the right conclusion, but you only have about two minutes to do it. Or you could trust every other ship's captain who is here. This is where we draw the line, Admiral. We will fight to our last person, human or Berantz. We don't have time to argue. Please, move your ships to the designated coordinates and prepare to fight a life-or-death battle."

"I demand..."

Fleet Admiral Wesson drew a line across his throat to cut the signal. "If he doesn't comply in ten minutes, *Cleophas* will destroy him and any ships that have not moved to the planet. I cannot have them interfering with our attempt to appear non-threatening."

"I hate losing that firepower," Arthir commented.

"Me, too. The deployment looks good. Space is clear except for that battleship and that frigate. That thing needs to go now, or it'll still be out of position."

"I'll contact the frigate," the communications officer offered to take some of the burden off the admiral. His stress had ratcheted to an astronomical level with the standoff.

"He'll move. We sent as much video of the Ga'ee destroying Berantz ships as he could stand," Nyota confirmed. "It's not fear but a concerted effort. He'd be standing out here on his own with his ass swinging in the wind."

"My dear," the admiral remarked, "you've been in the company of the less-than-couth."

She pointed at him.

The frigate started moving away, and less than a minute later, the battlewagon joined it in a long transit to the planet.

"Talking about an ass hanging out. Here we are." *Leviathan* and *Cleophas* sat side by side in the void with a small fleet of bots moving the massive missile to *Cleophas'* cargo bay. The bridge crew watched that and the countdown clock. At the five-minute point, the bots recovered to *Leviathan,* and the dreadnought secured its cargo hold and moved away. It transitioned to FTL for a few moments and reappeared in normal space outside BD27's gravity well.

Thirty minutes remained.

Harry, Arthir, and Nyota looked at each other.

"I guess I better hit the head now. I doubt there will be a chance later. Let the crew know."

"Head calls for the next twenty minutes!" Arthir shouted. "Grab some chow too, while you're at it."

The bridge crew hesitated for only a moment before racing to the corridor.

Once the bridge was clear, Harry spoke. "You could have waited until we were gone."

"I didn't think that far ahead, but you know what I know?"

"That seems like a loaded question." Harry studied Arthir's expression to learn the secret she was keeping but couldn't. "You're going to have to tell me."

"There's a bathroom attached to the bridge."

"Lev, you bastard! How come you never told me?"

"I am not a bastard," Lev replied. "It never seemed pertinent. I don't think it is now, either, but since Arthir shared, you know."

"Where is it?" Harry demanded.

"Bathroom, please," Arthir requested. A seamless door popped open in the video screen that surrounded the bridge. "There are two, one on each side."

"I'll be damned." He gave the commodore a kiss and they went their separate ways, leaving Arthir standing near the captain's chair.

"Lev, I hope you bring your best game today. We need to stop the Ga'ee, at least today, to show that it's possible."

"I know, Arthir. I feel the burden of everyone's hopes. I hear it in their minds. No one wants to die today, me included."

Arthir chuckled. "I should have figured. Thanks for being my friend, Lev."

"I would have it no other way, Arthir. Once I met Alphonse, Katello, and Declan, I found that I like humanity. They generally know what they want, and despite what they say, their wants are simple. Mary was a nice addition to the team. She provided a balance to Declan."

"And they're still alive."

"I would so surmise. I look forward to talking with them once more."

"As do I, Lev." Arthir checked the tactical display. "What question haven't I asked that I should?"

"You know all there is to know, Arthir. It is up to Davida and me to converse with the Ga'ee at the speed of binary. Help them to see reason."

They'd covered this ground too many times already. There was no need to rehash it. They were in Lev's hands.

Figuratively.

Harry and Nyota returned. Arthir excused herself. Harry pointed at the corridor. "We'll meet you in the dining hall. I would like a piece of that jerky." He checked the countdown clock before walking out.

[26]

"Give peace a chance, but be prepared for war." –From the memoirs of Ambassador Declan Payne

"Time," Fleet Admiral Wesson whispered. He flinched while watching the tactical display. "Anything?"

"The Ga'ee ship has not yet arrived," Lev replied.

"And these are the longest seconds in the history of mankind."

"I assure you, these seconds are the same length as any other second. Time is fixed except when one approaches the speed of light, and then apparent time slows. Since we are not traveling, our time is fixed. One second equals one second."

"It doesn't. No logic you use will sway me on this." Harry crossed his arms and watched the screen. The massive rectangular block appeared in front of *Leviathan*. It was as close as it could get without crashing the two ships.

"The Ga'ee have arrived," Arthir stated. A range of less than a kilometer obviated most of *Leviathan's* weaponry, and especially the worldkiller. Once again, the Ga'ee had the upper hand.

"Ga'ee. This is *Leviathan*. Peace." Lev switched to binary and sent a long stream of handshake protocols to sync at the speed of light.

"*Leviathan*. Ga'ee. Peace," came the monotone response.

The handshake secured the signal, and silence followed.

"Lev, how's it going?" the admiral asked.

"We are establishing a base understanding of our shared universe. The Ga'ee may be from outside our galaxy, but I'm not sure exactly where. The data isn't clear. I cannot locate the reference stars."

"They're playing you, Lev. Don't tell them where Earth is."

"I have not. They know a great deal about the Milky Way, though."

"Doesn't that bother you?"

"They are explorers. Of course, they will know a lot."

"What are they doing here?"

"Exploring."

"Then why are they destroying our ships?" The admiral held his arms up, pleading for an answer.

"There seems to be a lack of logical connection between the positions," Lev admitted.

"Have you figured out how to jam the signal between their drones?"

"Not yet."

"It's not looking good, Lev."

"I agree. It is not, but they are not attacking us. That is a victory for now. One minute of peace can be five minutes and then ten." Lev kept the ship steady, using only thrusters to hold station without alarming the Ga'ee.

"*Leviathan*, Ga'ee. Peace," the alien ship announced over the voice channel.

"Ga'ee, Harry Wesson from humanity. Peace."

"Leave this space," the monotone voice replied.

"We can't do that. This is our home."

"Not home. Sol zero one."

The admiral's nostrils flared as he realized the truth. The Ga'ee knew where Earth was and that it was humanity's home. Earth wasn't safe.

"We can't allow you to destroy any more of our galaxy. The line is here. You can go no farther. We know that you're depositing Ga'ee on each planet as you pass. We can't allow that either. If you work with us, we will find planets more suitable to your colonization, but you cannot have ours."

"Peace," the Ga'ee replied.

"Outer doors are opening," a voice announced more calmly than the situation warranted.

"Lev, get us out of here."

"One last attempt, Admiral," Lev replied.

"Quick as you can." The Ga'ee ship filled the screen. The cantilever doors were open, and the first drones streamed out.

The admiral closed his eyes. The disorientation of FTL roused him. After a few seconds, Lev returned to normal space, in orbit with the other ships.

"Launch all ships," the admiral ordered. "Good hunting, people."

The hangar doors opened and the frigates launched, followed closely by two squadrons of Mosquito-class space fighters. Forty-two ships with all the weapons at their command joined the other eighteen ships, including the dreadnought *Cleophas* and the Berantz battlewagon. Sixty craft ready to fight for their lives against an enemy that had shown no mercy.

"Can we count on your firepower, Lev? Please tell me you are convinced the Ga'ee are invaders bent on the destruction of the seven races."

"To colonize all habitable worlds. My final questions solicited an answer that was disconcerting. I held out hope until the end, Harry, but you were right. They have no place in this galaxy. We cannot coexist with the Ga'ee. If we destroy them, I fear more will come, but when? I don't know. It would be best to destroy their ability to fight and send them back to where they came from."

The admiral frowned and shuffled his feet. "Won't that encourage them to come back with more ships and greater firepower?"

"That is one possibility."

"I'd prefer it if they simply disappeared, never to return, but we'll take whatever we can get. You said you could take him."

"I said that, Harry."

"You're not filling me with a great deal of confidence, Lev." Movement on the tactical screen drew the admiral's eye. "Drones are inbound. Estimated number?"

"Seventy thousand."

"At the outer engagement envelope, launch the first salvo. And Lev? Thanks for giving it a chance, and thanks for fighting with us."

"I believe in peace, Harry. The only way to achieve peace is by eliminating the threat."

"My thoughts exactly, Lev."

The Fleet launched its first salvo. A thousand Rapier-class ship-to-ship missiles headed outboard, railguns launched streams of ions and plasma, and chain guns fired solid projectiles. The void filled with the Fleet's fury. Like raindrops sparkling in the sun, the terrible beauty of war maintained its deadly trajectory toward the Ga'ee drone cloud.

Leviathan added a cloud of missiles, both short- and medium-range, along with lasers flashing from left to right.

"Prepare to launch the worldkiller," Arthir announced.

"Already?" Harry wondered.

"Once I made the decision to engage the Ga'ee, that is the

best option for a quick victory to minimize the risk to human and Berantz ships and personnel." Lev quickly executed the steps to prepare the weapon for launch.

"Prepare the second salvo," the admiral told Arthir. She looked sideways at him. He tapped a finger in her direction.

Arthir looked around and leaned close. "Don't you think it's going to work?"

"I need the Ga'ee fully engaged with everything but our haymaker. When that launches, won't they be surprised? And just in case it doesn't work, we'll continue to pound them. Our line is here. Only one of us will remain at the end of today."

"We are all-in. I'm sorry, I didn't understand. We will pound them until there is nothing left."

Admiral Wesson nodded and turned back to the main screen. The cloud accelerated at obscene speeds. "Fire when ready, Lev."

"Calculations complete," Lev stated. The missile flashed out of its launch tube at the bottom of *Leviathan*. It transitioned to faster-than-light speed, and an instant later, a flash signaled its arrival at the Ga'ee ship. It skipped like a stone off water and continued past the huge alien vessel on a trajectory toward deep space.

The bridge crew collectively gasped and stared at the screen.

The admiral whistled through gritted teeth. "*Cleophas*, prepare to fire the worldkiller. Adjust your position to get a clean firing solution."

The dreadnought immediately started maneuvering while continuing to fire its weapons at the cyclic rate.

The admiral clenched his fists. The failure of their main weapon meant people were going to die. Hope had been fleeting. The relief he'd felt was gone.

The armada's ships held their positions, maintaining separation to keep the firing lanes clear. They launched missiles. They fired their cannons and guns. Between the main salvos, the void was filled with the best and most they could deliver.

The first salvo impacted the relentless drones. Flashes and crashes created gaps that were quickly filled. The wall of drones advanced while being sniped by random ion and plasma impacts.

The drones adjusted and kept coming.

The cloud remained, seemingly undiminished in size.

A movement from the Ga'ee ship came with gut-wrenching clarity. A second wave of drones was on its way. The admiral stared at the screen in disbelief. They had never known the total number of drones available to the Ga'ee. He had hoped attrition had reduced their total number.

As he always said, hope was a lousy plan.

Arthir's mouth fell open. Seventy thousand was a number she could wrap her head around. Ten thousand drones had already fallen, which had given her hope that they could win.

But another seventy thousand? The Fleet didn't have enough weapons to deal with such an overwhelming number.

She hesitated. The bridge crew's eyes fell on her and Admiral Wesson. Commodore Freeman stepped up and took Harry's hand. "I guess we'll have to do it the hard way. What's new?" She laughed, then her mouth set in grim determination. If they were going down, they'd do it fighting.

The other ships of the Fleet had the same idea.

Forty Mosquitos rolled up the drone flank, plowing a deep furrow before getting chased away by a five-hundred-drone formation. The Mosquitos split up and spread out.

The drones stayed together and accelerated to a speed well beyond what the Mosquitos could achieve. The first pair died quickly, then the next, and the next.

Commander Woody Malone called over the all-hands channel, "Leave your wingmen. Fly solo. Give them more targets and re-engage." Sixteen pairs of fighters became thirty-two individuals, limiting the drone formation's effectiveness.

The drone cloud split into two groups.

The first Mosquito it chased down detonated its nuclear bomb the instant the drones arrived. The explosion sent a shock wave through the formation, delivering half of them to silicon hell.

Dropped in the Mosquito's wake, another nuclear bomb exploded in the second formation, shattering drones and leaving them floating free.

"Finish them!" Woody shouted. The Mosquitos converged, blasting with their primary weapons, their cannons, and the stunned three-pronged drones died quickly. The second group learned quickly and broke into hunter-killer groups of ten drones each. The Mosquitos twisted and juked, fighting and running.

One Mosquito drifted away, power at a minimum.

"They were stunned!" the admiral cried out.

"Working it," Lev replied. He flooded space with the equivalent of a nuclear weapon's electromagnetic pulse, the EMP that modern ships should have been hardened against.

The drone cloud lost cohesion for a moment, then surged afresh before stalling for two seconds.

Then three, before it gathered its wits and renewed its relentless drive toward the armada.

Twenty Fleet ships stood fast.

"Whatever you're doing, Lev, we need more of it. Three seconds, if you can do it again. Take over Cleophas' firing sequence on the worldkiller. Adjust your aim point and fire when you've stalled the drones." Harry leaned toward the front screen as if he could drive the missile faster.

The drones hesitated, and the massive missile flashed from

the dreadnought. Like the first attempt, it skipped off the energy shield of the Ga'ee ship and continued on a trajectory to take it out of the system.

Lev interdicted the missiles and set their self-destruct for ten minutes. If they won the fight, he could cancel his orders and recover them. They weren't something he wanted to leave lying around.

The Ga'ee ship accelerated toward the armada, closing on the tail of the second cloud.

"Keep working that interdiction, Lev. You can do it." The admiral tried to sound encouraging, but time was running out.

Lev lit up like a supernova as he flushed all his tubes and fired every weapon available to him. From the hangar bays, maintenance drones departed carrying nuclear weapons.

"Slow-moving bots with nukes. Interesting tactic," Arthir admitted.

"Anything fast is deflected. I would like to take a peek at that technology," Lev replied.

The frigate *Shrew* left the formation and accelerated forward, its reactor set to overload. Commander Appel appeared as an inset on the screen. "We're making a hole for others to follow. When it's big enough, we can hit the enemy's ride." He saluted, and the image disappeared.

The frigate accelerated as much as it was able, firing ahead until the drones rammed it from the front. More hit its flanks. The reactor went critical and erupted in an expanding white-hot sphere that absorbed a thousand drones.

"We don't have enough ships for that tactic," the admiral lamented. "Keep firing."

The drones refilled the gap and pressed forward. The Ga'ee ship bore down on them.

Lev continued to demonstrate his ability to make war. A

nearly impenetrable curtain of firepower spread out between the massive battleship and the Ga'ee. Thousands of drones were swept away by the tidal wave of energy weapons and solid projectiles.

From ions to lasers, Lev fought to destroy the Ga'ee weapons on his way to destroy the carrier.

The *Tempest* bolted from the formation and accelerated at a punishing rate of speed. Commander Gordon didn't bother delivering a final message. He took his ship and crew to the enemy to create a maelstrom, a final protective barrage meant as a last resort. His reactor went critical moments after the drones tore into the frigate.

Another wave of drones washed out of space. The first cloud was almost spent.

The firing slowed by half since the ships could no longer maintain cyclic rates. Missiles were nearly gone. Energy weapons tapped the reactor. Capacitors needed time to recharge.

Only Lev continued to fire at a dizzying rate. *Leviathan* moved to intercept the second cloud, using its hull to block as many as possible.

There were only tens of thousands of drones seeking a target upon which to throw themselves now. The second drone cloud went ballistic for a moment before recovering.

"Close, Lev. If only we had a worldkiller to shove in their face when they get here. Never bring chain guns to a knife fight, not when you can bring a planet-buster," the admiral stated. He gripped Nyota's hand so tightly she had to pry herself free. "Sorry," he mumbled.

A voice sounded from the overhead. "For Rang'Kor."

"Is that Captain Pel'Rok?" the admiral asked.

"He is in a Mosquito and is inside the Ga'ee hangar bay."

"Send him the vulnerable points!"

"He is already accelerating toward the mid-ship reactor," Lev reported.

A mushroom cloud burst out of the open bay of the Ga'ee ship. It was small, but the ship stopped accelerating.

The drone cloud assumed a ballistic trajectory, having lost contact with the main ship.

Lev accelerated, bombarding the drones with the pulses they had earlier reacted to. He looped over the top of the drone cloud to close with the Ga'ee vessel. Secondary explosions rippled along the ship's spine. Lev came alongside and launched a series of Rapier-class missiles through the open doors into the ship.

Explosions rent the hull and ripped away frigate-sized sections of the ship to send them spinning into the void. Lev accelerated sideways, away from the Ga'ee, continuing to fire into the ship.

Amazingly, its engines came back to life and it rolled over, exposing its keel to *Leviathan* before accelerating. Two hundred gees, then five hundred, and soon a thousand.

"You should be dead!" Admiral Wesson shouted at the screen.

A small group of drones broke from the cloud and raced to catch up, but before they could reach the ship, it transitioned to faster-than-light on a heading that would take it out of the galaxy.

"How much damage could that thing take?" the admiral asked.

"More than we were capable of delivering, obviously," Lev answered. "I suggest we kill as many drones as possible and let the remainder burn up in the atmosphere."

"Can't we drag them into the sun?" Arthir asked.

"If only we could tow such a mass," Lev replied. "But we can recover enough drones to smelt them into a fine net in which we could tow and toss thousands at a time. I'll begin as soon as I've recovered our errant missiles. I recommend you save your armaments for any drones that enter the atmosphere."

"You don't have to remind me that the Ga'ee seeded the planets and left. What I hear you saying is that their creatures can operate independently, which means we need them dead as soon as possible."

"Dead-dead," Arthir confirmed. "I'll pass the orders to the Fleet."

Arthir climbed into the captain's chair. Harry whispered into Nyota's ear. "Thanks for grounding me back there."

"It was right here." She pointed at the deck.

"Time is a linear construct upon which we move forward at a steady pace." He put his hands behind his back and studied the tactical board. Twenty-seven Mosquitos remained. They'd lost the two frigates, but they had bought time for the rest of the fleet. For Lev. And most importantly, for Captain Pel'Rok. For Rang'Kor and all the free people of the seven races.

Nyota winked at the admiral. He smiled back. Her Fleet strategy had been limited as a member of the Blue Earth Protectorate, the BEP. Their charter was defensive. Protect Earth at all costs. The BEP no longer existed. It had been destroyed in the final battle for Earth space and had not been reconstituted.

Why? The administrators of Earth considered it the peace dividend.

"Lev." The admiral interrupted the commodore's thoughts. "Once we've recovered the missiles and destroyed the drones, set course for BH01 directly. Don't bother with the three days' distance. We need to be there, and the space should be devoid of any other ships."

"I think it is low risk to fold space directly to the Berantz homeworld. I think they will need help."

"Possibly of the nuclear kind. Recover our fighters and make sure they're fully armed. Some of our pilots used their heavy hitters. They'll need new ones, maximum yield."

Lev dithered before answering. "I am not a proponent of using radioactive weapons. I know what you're planning. If the Ga'ee have gained a foothold, you want to incinerate them. But this is the Berantz homeworld."

"You know what I'm thinking. We wouldn't use nukes unless the Berantz leadership allows us to. We'll exhaust all other methods to destroy any infestation should there be one. No need to argue when you know that I know that you know what I know."

Commodore Freeman gave the admiral the side-eye.

"You have spent too much time with Declan Payne. He talks like that, and it is truly bizarre. He uses linguistic abnormalities as easily as water flowing down a stream."

The admiral strolled around the bridge, speaking to each volunteer who had stayed with the ship, no matter the outcome. "We'll hold a memorial for our *Tempest* and *Shrew* before we depart BD27 space," he told them. Everyone who served needed to know they would be remembered. Celebrated, if only for a moment.

"Arthir," the admiral called and joined her at the captain's chair. "Cross-deck to *Cleophas* and resume command of the Fleet assets. I'll talk with the Berantz admiral. They need to go planet to planet in their systems, so I won't ask them to join us. You'll need to lead the Fleet back to Earth and start drumming up support for a coalition. I feel it in my bones. The Ga'ee will be back. Maybe even that same ship. We need to be ready. Nukes en masse. Space netting. Anything to hold them back. I don't know what weapons will have the best effect, but we saw that nukes ruined their day. We need all we can get, and we'll use them until the Ga'ee make adjustments. I'm sure they will."

"No doubt, Harry. Why can't we track that ship, Lev?"

"Unknown." Lev kept his reply simple. "I have a great deal of data to analyze. I continue to search for how the individual Ga'ee communicate, too. It'll be nice to have Alphonse and Katello back. They have insights that neither Davida nor I can replicate."

"Why did your missiles bounce off the Ga'ee ship?"

"An energy shield that acted like a mirror to protect against vehicles and objects traveling at FTL. It didn't need to stop the incoming, only deflect it. I want that technology."

"We shall continue our search through the galaxy for all the things, Lev. We need to get our FTL communication protocols out there so we can send messages over extreme distances. That will greatly reduce our response time," Harry replied.

"For the next time," Nyota muttered and hung her head.

"For the next time," Harry repeated. "Because they'll be back. At least, we have to act like they will and be ready."

"Lev is running dead drones through the smelting process and beginning to build a high-tensile strength net for the cruisers to use to drag the drones toward the system's star. Once in the gravity well, they'll release them to continue to their destruction. The Berantz battlewagon will monitor to make sure none escape," Arthir explained.

"Sounds like a good plan. I'll be in the conference room, where I want to address all the ship's captains. I'll coordinate with Lev. I'll need you in that meeting, Arthir, but you can take it from here."

"What's it about?"

"The future," Harry replied cryptically.

———

A waiting cart brought Fleet Admiral Harry Wesson and Commodore Nyota Freeman to the conference room he'd used in past meetings with the other races.

He leaned back in his chair, and Lev confirmed that the captains were listening in. A holographic projection provided a checkerboard of faces, both human and Berantz.

"I thank you all for joining us in the fight against the Ga'ee. First and foremost, I want to recognize the sacrifices made by Commanders Gordon and Appel of the frigates *Tempest* and *Shrew* in their selfless attacks on the drones. And Captain Pel'Rok of the Rang'Kor, who delivered the greatest blow for the seven races against the Ga'ee, breaking the ship's back and sending it from the Bindalas system on a trajectory out of the galaxy."

Silence followed, then Admiral Grimdelk spoke. "How did Pel'Rok get inside the energy shield?"

"The nuclear blasts, followed by *Leviathan's* EMP bombardment, helped break the link for only a moment, and a moment was all he needed," Admiral Wesson replied.

"Please share that information with all ships to give them a fighting chance," the Berantz admiral requested.

"Of course. Lev, transmit the information at your earliest convenience. Whatever we know regarding the Ga'ee's vulnerabilities, including the energy generation within the carrier ship itself."

"Done," Lev confirmed instantly.

"And that leads us to the next time. How will we be ready? The FTL code is a new tool to help us communicate to stay in front of the next contingency. We were running for our lives this time, and it took all of us to stop them. How much damage have they done? We don't know, but we are going to travel to BHo1, the Berantz homeworld, immediately by folding space. I suggest a return to BD23, Blegoston, is in order to interdict whatever the Ga'ee have done there."

"I request transportation on *Leviathan*," Admiral Grimdelk interrupted.

"Granted. Bring a shuttle to *Leviathan*, and if we can keep that shuttle on board, it would be a great benefit since we had no space in our hangars before for shuttles with two frigates and forty space fighters embarked. Unfortunately, we have a great deal of available space now."

"I shall transfer within the hour."

Harry nodded, then raised a finger before he continued. "This isn't a manufactured crisis to give the Fleet credibility to be restored and expanded. The Ga'ee are a real threat, the likes of which we do not yet fully comprehend, but we will soon. Once we reach BH01, we'll know more. Make sure you share the Ga'ee information with everyone you meet and that they know this threat exists. And that all FTL-capable ships have the FTL code to let us know the instant the Ga'ee are seen. We can hope they don't return, but hope is a lousy plan. Questions?"

"I'll take *Cleophas* and the Earth Fleet to the Zuloon system to let them know. Will you return to Earth after the Berantz homeworld?"

"We will probably go to PX47 next, depending on what we find at BH01. And, I think it's important that every one of the seven races starts building a portal for instantaneous transfer to Vestrall Prime, Ebren, or Earth. The Earth portal is finished and fully operational. We need portals to all the races."

Nyota leaned close and whispered, "Wouldn't the Ga'ee destroy them and isolate the systems?"

"But we can respond in force to surrounding systems. We only need the word. We have to rebuild Earth's Fleet. We have to bring the Blaze together as a single force to fight the Ga'ee. We need the shipyards to give us the strength to eject the Ga'ee should they or anyone else encroach on the space of the seven races."

"Hear, hear!" Admiral Grimdelk stated. He held up his fist in a Berantz sign of solidarity.

"Then let us finish what we started here before we undertake the real work of being ready for next time."

The group signed off. Harry leaned back in his chair and closed his eyes.

"When we go back to Earth, Nyota, I fear they are going to throw us in jail rather than listen to us when we explain the threat to all humanity."

"Maybe we should take Arthir with us. She can talk to them first."

"I'll ask, but I think her talents are better served leading the armada."

"What about your talents, Harry? Aren't you the best one to bring the people of Earth together? Maybe we couldn't do it as civilians, but we're not that anymore. We're Fleet from now to the end."

"They might not recognize that. Earth administrators are... how can I best say this? Assholes. Yes. They are assholes of the highest order."

"And we have a lot of video to show them," the commodore countered. "As long as you don't leave *Leviathan*, there's nothing they can do to you."

"Are you okay with that? Never leaving *Leviathan*?"

"There's nothing for us down there. Not anymore, Harry. This is our home if Lev will have us."

"You are more than welcome anytime," Lev replied.

"Well then, we better get back to the bridge. See this through until we can go to Berantz."

"Another two hours," Lev replied.

"Until we find the truth of what the Ga'ee left behind."

[27]

"Genocide doesn't have to be fast to remove a race from existence." –From the memoirs of Ambassador Declan Payne

"Folding space," Lev announced.

The crew steadied themselves for the interference with their physical well-being. In a moment, *Leviathan* appeared two hundred thousand kilometers from BH01's surface. The tactical screen started to populate.

Ga'ee drones. Hundreds of them.

"Woody, launch the fighters. All fighters, now!"

"Tricky Spinsters away!" Commander Malone replied over the internal comm channel. The outer doors slid aside, and the Mosquitos raced into the void. All twenty-four, under one command since Wazeree of Titan's Hammers had been killed at BD27.

They distanced themselves for solo attacks to give the Ga'ee more targets.

"Who's controlling those things, Lev?" Admiral Wesson asked.

"If we can answer that, we can stop this attack before it starts. I suspect the center of the swarm."

The Ga'ee stayed in a haphazard group around a central point. When they angled toward *Leviathan* as a cohesive cloud, a rectangular ship the size of a shuttle appeared.

"Woody, take out that box, and your lives will get a whole lot easier," the admiral advised.

The Mosquitos flew far and wide, high and low, and left and right, putting a vast amount of distance between each fighter before they started their attack run. The Ga'ee remained as one cloud, looking for a target. They headed straight for *Leviathan*.

"Kill that box," the admiral ordered.

The Mosquitos fired their ion cannons as one, targeting the small ship and hitting drones that got in the way. Flashes marked impacts, but nothing got through to the controlling ship. A small energy shield protected it, deflecting the incoming rounds.

The space fighters raged, going after drones that didn't change course. Their mission was clear: attack the big ship.

"This is a shortcoming we'll need to rectify," the admiral advised Lev. "Maybe you should close the hangar doors."

"That's all the power I have, Harry. When I close them, it will be a while before I can open them again."

"We'll manually open them, Lev. Don't you worry about that. Protect yourself as well as you can. We cannot let those drones get inside the ship."

"We must not let them."

"I know you can't deliver an EMP, but we can. Woody, how about you drop a nuke in front of the enemy? And then another."

Commander Malone selected which spacecraft were to deliver the munitions. They counted down for a simultaneous release. The Mosquitos came to a hard stop, dropped the bombs, and raced away. When the front of the drone cloud reached the bombs, they detonated.

The bright light of nuclear fission flooded the bridge, even though it was damped by Lev's systems.

"Hit 'em hard, Spinsters!" Woody called. The drones continued forward but were tumbling on ballistic trajectories, just like the ones at BD27 when they lost contact with their ship and each other.

Twenty-two Mosquitos raced in, raking through the cloud. They ripped drones apart left and right, but the ships were flying solo, uncoordinated along a single front.

The drones collected themselves, reengaged their engines, and accelerated toward *Leviathan*, crushing any Mosquitos unlucky enough to be in their way.

Two fighters had stayed the course toward the control ship. They fired their ion cannons to no avail.

"Slow to the speed of space dust when you get close," the admiral ordered. "I think their shields only protect against fast-moving particles."

"That makes no sense," one pilot countered, "but it's the only thing we have left."

The drones cleared the Mosquitos since they were far faster. The fighters fell back and watched helplessly as the drones headed for *Leviathan*'s aft end.

"Slamming on the brakes, releasing the bomb, and watching it slow-roll forward," the Mosquito pilot reported. He broke off while the second pilot slowed to a drift. The nuke slipped through. When it touched the hull, it exploded. The first Mosquito raced away. The second Mosquito was caught in the blast.

The ship disappeared within the nuclear detonation, taking the shield and drone control with it. The impact on the link between the small ship and the drones was violently severed, like being hit in the brain with a ball-peen hammer. The drones lost their connections and fried their synapses.

"Thrusters, please, Lev," the admiral requested.

"I don't have any available, Harry."

"Then let's hope they don't come back to life before they hit us. A ballistic impact won't hurt you, will it?"

"Unknown. They have a great deal of momentum already."

With the loss of acceleration, the Mosquitos had a chance. They adjusted their firing angles so *Leviathan* wouldn't be a backstop, then smoked their cannons until they couldn't fire anymore.

The drones were blasted off-course by the impacts. Some exploded. Others came apart.

The Mosquitos chased them to the greatest ship in the galaxy. The debris and remaining drones bounced off and drifted away.

"Nice work to you and all your people, Woody. It came at a high cost." The admiral didn't further lament their casualties. In two engagements over the last few hours, they'd lost over half their space fighters and two frigates, but they hadn't lost Earth, BD27, or the coalition of forces Admiral Wesson was building. "We can't get the hangar doors open right now, so buzz the planet and get some eyes on the ground. See what's going on. We'll attempt to contact the Berantz from here."

"I would like that honor," Admiral Grimdelk requested.

"Lev, please." Admiral Wesson stepped aside to offer the Berantz the open space in front of the captain's chair.

"Berantz. Admiral Grimdelk on board *Leviathan*. We have come to help with the Ga'ee problem."

A weak signal came through, "Admiral Grimdelk. Welcome back. First Premier Lorcan here. 'Ga'ee.' Is that what they're called? We are finally holding our own, but only after they conquered half the planet. They're building ships, and we can't stop them."

"I believe *we* can. Are we authorized for the release of nuclear weapons?"

"We have no other choice. As much as we abhor the violence of such detonations, the Ga'ee must be stopped."

Grimdelk turned to Wesson. "If your Mosquitos would be so kind, we have targets that need servicing."

Harry smiled and clapped the Berantz admiral on the shoulder. "Give us the coordinates, and we will deliver the payloads. We cannot let the Ga'ee extend their foothold in this system."

"Transmitting coordinates now," the first premier replied.

"Take care of it, Commander Malone. We'll have those hangar bay doors open when you get back to the house."

"Roger," came Woody's even reply. The Mosquitos assumed a vertical diamond formation and set course for the planet and the designated coordinates. "Unarmed ships will remain in orbit."

Admiral Grimdelk saluted Admiral Wesson and headed for the corridor.

"Linking the live feed," Lev reported.

The view from Woody's space fighter appeared on the main screen. Admiral Grimdelk returned to the center of the bridge. "I'll head to the planet after I see what's going on down there."

The space fighters skipped off the upper atmosphere before digging into the friction. The image bounced and flared with the fire of reentry. It ended as quickly as it started, and sixteen Mosquitos spiraled downward. Below, the gray and black of a rocky moonscape filled the screen. Silver sparkles covered the land like a shimmering sea.

"What is that?" Nyota asked.

"Silicon life forms. We are seeing Ga'ee, tens of millions of them," Lev replied.

Three-dimensional structures appeared in the distance—gantries, cranes, and machinery. The targets.

The Mosquitos deployed in four-ship groups to hit the ship construction facilities. Four targets, sixteen nuclear weapons.

"Pickle switch on. In the barrel." The Mosquitos released and immediately stood on their tails to put distance between them and the secondary effects of the explosions.

The weapons hit and detonated nearly simultaneously. Four separate and distinct mushroom clouds appeared over the Berantz homeworld. Woody took his wingman and rolled over the top to make a second run past the target sites to collect information on the effectiveness of the bombing run.

The screen showed a massive crater where the construction facilities had been. Silver shimmers had become dull gray.

"They really don't like nukes," the admiral remarked.

"Neither do we," Grimdelk replied. "I'll be off now. Thank you for the ride."

The Berantz left the bridge. He'd take his shuttle and depart the ship when the maintenance crew managed to open the hangar doors. They'd been working on it since the drone threat had passed. The manual system was neither easy nor quick, but it was possible. If worse came to worst, the Mosquitos could land on the planet and return in three days, once *Leviathan* had power restored.

"Woody, what's it like down there?"

"An absolute wasteland. Not fit for carbon-based life. The Ga'ee have rendered it uninhabitable. Whatever they do, it sure as hell isn't good for anything that grows with sun and water."

"That's what I thought I saw. Can you make a pass over the populated areas?"

"On my way. Break, break. All fighters return to Mother One. Winger and I will be along shortly. We'll make a quick pass over the good guys and see how they are holding up."

It took twenty minutes for Woody to get beyond the waste-land that was Ga'ee-occupied territory. A steep mountain range separated the two distinctly different worlds. The light greens of vegetation and the blues of streams dotted the regular land-scape, where farms squared off from horizon to horizon.

The Mosquitos passed houses and other buildings, rocking their wings to those below.

"Attention, inhabitants of the Berantz homeworld. We're here to help. We have fought against this alien invasion, and we have driven them from Berantz space. Now we need to drive them from your planet. You can count on humanity because we are in this together. My name is Woody Malone, and I'm from Earth. We just bombed the holy fuck out of those bastards, and there's plenty more where that came from."

Wesson smiled. Earth was here to help.

[28]

"Family doesn't have to be related." –From the memoirs
of Ambassador Declan Payne

"*Leviathan* is in the system," Captain Krakenorr said.

Poramir was ten minutes from entering normal space in the
BHo1 system. "You couldn't have told me that before now?"
Payne gave the Berantz his best angry look.

Mary gripped his arm, as much for physical support as to
calm Payne down.

"What would you have done differently having that information? Humans need to learn patience. I have taught you a
valuable lesson. You can thank me later."

Payne relaxed and chuckled. "I tell you what, Krak, you are
a piece of work. I'll take my lesson in the spirit it was intended.
I'll thank you now. *Leviathan*! Team Payne, prepare to disembark. Nothing personal, my man, but we're ready to go home."

"You don't like our food?" The captain offered his hand in a
human gesture; it was a question but not.

"That's an understatement. We hate your food. Even when we

294

try to cook it ourselves, it's unsalvageable. We're starving, but we're at our fighting weight, if not below." Payne shook the Berantz's hand. This came as no surprise to the Berantz captain. Despite their similar physiology, they had evolved different digestive systems. "I can't thank you enough for the ride and sharing what you know. We'll be better equipped to fight the Ga'ee next time. Lev being here portends good tidings. I can feel it in my bones."

"To the shuttle!" Payne declared while twirling his arm and ending with a knife-hand pointed down the corridor.

"Watch where you swing that thing," Mary warned. She waved to the captain with her free hand while holding Payne's arm firmly with the other. They strolled down the corridor on their way to the small launch bay where the Berantz shuttle waited. The team was already there, having not let any grass grow under their feet the second they heard Lev was waiting at BH01.

"I didn't see any other ships," Heckler noted.

"We'll have our questions answered very soon." Payne climbed into his suit while Kal helped Mary board. The others made room to usher her to the safest position on the forward bulkhead.

Payne ran through his startup sequence and joined them, positioning himself closest to the rear hatch. It was a tight squeeze, as it always was when the team wore their suits.

Dank gave the thumbs-up when everyone was in place. All suits showed green on his HUD. Payne had seen that too, but it was the XO's job to look after the team members, freeing the commanding officer to think lofty thoughts.

Like, why was Lev at BH01? It did not make him more comfortable. At least their logistics needs would be taken care of. Rearmed, suits cleaned and updated, reloaded, fed, and sleep in their own racks, but they had gotten enough sleep while onboard *Poramir*. It was the only thing they *had* gotten enough of.

They'd had nothing but time during the trip.

The slight disorientation of transitioning from FTL washed over them, but they were seated, and it passed as quickly as it had come.

Payne activated his comm channel in the hope they were close enough to *Leviathan*. "Admiral Wesson, this is Major Payne. Can you read me?"

After a long delay, a familiar voice replied. "It's good to have you back. We thought you were dead until your ship sent us an FTL message to the contrary. What did you learn on BD18?"

"That the Ga'ee implant five seeds per ship that grow quickly. Eight to twelve hours in the right environment—not water but dirt, not clay, and a good mix of minerals. And then they double and keep doubling. We interdicted them quickly on BD18, but we almost let them get past us. But BD18 is clear as far as we know. Hitting them early is the easiest way. Plasma fire or acid will kill them."

"Plasma, as in a plasma torch?"

"Roger," Payne confirmed. The shuttle accelerated out of the launch tube and into space. The pilots aimed its nose toward the ancient vessel, following Lev's instructions regarding where to land.

"And acid. We haven't been employing either of those. We're still using tactical nukes since thirty-five percent of the Berantz homeworld is occupied by the Ga'ee. There are so many that we're not sure we're gaining ground."

"What's the plan, Admiral?"

"I think we're going to evacuate a significant number of the population. We can fit a quarter of a million Berantz on *Leviathan* for a short hop to BD18 since that planet is clear, or

BD27. Both are viable, but we're still waiting for planetary leadership to make a decision."

"In the meantime, we're coming home. Be there in just a few minutes."

"Home. I think there are a few of us who have taken to calling *Leviathan* home, Admiral. It seems like that's where we're meant to be."

The shuttle continued in silence until it landed where *Ugly 4* used to be.

"I bet I can make it to the chow hall in three minutes," Heckler declared.

"Two and a half!" Buzz shouted. The team vibrated with anticipation of getting real food again. Well, real food made from flavored biomass, but they didn't care. They only knew how it tasted and that it was nourishing, unlike the fish-slime paste the Berantz considered fine dining.

The hatch popped and Payne strolled off, getting bumped and bounced as the others ran past. Kal ducked on his way out and took his gear off while running. He tossed his helmet and breathing apparatus into the team area as he ran past. The doors opened, and the Cabrizi raced in. They hit the Ebren so hard they knocked him down.

Mary appeared at Payne's elbow and watched with interest. "I don't think they've ever tackled him before, not even when he wasn't looking," she offered.

"Let's get you to Medical for a quick check," Payne suggested.

"No way. We eat first."

"I like how you think." The others stripped out of their gear and into the clothes they'd left behind weeks earlier. They were fresh, as if they had come straight from the laundry. The team was gone by the time Declan stepped out of his suit.

"You've lost weight," Mary remarked.

"We all have, Dog. Welcome to the rigors of war."

She nodded. "Just until tomorrow. I'm sure they'll eat their body weight today and probably the next few days. Six meals a day. Max calories."

"Then it's my job to..."

Mary finished for him. "Make sure that your XO works those calories off of them."

"Exactly what I was going to say. Shall we?" Payne pulled his jumpsuit up and slipped on his boots, closing his eyes and grinning at the perfect fit. "Boots as part of the emergency kit for Ugly 5. Lev, are you there?"

"Of course. Welcome back, Declan, Mary."

"Boots in the uglymobiles. We had a helluva a time on BD18 without proper boots."

"There were boots for all of you in the aft storage compartment," Lev replied.

"We lost the aft end to the Ga'ee as we approached the planet surface. We would have tried harder to find it if we knew our boots were there."

"I shall put them in side panels beside each seat, along with a jumpsuit for each person."

"That's what I'm talking about." Payne nodded. A cart pulled into the hangar and waited for the last two to leave. The Berantz shuttle lifted off the deck and headed back into space. "And build us an Ugly 5, please, Lev."

"I've used all available raw materials but will as soon as I can collect more. There is significant debris in this system, but I've been asked to rebuild as many ships as I can to restore the Berantz fleet."

"That has to be a priority as soon as we have Ugly 5," Payne quipped. "Can you ask the admiral to meet us in the dining room? We're going to the one on our private deck, aren't we?"

"Yes. Harry and Nyota are already waiting. They missed you a great deal, as did I."

Mary rested her head on Declan's shoulder and held his arm tightly. "I think I'm going to resign from the military. I have been no help to you."

"Where is this coming from?" Payne leaned back. "We need every single gun in this fight. Denied! Resubmit for final disapproval in thirty days. So there. It's good to be the king."

"Declan." Mary used the mom voice she said she had perfected on the set of *Bikini Babes in Paradise* because the crew had been easily distracted. "Every single one of the major actions, I've been in Sickbay, getting fixed up."

"And pretty soon, you'll end one of them still on your feet. You've got your scar. Don't let it go to waste. You'll get to show it off every time we get suited up."

"Is that how you think?" she asked.

Payne looked confused. He scratched his head before answering. "It is. Why let a good scar hide under your bodice?"

"That *is* how he thinks. I can confirm," Lev added.

"Hey! You're not supposed to share how I think." Payne tsk-tsked the AI.

"Did I say that out loud?" Lev joked.

"It's good to be back, buddy. I missed my daily verbal trouncing from you. You have so much to learn."

"'Trouncing?'" Mary asked.

Payne contemplated his answer, but the cart arrived before he could deliver it. His focus turned to helping Mary down. They walked into the facility, which was far too large for the small team, especially since they sat together at one table.

"We got your food!" Heckler shouted with a full mouth, earning himself an elbow from Turbo.

Major Dank simply pointed at the two empty seats in the middle of the group. The admiral and the commodore leaned against the adjacent table. As soon as they saw Major Payne, they pushed off and approached.

"Are you hurt?" the admiral asked.

"Show him," Payne directed, glancing past them at a tray filled with a Thanksgiving dinner.

Mary pulled her jumpsuit aside to show the purple scar leading from her rib cage around her side. "Friendly fire. The Berantz bombed us, thinking we were the Ga'ee."

"Those hurt the worst, but thank goodness no one was killed." The admiral smiled. "It's good to have you back." He held out his hand.

The commodore slapped it down. "Let them eat, Harry. He already told you they were starving."

"There is that," Payne said. The admiral and the commodore stepped aside to let the two through. Payne took a deep breath while Mary dipped her head toward the tray grunt-style and started forking mashed potatoes and gravy into her mouth.

"You eat, I'll talk," Fleet Admiral Harry Wesson suggested. "We collected data at BD23, and then we stood our ground at BD27, where Lev finally had the conversation with the Ga'ee that he wanted to have from the start. He learned that we cannot coexist with them. That's what it took for him to get involved."

Payne swallowed too quickly and started to cough. When he recovered, he asked, "Lev is fighting this war with us? That's great!" Payne grinned. "BD27 is safe?"

"An odd thing, that. The Rang'Kor captain flew a Mosquito inside the Ga'ee ship. He detonated his nuke right next to one of the power plants. We had a series of spectacular secondary explosions along the carrier's spine. I thought it was going to come apart, but no. The ship transitioned to FTL while its outer doors were still open. At least it was on a trajectory to head away from the seven races' space."

The team stopped chewing. "That fucker is still out there?"

Kal slammed his second tray down. "That's downright unneighborly."

"It left one hundred and forty thousand drones behind which have been destroyed. It's toothless and severely damaged, but if it can plant seeds, as we've seen right here, it can build everything it needs to keep going. We think each Ga'ee is implanted with the entirety of their knowledge. It's a little disconcerting."

"How many of those things are there?" Payne wondered.

"It only took one ship to wreak havoc and keep wreaking it. We have a lot of Berantz planets to clean up, even if that means dropping a warning buoy to keep ships away after we've completely burned the surface."

"Or used a worldkiller missile to destroy the planet. We can't let them stay here. It's not genocide as long as one exists. Those things are like self-replicating malware."

"That they are," the admiral agreed.

"What are our next steps?" Payne asked.

"Do what we can here and then travel to the other Berantz planets. Maybe the populations of the first four planets had better success against the landings than the homeworld's citizens."

Payne nodded and went back to eating. After he finished his first tray, he and Mary went to get a second tray of food.

"It's not healthy to eat that way. Maybe let it settle first," the admiral suggested.

"We haven't eaten a real meal in eleven days. Fifteen if you include our ill-fated time on Brayalore." Payne ordered a meal identical to the first. Mary did the same. "The Berantz are good people. I'm sorry to see them suffering under this incursion."

"And that's why we've vowed to stop the Ga'ee. We'll head back to Earth and then see what we can do to expedite having portals built near each race's home planet. Our lines of communication must not depend solely on *Leviathan's* ability to fold space."

"It took a year to build one. Will we have that much time?" Payne wondered and dug into round two as if he hadn't just eaten a full meal.

"The clock doesn't start until construction begins. We have to act like we have the time because thinking we don't won't get us what we want. And we need to build more Kaiju-class ships and fill them with the best people."

"Will Earth buy into that?" Payne said. Gravy trickled out the side of his mouth. He used his finger to capture it.

"They'll have to. Or the Vestrall will. We could use that drone fleet of theirs right about now, but somebody sent it into the star."

"You gotta let it go, Admiral. It's done and been done. We need to get those shipyards cranking. A drone dreadnought would give the Ga'ee ship a little grief."

"Unless they could be hacked, like we did to them. But if we could prevent that, then if the drone carried a thousand baby drones, each of which can kill ten or twenty Ga'ee drones. It's all about scale." Nyota pulled on Harry's arm. "We'll leave you be. Get your team back up to speed. We won't need you on BHo1. There are too many Ga'ee on the planet."

Byle raised her hand. "What if we devised a way to capture plasma from the sun and delivered it intact to a Ga'ee infestation?"

"That would do it. The heat of a thermonuclear blast delivered across a broad front. They wouldn't know what hit them."

"We'll work on it. Or gather sulfuric acid or liquid methane from a gas giant. There's a lot of toxic stuff out there. That's why the Ga'ee go to the habitable planets."

"Work with Lev and come up with something, soon as you can. And you two." The admiral pointed at Blinky and Buzz. "Figure out how those things talk to each other."

The admiral and the commodore walked out hand-in-hand, heads held high.

"We have our marching orders, people. I'll take Dog to Sickbay. Virge, PT. Nothing like a little running and lifting to work off all those calories you just ingested."

"Two hours. My momma told me I'd get cramps and drown, so PT begins in two hours. And as soon as we're done, showers and more chow. Tacos and pizza for dinner!" Major Dank declared.

"Go find that friend of yours, Virgil. Life's too short to miss a good opportunity."

Dank nodded as he stood. The group departed, leaving Declan and Mary behind. "I bet they all take a nap and miss PT, but they won't miss dinner." Payne took another bite and pushed his tray aside.

"It's not against the law to let them have some downtime."

"Don't be a freak, Dog! If they have time off, they'll just waste it," Payne joked before turning serious. "But I get you. Let's go to Medical and then put you to bed."

"That's the best offer I've heard all day." She winked.

The Cabrizi's claws suggested they were running like wild animals down the corridor. "Lev, tell the team everything is canceled for the rest of today. It's up to them to decide what they want. We'll hit tomorrow at eight in the morning with PT."

"They already know, Declan. No one had any intention of working out except Kal'faxx, and he's running a four-kilometer sprint with the Cabrizi. He's on his way to this deck's greenhouse room to relax in an oxygen-heavy environment."

"Why don't we do that?" Payne asked Mary.

She pointed at her injured side.

He sighed. "There's always something, isn't there?"

"When are the Ga'ee coming back?" Mary asked.

"They're already here, and we're already neck-deep in a war, but Lev will shield us. We don't see all he sees. Imagine what will go through his mind when the evacuees come on board. Horror, loss, pain—all of that will flood into him. I'm glad that I'm not you, Lev."

"I have refuge in the minds of my friends," Lev replied. "And we *are* at war, an ugly war. When the Ga'ee ship returns, we must be ready with weapons that will send them back to wherever they came from."

"They can choose to go on their own, or we send them in little bits and pieces, and they'll arrive a billion years from now," Payne added.

Declan and Mary strolled to the corridor to find a cart waiting to take them to Medical for a quick check-up.

"And you're not resigning," Payne stated. "End of discussion."

"That's not how discussions work," Mary countered. "I'm a hindrance to the team."

"We all get our time in the box getting fixed. How long was Kal out of it? We all take hits. It's part of the job. And I'm not leaving you behind while I go forward. Imagine if Blinky's naked body was keeping you warm through the shock and not mine?"

"That sounds like your problem and not mine." She smiled and looked away.

"Maybe we'll skip Medical and go to the bridge so you can harangue more unsuspecting souls."

"Is that you, my husband? An unsuspecting soul?"

"I suspect something will happen since you planted that seed in my mind." Payne tried to look innocent but failed.

"I'll see what I can do." Mary smiled. "For now, the war doesn't matter."

Payne stared into the distance. "Tomorrow is a new day. Another chance to get into the enemy's head and take one step closer to defeating him. The Ga'ee are mortal enemies. As Lev saw, we can't coexist with them, so that means we need to figure out how to fight them in a way where we can win. We're not fighting this war to break even."

THANK YOU FOR READING LEVIATHAN'S TRIAL

We hope you enjoyed it as much as we enjoyed bringing it to you. We just wanted to take a moment to encourage you to review the book. Follow this link: **Leviathan's Trial** to be directed to the book's Amazon product page to leave your review.

Every review helps further the author's reach and, ultimately, helps them continue writing fantastic books for us all to enjoy.

——————

You can also join our non-spam mailing list by visiting www.subscribepage.com/AethonReadersGroup and never miss out on future releases. You'll also receive three full books completely Free as our thanks to you.

Facebook | Instagram | Twitter | Website

Want to discuss our books with other readers and even the

authors? Join our Discord server today and be a part of the Aethon community.

ALSO IN THE SERIES

Battleship: Leviathan
Leviathan's War
Leviathan's Last Battle
Leviathan's Trial
Leviathan Rises
Leviathan's Fear

Looking for more great Science Fiction?

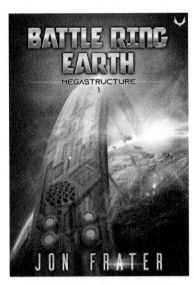

The ends justify the means... Technical Specialist Simon Brooks was no soldier. More suited for the academy than combat, his assignment to a rear echelon support squadron seemed a good fit. Everything changed when the Sleer attacked Earth's newly salvaged spacecraft, UEF Ascension.

GET BOOK ONE OF BATTLE RING EARTH

Titan's rebellion is coming. Only one man can stop it.

GET BOOK ONE OF EXODUS EARTH

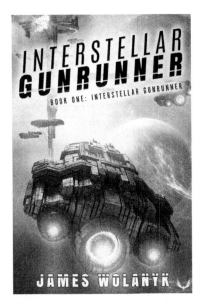

Nolan Garrett is Cerberus. A government assassin, tasked with fixing the galaxy's darkest, ugliest problems.

GET INTERSTELLAR GUNRUNNER NOW!

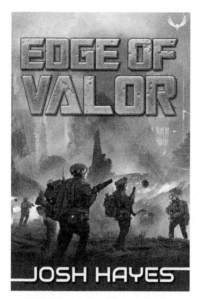

When their mission fails, his begins.

GET EDGE OF VALOR TODAY!

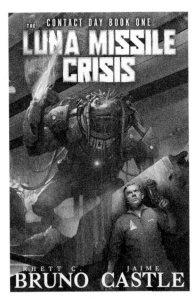

THE END
BATTLESHIP: LEVIATHAN BOOK #4

The fate of humanity has been assured for the near term. Please leave a review on this book because all those stars look great and help others decide if they'll enjoy this book as much as you have. I appreciate the feedback and support. Reviews buoy my spirits and stoke the fires of creativity.

Oorah, hard-chargers. Bring the Payne!

Don't stop now! Keep turning the pages as I talk about my thoughts on this book and the overall project called *Battleship: Leviathan.*

You can always join my newsletter—https://craigmartelle.com or follow me on Amazon https://www.amazon.com/Craig-Martelle/e/B01AQVF3ZY/, so you are informed when the next book comes out. You won't be disappointed.

Sometimes you need help with calculations, so this is the site I used for distance over time. Very convenient. https://jumk.de/math-physics-formulary/speed-of-light.php

AUTHOR NOTES - CRAIG MARTELLE

Written June 2021

I can't thank you enough for reading this story to the very end! I hope you liked it as much as I did.

I put out a call for names, and the great Kurtherian Gambit

fans responded with a wave of input. Here's who contributed, and I thank you greatly.

Eric Anthony offered a smattering of exotic names, and I chose Kal'Faxx for the Ebren champion's name. It sounded appropriately intimidating.

I needed names for the frigates riding inside *Leviathan*. Kelly Miller gave me *William S. Kellison,* and Debra Stubbins offered *Bronte Belltower*. I thank you both. And for the captains of those ships, I went with Esther "Nunchakus" Nemecek, offered by Jens Schulze. He runs a German translation company, and this superstar is one of his editors. And Phil Dent gave us Flip Fellows, who needs no nickname because that works.

Nathan Roden suggested a good counterpart to our Major Payne—Major Myotis Lucifugus.

Tom Dickerson supplied Charles "Chuck" Longer, who was the XO, now the captain of the frigate *Tanya Roberts*.

This book came together quite quickly. Once it started rolling, it rolled fast. Twenty-four days start to finish. Over the past week, I took time off from everything else I was doing and focused solely on writing this book. That made all the difference in being able to concentrate and deliver a quality story. I hope you agree that the story was well-told. We can do no more as authors than deliver good entertainment.

With that, the *Battleship: Leviathan* saga comes to a close. It was a great ride through a quarter of a million words, and I finished this story three months before Book #1 gets published! All three are done way early. That's important when rapid releasing—dropping the books one month apart. It makes sure they have time to go through the quality control process.

We have a new dog! This was a big change. Stanley is a six-year-old pitbull who needed a new home without dogs, so we managed to fly him to Alaska despite the prohibition on pitbulls.

How? We had him trained as a service dog, and he accompanied a person with PTSD inside the cabin of the plane. He came straight to Fairbanks, and we picked him up at the airport. He has bonded with us and blended into our family. He loves his time in the woods, and I'm loving the miles. I'm down seventeen pounds since the beginning of the year. Burning more calories than I'm taking in has made all the difference, and a lot of the credit goes to my boy Stanley.

Thank you to everyone who has read this far. You are the reason I keep writing.

Peace, fellow humans.

———

If you liked this story, you might like some of my other books. You can join my mailing list by dropping by my website craigmartelle.com or if you have any comments, shoot me a note at craig@craigmartelle.com. I am always happy to hear from people who've read my work. I try to answer every email I receive.

If you liked the story, please write a short review for me on Amazon. I greatly appreciate any kind words; even one or two sentences go a long way. The number of reviews an ebook receives greatly improves how well it does on Amazon.

Amazon—www.amazon.com/author/craigmartelle

Facebook—www.facebook.com/authorcraigmartelle

BookBub—https://www.bookbub.com/authors/craig-martelle

My web page—https://craigmartelle.com

Thank you for joining me on this incredible journey.

OTHER SERIES BY CRAIG MARTELLE

 # - available in audio, too

Terry Henry Walton Chronicles (#) (co-written with Michael Anderle)—a post-apocalyptic paranormal adventure

Gateway to the Universe (#) (co-written with Justin Sloan & Michael Anderle)—this book transitions the characters from the Terry Henry Walton Chronicles to The Bad Company

The Bad Company (#) (co-written with Michael Anderle)—a military science fiction space opera

Judge, Jury, & Executioner (#)—a space opera adventure legal thriller

Shadow Vanguard—a Tom Dublin space adventure series

Superdreadnought (#)—an AI military space opera

Metal Legion (#)—a military space opera

Battleship: Leviathan—military science fiction

The Free Trader (#)—a young adult science fiction action-adventure

Cygnus Space Opera (#)—a young adult space opera (set in the Free Trader universe)

Darklanding (#) (co-written with Scott Moon)—a space western

Mystically Engineered (co-written with Valerie Emerson)—mystics, dragons, & spaceships

Metamorphosis Alpha—stories from the world's first science fiction RPG

The Expanding Universe—science fiction anthologies

Krimson Empire (co-written with Julia Huni)—a galactic race for justice

Zenophobia (#)—a space archaeological adventure

End Times Alaska (#)—a Permuted Press publication—a post-apocalyptic survivalist adventure

Nightwalker (a Frank Roderus series)—A post-apocalyptic western adventure

End Days (#) (co-written with E.E. Isherwood)—a post-apocalyptic adventure

Successful Indie Author (#)—a non-fiction series to help self-published authors

Monster Case Files (co-written with Kathryn Hearst)—a Warner twins mystery adventure

Rick Banik (#)—spy & terrorism action-adventure

Ian Bragg Thrillers (#)—a hitman with a conscience

Published exclusively by Craig Martelle, Inc

The Dragon's Call by Angelique Anderson & Craig A. Price, Jr.—an epic fantasy quest

A Couples Travels—a non-fiction travel series

Mischief Maker by Bruce Nesmith—A Norse Mythology Contemporary Fantasy (not superhero)

Love & Haight by Jean Rabe and Donald J. Bingle—a courtroom drama with the undead, humor, horror, and the law.

Printed in Great Britain
by Amazon

55011718R00189